"Keep her quiet."

Terror swelled within her, and Allie kicked and thrashed at the man until he tightened his hold, squeezing the breath from her body. Weakly, she squirmed, but his viselike grip convinced her of the futility of struggling. With a flash of realization, she knew what they were waiting for, and she made another attempt to rip herself from the bruising hands that held her.

"No," she whimpered as the man pulled her painfully back. In a wave of dizzying panic, she heard the click of the key turning in Josh's lock next door, followed instantly by a second terrifying click very close to the side of her head.

"Allie," Josh called out. "Their pastrami looked like hell. I got you ham and Swiss instead. Allie?"

The light blazed on, momentarily blinding her, and Allie slumped limply back against her captor.

"Mercer," the big man said, holding a gun within inches of her temple. "Put your hands on your head and walk slowly into the room."

ABOUT THE AUTHOR

Catherine Judd's imagination has been working overtime. Following on the heels of her first novel, *Dance of Deception,* comes *Indiscreet,* the story of a couple hot on the trail of a forty-year-old mystery who manage to fall in love in between adventures.

"I've always loved old movies," says Catherine, "so it made sense to pattern my characters after two of my all-time favorites, Spencer Tracy and Katharine Hepburn. Like those two greats, my characters, Allie and Josh, can't live with—or without—each other."

Catherine, still a newlywed, lives with her husband and shelty collie in Mesa, Arizona.

Books by Catherine Judd

HARLEQUIN SUPERROMANCE
587—DANCE OF DECEPTION

Don't miss any of our special offers. Write to us at the following address for information on our newest releases.

Harlequin Reader Service
U.S.: 3010 Walden Ave., P.O. Box 1325, Buffalo, NY 14269
Canadian: P.O. Box 609, Fort Erie, Ont. L2A 5X3

Catherine Judd

Indiscreet

Harlequin Books

TORONTO • NEW YORK • LONDON
AMSTERDAM • PARIS • SYDNEY • HAMBURG
STOCKHOLM • ATHENS • TOKYO • MILAN
MADRID • WARSAW • BUDAPEST • AUCKLAND

ISBN 0-373-70603-0

INDISCREET

For my mother, Carol Ann Krziske,
with friendship, gratitude and love

If thou remember'st not the slightest folly
That ever love did make thee run into,
Thou hast not lov'd.
                              —*As You Like It*

CHAPTER ONE

"JOSH, I'M QUITTING."

"—although I'd say this guy knows what he's talking about. I'm telling you, Allie, it's the biggest story we've ever done. The biggest. Lena LaLorne. Think about it. That old crocodile Crombaugh is going to hate your guts. I can see it now—the parties, the press, the free champagne, the trips. We'll be back on top, Allie. We'll be the cream of the publishing milk bucket again. Rising to the top with all the grace and goodwill—"

"I'm quitting, Josh," Allie Shannon repeated.

The restaurant hummed with laughter and conversation from the lunch crowd. For an instant Allie thought her words had penetrated the din, but Josh only continued on relentlessly. When Joshua Mercer got hold of a subject, he didn't let go easily. Persistence was one of his trademarks.

"—for which we're so well known."

Josh leaned toward her, his strong, angular face handsome and eager, the minute flecks of gold in the dark depths of his brown eyes shining. Absently he moved his plate of untouched pasta with clam sauce to the side.

"This is the big one, Allie. I can feel it." He raised his hand as though to fend off her objections. "I know, I know. I've said that before. So my last few books didn't go over as well as we'd thought. I admit I've been in a slump for a little while, but I can almost taste it this time. The *New York Times* bestseller list. Think about it.''

"I'm quitting, Josh."

This time Josh paused to squint at her, seeming to consider. Then he smiled the same famous, slightly crooked smile that had graced the back covers of all his books and fueled the imaginations of women across the country. In his denim jacket and black T-shirt, the tie he'd borrowed from the restaurant hostess looked ridiculous. But then Joshua Mercer never cared very much about his appearance. Of course, Allie thought with just a twinge of irritation, he'd never had to.

Tall and dark-haired, powerfully built and broadshouldered, with a rugged face that sported a scar over one eyebrow and another beside the cleft in his chin, Joshua Mercer looked as dangerous and handsome as a renegade sea captain and about as much like a writer as Muhammad Ali. Still, his readers were always amazed to learn he'd actually been a boxer at one time—still boxed, in fact.

Nothing could have surprised Allie less. There was a stubborn streak a mile long in him—some called it ruthlessness—and he had an infallible sense of when to go in for the kill. It was those two attributes that had made him so successful as an investigative reporter and later as a true crime writer.

"Did you hear me?" Allie asked. "I said I'm quitting."

"Sure, Allie. Sure you are. So what do you think? Should we go for it? We can catch a flight to Seattle this evening—"

"In fact," she interrupted him, stabbing at her Caesar salad, "I'm handing in my resignation today."

Josh hadn't even paused. "—which means we'll be there before morning. We can visit Tory and Val, then hit the road again, hot on the trail of another sensational story. It'll be great. Remember the Trimaldi story? You and me, Allie. It'll be just like old times with—"

"Since you ask, I've decided to move to Charleston. That's South Carolina. I've always wanted to live in the South. Antebellum homes. Quiet lazy days. I'll be sharing a house right on the shore."

"—all the old thrills and spills and high jinks. Where do you suppose that phrase ever came from? High jinks." Whipping a small, battered leather notebook from the pocket of his denim jacket, Josh scrawled the phrase on a page with the stump of a yellow eraserless pencil and stuffed the notebook back into his pocket in one smooth movement, never missing a beat of his running dialogue.

"Of course, Lena LaLorne's an old lady," he went on. "Hope you don't mind missing out on getting shot at this time. I can't see Miss LaLorne toting an Uzi around like that Unger character. Remember him? Trimaldi's bodyguard. The one with that—"

"Naturally I'm a little apprehensive about the move," Allie tried again. "But after a great deal of thought, I've decided it's the best thing for me."

"—hideous purple birthmark on his bald head. You said it reminded you of the map of Turkey."

"Josh." With palms pressed flat against the table, Allie glared at him. "Shut up, would you? I'm trying to tell you..." She faltered as a sudden bleakness washed over her. "I'm trying to say goodbye."

Leaning back in his chair, Josh eyed her skeptically. "Goodbye? That'll be the day. Sure you're quitting. Of course you are. You're always on the brink of resigning and moving away. Last winter it was London. The year before it was San Diego. You've been threatening to quit Grauber Publishing for the past ten years."

"Eleven. This time I mean it."

Noticing the plate of pasta before him, Josh shrugged and picked up his fork. "Sure, sure. This time you mean it. But could you wait until I track down Lena LaLorne?"

Allie closed her eyes and breathed deeply in frustration. Joshua was her older brother's best friend from college, and she'd known him for half her life. A year or so after she'd joined Grauber Publishing fresh out of college, Josh had shown up with the manuscript for a true-crime story. She'd read it in one sitting that very night. They'd sold more than a million copies. Josh became a big name and quit the newspaper. And because he insisted on working with no one but her, she'd received a steady series of promotions.

It had seemed an arrangement made in heaven. For ten years as editor and author, they'd been a team, a winning team, and for a while it looked as though they would always be on top. Unlike the other authors on her list, Josh involved her to an unusual degree in the research and writing process, never bothering to question whether it was part of her job or not. She'd huddled outside dark warehouses acting as lookout for him, she'd kept a security guard occupied in the

Cleveland City Hall while he searched a file room of records, she'd patched up his face when he ran into the fists of a couple of Trimaldi's men, and together they'd shared innumerable thermoses of hot coffee and bottles of malt whiskey.

Yet now, after ten years, it was all over.

Josh's last three books had languished on the shelves, and she'd made a few mistakes—pushing for the autobiography of a politician, who shortly after publication was arrested for child molesting, not to mention buying a series of books about magicians that none of the marketing people could sell and no one wanted to read. She hadn't been asked to represent the company at an important booksellers' convention that spring. In fact, she hadn't even been asked to go along.

They were on the way out, Allie knew, but that wasn't the worst of it. What smarted most was finally admitting that, all along, she'd been lying to herself. Oh, she'd gotten just as caught up in each story as Josh had. The icy rush of fear at the possibility of danger, the breathless triumph of discovering missing evidence and the satisfaction of publicly revealing injustices all made for heady stuff. She'd been intoxicated by the thrill of the chase and lured by the idea of success.

But she wanted more, much more, and goaded by her recent failures, she'd finally forced herself to confront the hard truth. After ten years of waiting for Joshua Mercer to look at her in any way other than as the kid sister of his best friend or as his editor and colleague in adventure, after ten years of hoping, she'd finally admitted the biggest defeat of all. Josh didn't love her. And she was finally tired of waiting for him to start.

"I hope it's a great story," she said graciously, avoiding his eyes. Goodness, she wasn't going to start crying right here in the middle of Le Madri, was she? "I really do, Josh. But you'd better discuss it with Nancy. She'll be taking over for me. I already talked to her about you."

"Nancy? Nancy Dorgen? Dorgen the Dragon? Are you out of your mind? Not in a million years. She was the one who dreamed up that idiotic series with the veterinarian detective, wasn't she? Listen, Allie, you just need a change of scenery. Let's go to Seattle. You'll feel better before you know it."

"I'm not going to Seattle with you, Josh. I'm quitting. I'm moving to Charleston. I'm going to live a *normal* life."

Wiping a speck of clam sauce from his bottom lip, Josh smiled indulgently at her. "Right. Sure you are, Allie. You're moving to Charleston. For about five minutes, you think you're moving to Charleston. I'd give you five minutes—no, as much as three days—in the deep South. Three days of stultifying quiet. Three days of watching the tides ebb and flow. And three days of oppressive heat and listening for things that go bump in the night. Face it, Allie, a woman like you isn't pioneer material. You're a New Yorker."

"Pioneer? Josh, I'm moving to Charleston, not the Amazon. Besides, I think it sounds wonderful."

"Wonderful? Don't be a dope. What about the smog, the traffic, the wail of sirens, the endless lines, the crush of people on the subway? You couldn't live without all that. You thrive on it. It's in your blood. Allie, think a minute. You can't even stand visiting me on Long Island. Charleston would be like Chinese torture for you."

"That's your opinion. But I'm going all the same. Walker is expecting me."

Pausing with his mouth open to take in a large forkful of angel-hair pasta, Josh's brown eyes flickered, then narrowed. He lowered the pasta, untasted.

"Walker?"

Uneasily Allie cleared her throat. This was going to be the hardest part, she knew—the part she'd been dreading. "Yes, Walker. Walker Claremont-St. John."

A suspicious look crossed Josh's craggy face. "Claremont *Hyphen* St. John?" he asked sarcastically. "Do I know this Walker Hyphen?"

"No, I doubt it. He's a…an orthodontist. I met him at the tennis club. He comes up to the city a lot for symposiums and stuff."

"I see." Josh reached for his wineglass, his eyes never leaving her face as he considered. "So, how long have you been seeing this Walker?"

"For a month or so." Allie paused, took a deep breath and blurted, "I'm moving in with him."

"Moving in with him?" Josh looked taken back. Then he looked a little sick. "You mean like living together?"

"Well, yes. I mean, I think so."

"You *think* so?"

"Well, I haven't really known him very long. He has a house outside Charleston on the beach. It's just a trial thing, you know. Roommates at first. I mean, neither of us is getting any younger."

"Neither of you is getting any younger? Let me get this straight, Allie. You're moving to Charleston,

South Carolina, to live in a man's house, a man you've only known a month, and an orthodontist of all things. Does Tory know about this?''

"Tory? Good heavens, no. Why should he?"

Josh looked away, shaking his head as if he could scarcely grasp her logic. "Don't you think he'd have something to say about this?"

Allie gaped. "Like what? I'm thirty-two, Josh. I don't need my big brother's approval to move."

"Why didn't you tell me you were getting involved with this guy?" Josh's low voice was strangled. "We're friends. We've been friends for over ten years. How could you not let me know you were thinking about doing this?"

"I did tell you, but you were busy with that trip to Madrid." She paused. "Walker's a nice man. A real Southern gentleman, even. He's stable and reliable and," she finished weakly, "well, he has great teeth."

As soon as the words left her mouth, Allie regretted them. She'd made Walker sound so dull. But how could she tell the truth? What would Josh say if she told him that Walker was as different from him as day from night and that alone had been enough to convince her there was a chance for them?

"Terrific." Josh scowled. "What a recommendation."

"It's better than some. Look, Josh, I'm *thirty-two*. You know what that means."

He stared at her, obviously at a loss.

"My biological clock is winding down." Looking around her at the bustling restaurant, Allie felt a fluttered wave of panic and a brief ache of longing for New York—and she hadn't even left yet. "Naturally there are a lot of things I like about my life, but I'm not getting any younger, Josh. I don't want to live this way forever. Coming home to an empty apartment every night. I don't want to get old and . . . and lonely. I need a home and a family. Children. Noise and laughter and people who need me. Walker wants those things, too. Doesn't it make sense for us to give it a try?"

"No. It's the stupidest thing I've ever heard," Josh said with great feeling. "That's not the way it happens, Allie."

"Oh, yeah? How is it supposed to happen? Why don't you tell me? You've been such a paragon of success in relationships, Josh."

A confirmed bachelor, Josh hardly ever talked about the women who occasionally and briefly drifted through his life, but Allie knew enough about them to have ached with jealousy, anyway.

"Ouch. Don't get nasty." Josh looked uncomfortable. "Maybe I don't know exactly how it happens or why. But I *do* know it isn't like what you're planning. Hell, you're treating it like a trip to the market, picking out a prepackaged husband complete with ready-made braces for the kids."

"That's unfair. You can't judge my decision that quickly. Why, you don't even know Walker. If you met him, I bet you'd like him."

"I doubt it." Josh looked away, frowning. Unexpectedly a murderous expression came over his face. "Have you been sleeping with this Walker guy?"

"Josh!" Allie cried, then made a face as the group at the table beside theirs turned to stare. "I don't think that's any of your business."

"Hell, I know it's not. But I want to know, anyway."

She had a good mind to dump his plate of pasta over his head. "No," she fumed. "There. Are you satisfied? I haven't. Not yet."

The lines of Josh's face softened, and his jaw unclenched. "So, what's he like, this Walker?"

"Would you quit calling him 'this Walker,' as though he's another species or something? Really, I thought you'd be pleased. I thought you'd be happy for me."

"I'm thrilled. What's he like?"

Allie shrugged. "Nice. Okay, I guess. He's tall. Blond. He beats me at tennis, and he owns a sailboat."

"Terrific. I suppose he belongs to the local country club down there?"

"Well, yes. I think he does."

"Wonderful." Josh picked up his fork, still wrapped in pasta, and shoved it in his mouth. "I hate that kind of guy," he muttered, his mouth full.

"You're being extremely uncharitable," Allie said sharply. "What's wrong with you?"

"Nothing's wrong with me. Move to South Carolina if you want. You're going to hate it. I know you, Allie. How will you live without Chinese take-out? Without your work? You'll go crazy."

"I'm sure they have Chinese restaurants in Charleston. And I'm not going to quit working. In fact, that's the other reason I'm doing this. It's time I finally started that novel. I've been saying for years I was going to write it. Well, the time is now. After all, I'm not—"

"—getting any younger," Josh finished for her, scowling. "Yeah, yeah. You keep saying that."

"Well, it's true."

"Crap is what it is! You make it sound like you've got one foot in the grave. Thirty-two is not over the hill, Allie."

"I know that. But if I don't start doing some of the things I've promised myself to do, like starting a family, it *will* be too late. Why, just last week my gynecologist told me—"

With a pained look, Josh raised a hand to silence her. "No. No, that's all right. Don't start on that gynecologist stuff. I don't want to know about it."

Allie sniffed in disgust. "That is such a . . . a chauvinistic attitude."

"It's not," Josh protested. "I just don't want the mystique about women to be ruined with clinical details. Besides, it's too private."

Sighing, Allie rolled her eyes heavenward. "I was only going to tell you the risks of having a baby after thirty-five—"

Again Josh cut her off. "And what about Lena LaLorne?"

Allie blinked, momentarily confused. "What about her?"

"You're going to just walk away from a story like this? You, Allie? This is going to be the best book yet. You want Nancy to publish it?"

Once more Allie felt a pang, almost of regret, as she suddenly imagined Nancy and Josh working together. If Josh really had a story, it would be Nancy who experienced all the excitement and the success this time. She would only read about it in the book section of the Sunday papers.

"Lena LaLorne's supposed to be dead," Josh went on. "After forty years, I think I've found her. After *forty years,* Allie. We might even learn what happened to her lover, Sid Calentro."

For a moment Allie let herself consider what that could mean. If Josh had really found Lena LaLorne and if the woman was willing to talk, a forty-year-old mystery that had stumped police, tantalized the media and enthralled the public would be solved. Just learning what had really happened to the famous couple after all these years would be reward enough.

"This could be the biggest thing since the Kennedy conspiracy," Josh added. "Think about it, Allie. They'll have to rewrite the history books. And you're going to let Dorgen the Dragon publish this book?"

A look Josh recognized came over Allie's face. Her lips tightened ever so slightly, and a tiny furrow appeared between her eyebrows as the possibilities occurred to her. Unconsciously, she pulled at a wispy strand of dark auburn hair that had escaped the sleek coil at the back of her head and curled at her chin. She'd had that look when he'd first told her about the Sharpe kidnapping story and the Trimaldi family story. The look gave him renewed hope.

Reluctantly Allie asked, "How can you be so sure she's still alive?"

"Because Walt Quinn—remember he did some work for us on the book about the Dawson triple murders?—he knows the guy who was Albert Freuboldt's lawyer. Used to work in the same firm as him?"

"Albert Freuboldt?"

"Lena LaLorne's agent. She and Freuboldt were as thick as thieves," he said. "When Albert kicked off, his lawyer found some pretty interesting things in old Al's personal papers. He mentioned it to Walt, and

Walt mentioned it to me. Seems dear old Albert might have been keeping in contact with Lena all these years."

"Seems?"

"Well, Walt's friend wasn't sure. But that's the impression he got. Besides, I've been doing a little discreet checking on my own. There's a possibility—"

"Discreet checking?" Allie narrowed her eyes. "The last time you were discreet your source blabbed everything and they burglarized my apartment looking for your notes, if you remember."

"I said I was sorry, didn't I? Don't worry, I was careful who I talked to this time. Believe me, if there's something to this story, we'll keep the whole thing under wraps. Very hush-hush. There are a lot of people who'd like to get their hands on Lena La-Lorne...."

Josh paused when he saw Allie wasn't listening to him anymore. Her bright, unusually luminous green eyes were narrowed, and he knew she was already turning over in her mind the significance of publishing such a story. It would solidify both their reputations for life, and she had to know it.

"Can you get hold of those letters?"

Josh shook his head. "Impossible. They're private. But I did find out from Walt where they were sent from. In fact, I've got an address. Which is why I want you to come with me to Seattle. If Lena La-Lorne is at this address, she might talk to another woman. I've been known to scare people off."

Josh smiled his most winning smile. She was getting hooked, he could tell, and suddenly it seemed very important that Allie be interested in his LaLorne story. They'd worked so well together for so long he couldn't imagine sitting across a table like this with anyone but her.

Besides, he told himself, he was doing it for her own good. Some slick, smooth-talking, country-club orthodontist would never be able to keep a passionate, vital woman like Allie happy. The dull and proper life-style in the South would drain away everything that was captivating and dynamic about her. She would end up behind the wheel of a station wagon, driving snotty-nosed, blond-haired kids with perfect teeth and Southern drawls to Cub Scouts and ballet lessons. He'd seen it happen before.

No, if nothing else, he owed it to his best friend to keep his little sister from a fate like that. If Josh himself had a sister, he'd expect the same from Tory.

"It sounds...possible. You might really have something, Josh," Allie said slowly, then frowned. "Wait a minute. Seattle? I can't go with you."

"Allie—"

"I have to be in Charleston at the end of the month. Walker's planning a sort of welcoming party that I *have* to be there for. No, I'm handing in my resignation today, and that means no Seattle. How would it look if I spent my last two weeks at Grauber traipsing around the other side of the country? If you really need someone, I'll talk to Nancy."

"Nancy? Don't make me laugh. Nancy Dorgen would be about as much help to me as a water buffalo at a beach party. She wouldn't inspire confidence, let alone *confidences*, in a kid. You've got to go with me, Allie. I need you."

"I'm sorry, Josh. I wish I could. But I'm quitting. I'm not going to be working at Grauber any longer. I'm moving to Charleston, and you're going to have to get used to the idea sooner or later. You might as well start developing a relationship with a new editor now."

It wasn't working, after all, Josh thought in some amazement. He wasn't convincing her. She was serious about this moving business. Or was it Walker she was serious about?

"Listen, I'm not arguing with you about that. You say you're moving to South Carolina. Well, all right. *I'm* certainly not trying to stop you. I think it's—" Josh thought he might choke on the word "—wonderful. But you're still my editor, right? For two more weeks. Give me this, Allie, just this one last time. You may be leaving, but I'm not going anywhere. I've got to come up with this book, and it's got to be damned good. We both know that. Don't walk out on me yet. Two weeks, Allie. For old time's sake, that's all I ask. In two weeks, you can move to Charleston or anyplace else that strikes your fancy. But I *need* you to go to Seattle with me."

"I can't, Josh."

"Allie—"

She folded her hands on the table and leaned toward him. "You think I don't know what you're doing, but you're wrong. *I* also know *you*, Joshua Mercer. You think that if you get me to agree to go to Seattle with you, I'll forget all about Walker and Charleston. Well, it won't work, Josh. I'm leaving. This time I'm really leaving, and you're just going to have to accept it."

"You're my editor, Allie. I can't work with anyone else."

"That's ridiculous. Authors change editors all the time. It's just *our* relationship that's been—" she faltered, as though uncertain "—so unusual."

Something about the hitch in her voice and the way she turned her eyes away struck a chord in Josh—a chord of memory. For just a moment he let himself see her as she'd been on that terrible morning in Cleveland four years before.

They'd drunk too much malt whiskey that night, after he'd bailed her out of jail for "wandering" into the judge's chambers when no one was looking. They'd sprawled across his motel-room bed, passing the bottle back and forth between them and pawing through memories that stretched back to his freshman year in college.

Somehow they'd said things that night they'd never said before—hell, things he'd never even realized he felt. Without ever really knowing how it happened, she'd suddenly been naked and luscious in his bed, and he'd finally learned the meaning of *consumed*. That night there hadn't been anything or anyone in the world but Allie. What he'd felt had been devastating, bone deep, and more than a little frightening. Later he'd attributed all of it to the whiskey.

It had taken them five embarrassed days to conclude their business in Cleveland and another two awkward years before their relationship felt comfortable again. He'd hated himself for what he'd done. Getting his best friend's sister drunk and seducing her had left him with a bitter taste of self-loathing for a long, long time.

After that first morning they'd never talked about it again. He'd sworn he'd never repeat the mistake, and no matter how difficult it was at times, he'd kept his promise. Yet he'd never been able to completely forget how painfully, exquisitely right she'd felt.

He'd also never found the courage to confess what he'd done to Tory. Maybe if he had, maybe if he'd let Tory punch the hell out of him once, he'd have been able to handle it better.

Maybe he'd have been able to forget.

"I already bought the airline tickets, anyway," Josh lied. "So it's too late."

"It's never too late," Allie said cryptically, pushing back her chair. "I'm just learning that. You'll have to go to Seattle on your own, Josh. I'm going back to the office now."

With a strange sense of loss, Josh also pushed back his chair and stood. Towering over the other diners beside them, he hunched his shoulders uncomfortably. He hated restaurants like this with their small tables and dainty, prim chairs. They made him feel big and awkward, like a giant in Munchkinland. Allie always picked restaurants like this, never the ones with deep solid booths that a man could lean back in without fearing he'd knock something over.

"Listen, Allie, I'll cancel those plane reservations tonight. Seattle can wait a day or two. Let's go to dinner. Talk about this."

With a sigh she slipped her purse over her shoulder. "I can't, Josh. Walker's going back to Charleston tonight. You and I'll get together again before I move."

As he followed her through the restaurant, Josh's sense of losing control grew stronger and more bewildering.

"Tonight? Well, hey, that's great. Let me take the two of you to dinner. I'd love to meet this guy." God,

Josh thought, was that a pile of manure. "Let's meet at Sardi's. What do you think? About eight?"

"I don't know." She paused near the front bar as a group of dark-suited executive types mingled, blocking the entrance. "Maybe that's not such a good idea."

"Not a good idea? What's wrong? Don't you want me to meet him?"

"Let's just say the thought doesn't thrill me."

Josh followed close behind her as she headed toward the door. "Why? Is there something wrong with him you haven't told me about?"

That stopped her. With cool green eyes, Allie scowled at him.

"No. There's nothing wrong with Walker. It's you I'm worried about. I still haven't forgiven you for what you did to that trumpet player I went out with a few times. I don't think I want a repeat of that night."

"I was reminiscing. That's all. I thought he'd get a kick out of it."

"You weren't reminiscing, Josh. You made it all up. I was never hospitalized for violent behavior. Oh, yes, he told me about that one, too. And you pretended Tory worked for the Mafia."

"No, I didn't. I might have mentioned he was a slugger for some hotshot in Seattle."

"You said he liked to wreak havoc with a baseball bat, but you never said at the ballpark."

Josh gave her a wide-eyed look of innocence. "Can I help it if the guy didn't know the Mariners' lineup? What kind of guy doesn't know baseball? Where'd he come from? Under a rock?"

Taking a step back, Allie raised her hands, palms up. "See? This is just what I'm talking about."

"Look, I'm sorry about that. But the guy was a jerk, which you admitted later, if you remember. Tonight I promise to behave. I swear, Allie. Let me take you and Walker to dinner. It'll be, uh, great fun."

Shaking her head, she glanced heavenward. "Fun? For who?" she muttered. "Oh, all right. But you'd better be nice."

"I'll be the model of decorum. I'll even bring my own tie."

With a hand on her hip, Allie studied him, then offered a small, sad smile. "I'm going to miss you, Joshua Mercer. I'm really, really going to miss you."

When she put her arm around him, Josh thought the bottom of his stomach might fall out. For one tumultuous moment everything in the world dimmed and faded, and there was only Allie's closeness, the light touch of her small hand on his shoulder blade, the faint fragrant scent of her hair as she leaned her cheek against his breastbone, and the warmth of her slender body pressed to his.

She felt so small and fragile to him—an airy, delicate Irish pixie with her hair of dark burnished red like a low smoldering fire and her sea-green eyes as clear as the water in a still pond.

Fire and water. And about as elusive and unobtainable.

The next moment she was stepping back and away from him, her eyes suspiciously shiny and her face a little pale so that the faint sprinkle of freckles across her nose were more noticeable.

"Eight o'clock. Sardi's," was all she said.

Before Josh could reply, she was gone.

IN ONE OF New Jersey's most desirable secluded bedroom communities, carefully protected from the outside world by money and influence, two men sat under
a striped umbrella on the flagstone patio behind an
ivy-covered Colonial house. Despite its sheer size and
immaculate lawns, the house had a quaint, lived-in
homeyness, with its bright curtains and potted gera-
niums. Tricycles and plastic toy guns littered the flagstones, and the backyard was filled with the laughter
and happy cries of children.

Despite the tranquil setting, Victor Lazano anxiously rubbed a hand over his balding scalp and studied the man in the lawn chair beside him. He wished
he hadn't eaten the last of his antacids in the car on the
drive down. Already he could feel the burning rise in
his throat. As the silence stretched on, his stomach
lurched queasily.

The man beside him was in his late forties and
showing it. Thick prematurely gray hair was combed
back from a high forehead, accentuating his nose,
which looked like the beak of a hawk, and dark purple circles shadowed his eyes. Dressed incongruously
in green and orange plaid shorts and black silk socks
with garters, he continued to watch the children's an-
tics in complete silence, his face impassive as stone.

It wasn't only the lack of expression that made Joey
Riazzi his father's son, Victor thought. The two men
hadn't looked much like father and son, but just like
Frank Riazzi, Joey knew how to use silence to intimi-
date a man. Over the years Victor had seen them both
use that silent unblinking stare to reduce lesser men to
quivering idiots. He'd never been on the receiving end
of one of those silences, thank God. And although he

knew he wasn't the intended victim now, he was still
nervous enough to need to empty his bladder.

"Can we find out ourselves?" Joey finally spoke,
his voice unexpectedly high-pitched and sweetly mu-
sical, like a choirboy's.

Victor swallowed with difficulty. "I don't know,
Joey. It'd be tough, but—"

Joey barely shifted in his chair, but Victor knew
enough to shut up immediately. Furtively he rubbed
his sweaty palms on his pant legs. He'd known when
he drove down from Long Island that Joey wasn't going to like the news much. Hell, there were going to be
a lot of nervous people around once this got out, but
none of them was going to be as mad as Joey. None
was going to feel the responsibility Joey felt. In that
way, Victor acknowledged, they'd been lucky Joey'd
taken over after the old man passed away. Joey didn't
take his duties lightly.

"There's an easier way," Joey finally continued.
His high voice was soft, yet somehow that made it
even more threatening. "Less risky."

Joey turned in his chair then and finally looked at
Victor. Black eyes—still and cold as an insect's and as
devoid of emotion as his face—fixed on Victor, pin-
ning him to his chair.

"Get Willis and Scarpini to help you. I want this
guy followed. Everywhere. I want to know every place
he goes." Joey smiled, but it wasn't pleasant. "If the
tip-off we got from the lawyer was right, he knows
where Lena LaLorne is. If she and that bastard Calentro are still alive, he'll lead us to them."

Victor licked his dry lips and nodded. "Gotcha.
Willis and Scarpini are good, Joey. And I already been

by this guy's place. In the middle of nowhere on Long Island. We can probably be out there in a few hours."

Settling back in his chair, Joey closed his eyes. "If Calentro's alive, we're going to get to him first." He sighed, the sound regretful and malevolent at the same time. "He betrayed my father, Victor. Betrayal carries a heavy price."

Victor nodded in silent agreement. That betrayal should be punished—and punished brutally—was more than a rule. It was the most important law in a code of unwritten laws, the one tenet that held together everything men like Joey Riazzi represented. Without it, vast empires would crumble. Whole international organizations would cease to function. Calentro had betrayed the Riazzi family, and even forty years later, he would be made to pay. Victor didn't feel sorry for the guy. He'd broken the most important law of the underworld.

"You make some calls. Send Willis and Scarpini out there by themselves tonight," Joey said, reaching for the lemonade pitcher on the table beside him. "Then you come back and play with the kids. Joey Junior's been asking about his uncle Victor."

Victor rose obediently.

"You'll stay for dinner," Joey continued, his voice almost friendly now that business was momentarily over. "Evie's making *frutti di mare*. I could smell it all over the house. You love that stuff."

"Sure, Joey. Sure. Thanks."

With a flick of his wrist, Joey waved off Victor's thanks and took a long sip of lemonade, the signal that Victor was free to make his calls now.

As Victor turned toward the house, he heaved a sigh of relief. It wasn't as bad as he'd imagined, and there'd be no more business talk for the rest of the day. He'd been invited to dinner. He was an old family friend. What did he always get so damned nervous about? He was an old family friend.

Yet still, as he made his heavy lumbering way across the flagstones, he felt a shiver down his spine and an almost overwhelming urge to avoid turning his back on the man under the umbrella.

CHAPTER TWO

"THIS IS YOUR emergency? This is what you had me pulled out of practice for?" Tory Shannon sounded incredulous.

"I don't think you understand," Josh said darkly into the phone. Restlessly he got up from behind the desk and started to pace the thick carpet of his study, only stopping when he saw the phone inching precariously close to the edge of the desk. "She's serious this time. She really means it, Tory."

"I can't believe you, Mercer. You've finally gone off the deep end. Hell, I thought something terrible had happened to one of you, you damned—" In the background, low male laughter broke out, drowning his words. "Call me tonight at home, huh? I gotta get back to practice. We've got a three-day home stand starting tomorrow."

"Tory," Josh said impatiently, throwing himself into the leather chair and staring across his cluttered desk to the view of his sprawling backyard, ankle-high with unmown grass. "Aren't you listening to me, buddy? Allie's quitting. Chucking it. She's moving to Charleston, South Carolina, for God's sake, with an orthodontist. An orthodontist, Tory!"

"Well, so what? What do you want me to say? That's great. She finally hit a homer and I'm happy for her. I hope he's a nice guy. Mom'll be thrilled."

"A nice guy? He belongs to the country club, the tennis club and probably even the damn yacht club. I'll bet he doesn't know a ball stat from a schedule. This is your sister we're talking about. You want her involved with some flashy, sweet-talking, Southern hick who fixes teeth for a living?"

The phone was silent for a long moment. "What's gotten into you, Josh? If that's what Allie wants, why not? Besides, I think you're jumping the gun on this one. Allie's been threatening to quit that company for years. She'll never do it."

"She's done it." Josh pushed a stack of newspapers aside and propped his elbows on the desk, lowering his head to clutch his forehead with one hand. "I called her boss."

"You *what?*"

"All right, all right. I realize it was a lousy thing to do, but I had to know for sure. This is going to affect my life, too, you know. I can't work with anyone else."

"You mean no one else will work with *you.*" Tory was silent again, and Josh could hear the hollow ring of lockers slamming and players laughing in the background. "I have to admit I'm kind of surprised. I mean, she didn't say anything about this to either of us. But hell, Josh, she's a grown woman. If she loves this guy—"

"But that's just it," Josh interrupted, sitting up straighter. "She's not in love with him."

"How do you know?"

"I know. Take my word for it. When Allie falls in love, there won't be any question about it. All she could think of to impress me with was that he had great teeth." Reaching absently for his coffee, Josh went to take a sip, then looked into the mug and wrinkled his nose in disgust. "She barely knows him."

"That's kind of hard to believe."

"I'll say." Dropping the offending mug into an open drawer, Josh slammed it shut with a bang. "This guy could be a psychopath for all we know. Happens all the time. Maybe he makes a hobby out of luring unsuspecting women to that house of his, and no one ever sees them again until one day the little old lady next door reports a foul stench in the backyard."

Tory laughed, but there was a nervous edge to his voice. "Sounds like one of your books. Allie wouldn't do something stupid like that." Despite his words, he didn't sound completely confident. "Allie's no rookie. She's sharp, Josh. She's not going to go off with some guy she doesn't know. She might be impulsive, but not about something like this. She's got a good head on her shoulders. Runs in the family."

"Oh, yeah? Well, I'm not so sure about her lately. She's been on this kick about her hormones or her clock running down or something. Talking about kids and the fulfillment of motherhood and the American dream. Every since she got passed over for that promotion she hasn't been herself. I'm telling you, some men can spot that sort of thing a mile away. You know what I'm talking about," Josh said ominously. "They take advantage of a woman's vulnerability."

Josh could tell Tory was thinking about that, and he waited, letting the implication sink in. Around him the old rambling Tudor cottage was quiet and hushed. He'd bought the house when his first book was still on the bestseller list after four weeks. At the time the privacy, the isolation and the vast empty vistas of grassy marsh and sea had appealed to him. But lately the quiet had been more distracting than restive. In fact, it had started to annoy him.

"Well, even if that was true, what can anyone do about it? Allie's a free agent," Tory finally said. "She makes her own choices, and she's sure not going to appreciate anyone sticking their nose in her business."

"Naturally I would never think of interfering." More confident now, Josh leaned back in the chair and put his feet on the edge of the desk. "But as her brother and her friend, you and I have an obligation to her. We have to give her an opportunity to make sure she knows what she's doing. If she isn't herself right now, she could be making a terrible mistake. Then how would we feel? Like dogs, right?"

Tory's voice was hesitant. "Yeah. I guess."

"So look. This is what I was thinking. I've got a possibility for a great story in Seattle. I've been trying to convince Allie to come along, but she's digging in her heels. It'd be a terrific chance for her to think things over a little more, but she won't go for it. So I thought we could try another tactic. Since you're right there in Seattle, you could call her. Make up some story about—"

"Oh, no. Not that. I'm not doing any more stuff like that. Some of your past great ideas have already gotten me in enough hot water with Val."

"This isn't like that, Tory. Nothing like it at all. You just have to call Allie. Tell her you and Val are having some trouble or something and you've got to see her. You know. When she gets there, everything between you and Val has already been fixed up. Val won't have to know a thing. Allie, either. All I want you to do is get her to Seattle. I'll take it from there."

It'd be like killing two birds with one stone, Josh congratulated himself. He'd get Allie's help on the LaLorne story *and* keep her away from that Walker guy long enough for her to come to her senses. With a little time, her plans to move would disappear, just like they always did. He was a genius.

"No way. Forget it, Josh."

Frowning, Josh sat up. He hadn't been prepared for resistance from this quarter. It was time, he decided, to pull out the big guns.

"You remember that time in our sophomore year when you agreed to get in the ring with Raul de-Cortica? Who took your place so you wouldn't bust up your hands and get cut from the team?"

"I already paid you back for that one," Tory insisted. "It's not my fault that woman found out you stood her up for a hockey game."

"It was basketball. The Knicks. Two tickets on the floor. And you set me up. She knew I didn't have an aunt in town, dying or otherwise."

"Forget it, Josh. Not a chance."

"Did I say forget it when you were hung over and missed the team flight to Milwaukee?"

Silence descended over the line.

"Allie could be making the biggest mistake of her life," Josh continued for added impact. "We'd hate ourselves if we just sat back and let her do that."

At last he heard Tory sigh. "You really think this guy might be dangerous or something?"

Josh gave a relieved smile and leaned back once more. "Definitely. I wasn't an investigative reporter all those years for nothing. I've got good instincts about these things, you know. That's how I make my living."

"All right, I'll do it. But only because you've got me worried about this guy Allie's been seeing. I'm telling you, though, this is absolutely the last time, Josh. After this, no more of your harebrained schemes. Not one of them has ever worked out, and you know it. If Val or Allie ever found out—"

"They're not going to. And, anyway, our intentions are good, aren't they? We're just trying to do what's best for Allie. Give her a little more time to think things over. Make sure she's making the right decision. That's all."

"That's all, huh?" From the sound of Tory's voice, Josh could tell his old friend was smiling, despite his gruff tone. "I wasn't born yesterday, buddy. Nothing's ever that simple with you, Josh. Nothing. I'm telling you, though, if Allie ever finds out you're pulling her strings, you're in for it. You'd better run for cover because I am *not* going to bat for you on this one. I'll be hiding from her myself. As far away as possible."

After hanging up, Josh sat behind his desk for a moment longer, staring across the room. On the opposite wall of his study, next to the autographed photo of Joe Namath and a print of the Dodgers' old Ebbitts Field, a row of framed dust jackets from his seven books hung on the oak paneling. Rising to his feet, Josh gave the seven reproductions of his face a pleased grin.

"Lena LaLorne," he said, crossing the study and putting a hand on the worn black leather of a punching bag that hung in the corner. "Here we come."

With a smooth practiced uppercut, Josh hit the bag with a powerful blow.

IN A LACY pale pink strapless bra and panties, her head bristling with electric curlers, Allie scurried around her tiny one-bedroom apartment, shoving shoes and empty shopping bags, tennis rackets and armfuls of discarded clothing into closets and drawers. After Tory's strange half-apologetic, half-urgent phone call, she'd sat for a long time thinking about her brother and his wife, wondering if she'd been too quick to reassure him that he could work out any problems on his own. After all, Tory and Val *never* had trouble. They were the perfect couple.

Yet Tory had called to ask her advice and help. It must be serious, she told herself. Maybe she could fly out there for the weekend. She could easily be back for work on Monday.

As Allie had reached for the phone to dial the airline, she'd glanced at her watch and realized that, if she didn't get going, she'd be late. Again. She hadn't even dressed yet, and she still had three whole rooms of disorder and mayhem to hide in fifteen minutes. She'd have to call the airline tomorrow.

Brushing her teeth with one hand now, she yanked open the refrigerator, tossed in all the empty Chinese take-out containers from the kitchen table and slammed the door. Normally she wouldn't have gone to so much bother, but Walker, she sensed, wouldn't find the chaos very appealing. She didn't want him to get the wrong idea and think she was going to trash his house the moment she moved in.

If nothing else, Allie thought, that was at least one thing she and Josh had in common. They were both slobs. She never felt compelled to clean up if Josh was coming over. He said the mess made him feel more at home.

However, she told herself once again, a penchant for clutter and a shared passion for a good story were about all they had in common. She'd finally admitted that those weren't exactly enough to base a long-term relationship on, and she'd better just get on with her life. It occurred to her that, since Josh wasn't exactly busting down her door with proposals of marriage, it wasn't really a decision she had to make. But it still made her feel a little better pretending she'd made it, anyway.

In the bedroom Allie peered under the bed looking for the second shoe of a pair of black heels that would go perfectly with her new dress. Finally spotting it on the windowsill, she tossed the remaining piles of shoes and clothes and books and papers scattered around the room into the center of the bed and pulled the down comforter over them.

All afternoon as she'd worked in her office, a nervous dread had formed and grown in her stomach. Between finally handing in her resignation to her boss, Jack Gates, and imagining all the possible disasters that could occur at dinner that night, she'd worked herself up into a state of near panic.

The hurdle of resigning was over, leaving her with a feeling not so much of relief as of emptiness. She knew she'd have to address that empty feeling sooner or later, but right now she had what seemed an even bigger hurdle to cross. Having dinner with both Josh and Walker was not an event she was looking forward to.

Josh wasn't going to give up easily. That much Allie already knew.

If she'd been a less honest woman, she might have tried to convince herself Josh wanted her to stay because he secretly cared about her. But the truth was too glaring to gloss over. Joshua Mercer needed her for his career. Not, she told herself, that he didn't care about her at all. He'd be the first to admit how close they were, what good friends they'd grown to be. But friendship wasn't all she felt for him, and she couldn't allow herself to keep hoping in vain for something that was never going to happen.

Once, four years before, she'd wondered. For one incredible, unforgettable night in Cleveland, of all places, she'd believed Josh loved her. But that belief had lasted only one night. Stunned and mortified, she'd realized the following morning that he regretted making love to her.

They'd never referred to that night again. In four years they'd never mentioned it once, and perhaps that hurt most of all. It was as though Josh had forgotten it, chased it from his mind like a bad dream.

Pulling curlers from her hair and swiping at the bathroom counter with a white tennis sock at the same time, Allie studied her face in the mirror above the sink. There were faint blue smudges under her eyes and those darned freckles were showing again. Peering closer, she wondered if they were getting darker with each passing year.

Thirty-two. How had she ever gotten to be that age? She remembered thinking as a young girl that anyone who was over thirty was ancient. Now she was probably older than half her high-school teachers had been. She didn't feel ancient. She felt the same as she had when she was sixteen. Only she wasn't sixteen anymore, and time was running out.

For ten years she'd dated carelessly, without much interest, always telling herself it didn't matter. Even in recent years, when her mother cornered her in the kitchen at Christmas and Thanksgiving and grilled her about her "prospects," she'd always answered with a small, secretive smile. She hadn't needed to worry about it because Josh was always there, like an actor waiting in the wings to rush onto the stage and sweep her away in the final act.

It had taken ten years, but she'd finally woken up and admitted that there wasn't going to be a final act. Josh wasn't going to do any sweeping, and she wasn't going to get any younger.

Wriggling and squirming into the tight, sequined black dress she'd bought especially for dinner that night, Allie pulled it up over her narrow hips, snagged her nylons with the zipper and cursed out loud.

No, she wasn't getting any younger. Maybe moving in with Walker was a crazy thing to do, but at least she had to try it. She owed it to herself. It was time for her to go out and grab all the things in life she wanted. It was time to go for the brass ring, the whole pie.

So why, Allie moaned as she scrambled through her drawer for another pair of black sheers, did she feel as if she was leaving behind everything that truly mattered?

Just as she finished tugging her dress back down over her hips, the doorbell rang. Running her fingers through her loose hair, she raced through the apartment, trying to fasten an earring and slip on her heels as she went. By the time she pulled open the door, she was dressed but breathless.

"How's my favorite future roommate?" Walker greeted her in a low, charming Southern drawl, laughing as though the greeting was the cleverest thing he'd said all day.

Allie gave him a weak smile.

"For you, Allison," he said, handing her two fire-red anthurium blossoms. "One for each month we've known each other."

"Oh, Walker. They're lovely. Thank you." Taking the large hothouse flowers, Allie peered warily at them. Sure enough, she felt the familiar tickle in the back of her throat.

"They reminded me of you," Walker added. "Fiery and exotic. You look fantastic tonight, Allison."

Backing up, Allie gave Walker space to pass into the living room, closing the door behind him as the tickle rose in her throat. As usual, Walker was impeccably dressed. In a dark blue, well-cut jacket and snow-white shirt, and with his tanned, square-jawed face and blond hair—thick and just ruffled enough to look sporty—he might have stepped off the pages of *GQ*.

Allie fervently hoped Josh wore something more appropriate tonight than his usual blue jeans and remembered to comb his hair.

"I'll just put these in some water," Allie said around the threatening tickle that was growing more insistent in her throat. As inconspicuously as possible, she held the flowers at arm's length.

The sneeze caught up to her before she made the kitchen. At the fifth sneeze, Walker bent to peer at her.

"Are you all right?"

Nodding, Allie gave him a woeful look. "Fine. Just fine."

"You're allergic to anthurium?"

"Oh, no. Well, maybe a little. But they're lovely. Really. It's so... *Ha-choo!* So thoughtful of you."

With a concerned expression, Walker took the flowers. "I'll put them in something for you. Can you keep them in the apartment?"

"Of course," Allie called as he disappeared into the kitchen. She wondered if she'd live through the night if she didn't throw them out until morning. "It's so nice of you."

Grimacing at the primly polite sound of her voice, Allie watched him walk through the kitchen door. Oh, what was wrong with her? Why couldn't she relax around Walker? Look at him, she told herself sternly. He's gorgeous. He's stable. He's polite. He's respectable. He liked her. He had the straightest, whitest teeth of any man she'd ever dated.

Somehow, Allie suspected, that was part of the problem. If only he had an overbite or a gap in his front teeth. If only something was wrong with him, she could stop fluttering and cooing around him like a jittery pigeon.

"There you are," he said, holding up the crystal vase for her to see. "I'll put them over here on the table. Are you ready?"

"Um, yes. All ready." Allie hoped her smile didn't look as panicked and stiff as it felt.

"So, Allison, who is this we're meeting tonight? One of your clients?"

"Authors. One of my authors. But he's also an old family friend."

"Hmm. Looking me over, is he?"

With a sudden rush of terror, Allie swallowed hard and raised her shoulders in a shrug. *Good grief,* she nearly moaned aloud. *If you only knew.*

WHEN ALLIE and Walker reached Sardi's and the maître d' led them through the dining room, Allie thought at first that he was taking them to the wrong table. Rising to his feet was a man in a sleek Armani suit of black silk. His dark longish hair was slicked back so that it curled fashionably over his collar.

Even with his hard rugged face, Josh looked every inch the elegant and sophisticated, although slightly battle-scarred, host. Like a darkly aristocratic lord of the manor who'd perhaps been in one too many jousts, Josh stood patiently, waiting to entertain the commoners.

At the table Allie stood with her hand on the back of a chair and gaped. "Josh?"

He was staring at her with a similar startled look, as though he vaguely recognized her but couldn't quite place her. He started to look away, then gave her a second glance, longer this time, and she saw one dark eyebrow lift in surprise.

"Allie," Josh finally said. "You're on time."

Still at a momentary loss for words, Allie indicated Walker with a raised hand.

"And you must be Walker," Josh drawled benevolently. "Nice to meet you."

If she wasn't imagining things, Allie thought, she'd almost swear Josh sounded like an indulgent patriarchal uncle. She stared at him, mystified and not a little alarmed.

Taking Josh's hand, Walker smiled his straight and perfect smile. "It's nice to meet you, too, Mr. Mercer. I appreciate your asking us to dinner."

"My pleasure, but call me Josh." His tone was cordial, but when he turned back to Allie, a hint of sardonic, questioning laughter lit his eyes, setting off warning bells in her.

Whatever Josh was up to, Allie thought, she had a feeling she wasn't going to like it.

"Please," Josh said graciously, waving a hand toward the table behind them. "Sit down."

Before Walker could make a move, Josh already had a hold on her elbow and was pulling a chair out for her. Surprised at his unusual display of manners, Allie lowered herself woodenly into the chair, sneaking quick peeks at Josh as he settled in his own seat. Across from them, Walker was beaming in friendly ignorance.

When they'd ordered cocktails, Josh leaned back and eyed Walker perhaps a moment longer than was necessary. "So, Walker, Allie tells me you're a dentist."

"An orthodontist actually. Lots of people confuse the two."

"And you practice in South Carolina?"

Walker nodded. "Yes. I'm a partner in a large medical clinic just outside Charleston. Part owner, really."

Both Josh's brows were raised now, and he avoided Allie's eyes. "Must be...exciting work," he said, his voice thick with hidden laughter.

Under the table Allie gave his shin a firm kick.

Josh didn't even wince. "So how did you wind up wanting to be a dentist?"

Innocently, Walker leaned forward, his blue eyes enthusiastic. "I'm really more interested in maxillo-facial surgery. It's a fascinating field. You'd be amazed at some of the things we can do now."

Allie started to speak, but before she could get a word out, Josh continued his interrogation with, "Maxillofacial surgery? You mean like surgery for guys who get their faces blown off during hunting season?"

"Josh!" Allie complained. "Please. Not before dinner."

Walker smiled. "Allison can be a little squeamish sometimes."

Turning, Josh grinned in amusement and mouthed, "Allison?" Aloud he scoffed, "Allie? Squeamish? This woman can gut a fish faster than most men I know. And if you ever find one of those huge fat spiders in your bathroom, this is the woman to call. It's a tension release for her to—"

"Please, gentlemen," Allie said sweetly. "Let's talk about something a little more appetizing."

From across the table, Walker gave Josh an aren't-women-cute smile, and Josh returned it with a forced smile of barely concealed contempt. Allie thought she heard the air above the table begin to crackle.

"Allison tells me you're quite a successful writer," Walker said, accepting a tonic water with lime from the waiter. "I thought your name sounded familiar, although I have to admit I haven't read any of your books."

"I'm sure Allie would be glad to give you a copy or two."

Walker's smile turned rueful. "I wish it was that simple. In my line of work, I don't get much time to read anything but professional journals."

"Oh, so you don't read much? That's too bad. Isn't that too bad, Allie?" Josh's face was poker straight.

She could have killed him right there.

"A lot of professional people don't have time to read a great deal." Allie smiled kindly across the table at Walker. "In the publishing business, we tend to think the whole world revolves around books." Shooting a withering glare at Josh, she added, "Particularly one's own books."

"Well, I might not be up on all that, but I think what you and Allison do is wonderful. I'm lucky, I'll tell you. It's unusual to find a woman as beautiful as Allison who is also successful and brilliant." Walker gave her an adoring look. "But I suppose, knowing Allison as long as you have, you already know that."

"Oh, yes." Josh agreed, his tone mocking. "It's something I think about all the time." Quickly he buried his nose in his whiskey glass.

"I still can't believe my good luck." Walker went on. "It was fate, that's what my sister would say. Allison and I were fated to collide on that tennis court."

With a loud sputter, Josh choked violently into his glass.

"Are you all right?" Walker asked, half rising. "Here, take a few swallows of water."

Lowering the whiskey glass to the table, Josh shook his head. "Thanks. I'm fine now. Something just went down the wrong way, that's all."

Allie studiously refused to catch Josh's eye. "Don't mind Josh," she told Walker in a honeyed tone. "Usually it's his words he chokes on, not his whiskey."

With a burst of laughter, Walker sat down again, chuckling. "That's good, Allison." He turned to Josh. "She's always saying clever things like that. Keeps me in stitches."

"Yes, she's a real hoot, our Allie."

"They're going to love you at the club, Allison," Walker continued. "You'll make friends straight away, I just know it."

Before Allie could comment, Josh asked, "What club is that?"

"The country club. I know that you, being an old family friend and all, must be a little worried about Allison moving to a city where she doesn't know anyone. But I can assure you, while it might not be New York City, we have our share of sophistication in Charleston. She'll have plenty to keep her occupied, and there's an amusing little group at the club she'll fit right in with."

"How nice," Josh said, turning to her. "A clique, Allie. You'll love it."

Ignoring him, Allie smiled at Walker. "I'm sure it'll be wonderful. I'm looking forward to a few months of complete relaxation before I start my novel."

"And of course," Walker added, "there's always the yacht club."

Abruptly, Josh turned his face away into his hand, and Allie gave him a sharp look.

"I've got a thirty-two-foot yacht I'm just dying to teach Allison to sail."

"Sailing?" Josh asked, straight-faced again. "Allie? I don't know about that. She's okay with a fishing pole off a wharf, but she gets seasick pretty easily."

"I do not," Allie retorted.

"Yes, you do. Spent a whole night barfing on my shoes in the Keys a few years ago."

"I didn't!" Indignant, Allie glowered at him.

"Yes, you did. Ask Tory."

"That was because the lobsters we ate weren't fresh."

Josh smiled knowingly at Walker and shrugged. "Just bring plenty of Dramamine and wet towels."

Across the table Walker was looking from one to the other of them, a faintly puzzled, worried expression on his face, as though he'd just that moment noticed the friction at the table.

"I guess you two have done a lot of things together," he said slowly. "Being friends all these years."

"Inseparable," Josh said.

"Not really," Allie said at the same time.

Walker looked even more confused. "Allison mentioned you two have worked on several of your books together."

"All of them," Josh replied gruffly. "She's traveled with me all over the country, nursed me back to health a few times, practically wrote the books herself—"

"We really didn't work that closely," Allie broke in. "Josh is just being, er, modest."

Walker smiled at her with admiration. "Now, I don't believe it's Josh who's being shy, Allison. I had no idea you were so involved. I admire that sort of—"

From under the table came a faint beep, followed by several more, and Walker calmly paused and reached into his pocket. Josh frowned.

Taking out a small black pager, Walker pushed his chair back. "Sorry. If you'll excuse me, I need to make a call. This happens all the time. One of the hazards of the profession."

"By all means," Josh said too quickly. "Don't mind us."

Allie thought Josh couldn't have been ruder if he'd said, "Go, and don't come back."

Stopping by Allie's chair, Walker put a hand on her shoulder. "Would you mind ordering for me, Allison? I don't know how long this will take."

As soon as he headed across the dining room, Allie whirled on Josh. "What in the world do you think you're doing? You're behaving in the most obnoxious—"

"That dress you're wearing is a little much—or should I say, none quite enough—for Sardi's, isn't it?"

Taken back, Allie paused uncertainly. "It is?"

"It's too low. And with your shoulders bare like that, you'll probably catch cold."

"But you always said I looked good in strapless dresses."

Gripping his glass tightly, Josh glared at his whiskey before taking a long swallow. "I didn't mean *that* strapless."

Her eyes narrowed, Allie watched him. "Oh, no, you don't, Joshua Mercer. You're trying to change the subject. I want to know why you're acting like this. You promised you wouldn't."

"He's young," Josh commented calmly, as though she hadn't said a word. "You didn't tell me he was so young."

"He's twenty-nine," she protested. "That's not so young."

"He's nearly ten years younger than me."

"Well, then, it's a good thing *you* aren't the one moving in with him, isn't it?"

"Allie," Josh said in a tone that pleaded for reason and logic. "You can't be serious about moving to

Charleston with this guy. He looks like an undergraduate recruitment poster for Yale."

"*I* think he's handsome, and so do a lot of other women."

"We're not talking about other women. We're talking about you. Allie, he doesn't read. He probably spends every weekend on the golf course. He thinks Charleston is *sophisticated*, for God's sake." Finishing the remainder of his whiskey in one quick slug, Josh glowered. "Besides, he laughs funny. Huh-huh-huh," he mimicked, sounding like a congested mule.

"He does not. You're just jealous. Just because you choose to live in perpetual bachelorhood, you want all your friends to stay single, too. It's selfish, Josh. It's selfish of you not to want me to find someone. You acted the same way when Tory married Val."

"I didn't!" Josh nearly shouted. Lowering his voice, he added, "That was different. That wasn't the same thing at all."

"Oh, yeah? How is it so different?"

Josh glowered at her wordlessly, breathing hard. Closing his eyes, he looked away. "I don't know. It just is. Val suits Tory."

"You didn't think so at the time."

"Well, anyway, it's different. This is you, not Tory. You can't do this, Allie. I won't let you."

Astonished, Allie stared openmouthed at him. "You won't let me? Just what do you think you can do to stop me? I'm moving to Charleston, Josh. I'm moving in with Walker, and there's nothing you can do to stop me."

"Oh, yeah?"

"This is stupid," Allie said, snatching up her menu. Flipping it open, she swiveled in her seat so the menu was between them like a barrier. "I don't want to talk to you anymore," she said from behind it. "I'm too angry with you."

For several minutes they were silent, pretending to study their menus with great concentration. Finally Josh lowered his and asked, obviously trying for a reconciliation, "So how does he like the hovel?"

For another moment Allie stared at her menu, then sighed. "All right, I guess. I cleaned it up, though."

"You did? You never did that for me."

"That's because you live in a worse mess than I do."

Josh frowned. "No, I don't. I hired that housekeeping service, remember? Twice a week a team of six comes in and shovels me out."

Despite herself, Allie felt her lips twitch in a smile. "It takes six?"

"Those are the good weeks."

Just then their waiter glided noiselessly up, and out of habit Josh ordered for all of them, since Allie could never decide. As usual, though, he let her pick the wine.

"You know," Allie was saying as the waiter disappeared. "I got a strange call from Tory tonight. Have you heard from him lately?"

Wrapping his fingers around his second glass of whiskey, Josh raised his brows with a look of complete innocence. "Tory? No. Haven't talked to him in a week or so. Why?"

"Well, he was pretty vague, but the gist of his message was that he thinks something's wrong between him and Val. He didn't go into any detail, but it must be fairly serious for him to call me about it, don't you think?''

Blank-faced, Josh shrugged and took a long drink. "I don't know. What do you think?''

"Tory and I have always been close, but he's never talked about his relationship with Val to me before. Not like that. The way he was going on, I didn't even get a chance to tell him about Walker. The truth is, I'm worried, Josh. I can't see Tory asking me to come to Seattle over just a little tiff or something.''

"He asked you to go out there?''

Allie nodded, taking a sip of her gin and tonic. "Yes, he did. That makes it seem, well, sort of more serious, doesn't it?''

"Yeah," Josh said, looking away. "That doesn't sound good at all. Could be there's something pretty major going on.''

"But what? Tory and Val have always been so great together.'' Allie paused and glanced up as Walker rejoined them. "I was just telling Josh about that call from my brother," she said.

Settling across from them, Walker assumed a serious air. "I don't know him, of course, but he sounds like a great guy. I told Allison she should go to Seattle.''

Straightening in his chair, Josh gave Walker a surprised look. "You did?''

"Of course. It won't interfere with the party if she goes for a few days. Family's important where I come from. I think it's marvelous that Allison and her brother are so close.''

Turning to her, Josh shrugged. "He could be right, Allie. If Tory needs you, maybe you'd better go.''

"That's what I was thinking," she said. "I could fly out there for the weekend and be back by Monday."

Raising his glass to his lips, Josh gave her a serious look, careful to keep the smile of triumph off his lips. "You're a good sister, Allie. Tory's a lucky guy."

CHAPTER THREE

JOSH COULDN'T REMEMBER the last time he'd been so pleased with himself. He felt almost magnanimous. If the Dentist, as he'd dubbed Walker, hadn't still been sitting at the table with them, he might even have become jovial.

Good old Tory, he thought, chewing a bite of salad. What a buddy. Now that Allie had decided to go to Seattle, it would be an easy matter for him to trudge along in the name of friendship. Tory and Val were his oldest, dearest friends, after all. They might need him, too. Allie would be impressed by his selfless concern for her brother, and once he had her settled in Seattle and away from the Dentist, he'd manage to convince her of the folly of her decision. She'd see the danger before she fell into it.

"So, what's this new story Allison says you're working on?" Walker asked him.

"We're going to do a book on the LaLorne-Calentro case," Josh said briskly, hoping the Dentist took note of the "we."

Walker looked at him blankly. "Who? I've never heard of them."

"Lena LaLorne and Sid Calentro?" Josh asked. "Come on, it was one of the biggest stories of the forties. If it hadn't been for World War II, it would have been the biggest."

"I saw her the other night," Allie said, trying unsuccessfully to spear a cherry tomato. "On the late movie. *Streets of Peril*. She was great. Absolutely beautiful. Did you see it?"

"Yeah," Josh said, turning to her with enthusiasm. "With Everett Blaine and Clark Montague. What a movie."

"Not me," Walker said. "I'm in bed by ten every night. Early rounds at the clinic, you know."

Josh tried to catch Allie's eye, but she determinedly avoided his gaze.

"Lena LaLorne was one of the greatest motion-picture actresses of the thirties and forties," Allie explained. "Mostly the forties. But she got involved with a mobster named Sid Calentro. The Mafia killed them."

"They disappeared," Josh corrected, shaking his head. "No one ever proved they were murdered."

"Well, Vito Giuseppe was certainly murdered. He was supposed to testify at those hearings, too, but they found him in that hotel bathtub."

"Yes, but a lot of people thought Calentro had killed him, then disappeared with the mob's help. It makes the most sense, doesn't it? Both Calentro and Giuseppe are scheduled to testify, but Calentro kills Giuseppe to keep him from talking and disappears with his girlfriend on an extended vacation, compliments of the Riazzi family. I mean, what other explanation is there? That the mob killed Calentro, too, to keep him from testifying? That doesn't explain what happened to Lena LaLorne and her maid.... What was her name?"

"Elsa. Elsa something, I think." Allie propped her chin in her hand, no longer interested in her salad. "It certainly is a fascinating mystery. More baffling than Jimmy Hoffa. Calentro was high up in the Riazzi family, and the FBI tried a number of times to indict him for tax evasion, just like Al Capone, didn't they?"

Josh nodded.

"But Calentro was too smart for them."

"Not that smart," Josh countered. "The authorities must have had something on him because he was willing to testify, along with Vito Giuseppe. The information those two men possessed could've shut down organized crime in this country for decades. Calentro alone was reported to have known the names of mobsters involved in the St. Valentine's Day Massacre. It was said he even knew who shot Bugsy Seigel. Half the upper echelons of the Mafia would have been in prison after Calentro was done singing."

"Which is why he's probably dead. Anyway, we know they got Giuseppe." Allie shuddered. "What a grisly murder."

Josh could see that the Dentist was losing interest fast and had already begun to glance around the restaurant. Josh began to feel even more pleased. He hoped Allie noticed, too.

"Maybe the mob killed Giuseppe, Calentro and the two women, but I don't think so," Josh went on. "And neither did a lot of other people at the time. For instance, the cops. According to the law, without a body, there's no murder. They only had Giuseppe's, so that means they were short three corpses. But the thing that really convinced quite a few people was the lack of talk. I mean, think about it, Allie. Three famous people, one of them a world-renowned film star, disappeared. If they'd been killed, someone, sometime, would have talked. Killing those three would

have been too big a job for there never to have been a
rumor about who did it."

"But those three people couldn't have just disappeared, either," Allie argued. "Lena LaLorne and
Calentro were so famous and their faces were so well-
known it's hard to believe they could live undetected.
Not in the United States, anyway. Sooner or later,
somebody would've spotted them. No, I think the
Mafia killed them."

"What if Calentro killed Giuseppe and escaped with
the mob's help?"

"I don't know," Allie said, leaning back as a waiter
removed her salad plate and set her main course before her. "It's been over forty years, Josh. I'm not
saying it's impossible, but that's a long time to hide.
Do you really think those letters—"

Clearing his throat noisily, Josh cut her off before
she could say anything more about the letters. "It'll be
interesting to check back through the old clippings,"
he said, a warning in his voice.

Allie looked startled, then glanced across the table
at Walker, who was concentrating on his fish. She gave
Josh a disbelieving look, but only said, "Anyway, it
could be a great book. I have to admit I'm envious of
Nancy. I'd love to work on it with you."

Picking up his own fork, Josh merely smiled at her.

After dinner, when their coffee was nearly finished, Allie rose and left for the ladies' room, apparently judging it safe enough to leave him alone with
the Dentist. Josh wasn't so sure. The moment she disappeared from the dining room, Walker placed an arm
on the table and leaned closer in a confiding manner.

"I understand that you and Allison's brother are
best friends and that you've been practically a mem-

ber of the family for years," Walker began in a low man-to-man tone. "I want you to know that she'll be in good hands. I'll look after her from now on."

Josh tried not to stiffen and merely nodded.

"Even though Allison's moving into my house," the younger man went on, "I have no intention of rushing her into anything. I think we're going about this in a mature and rational way, and I want to continue that. Whatever Allison wants is what I'm prepared to give her. I realize you must be wondering about that. After all, Allison and I haven't known one another very long. We're actually still not much more than, er, friends."

For a brief instant an image of Allie and the Dentist as "more than, er, friends" popped into his mind, and Josh thought he might just push his fist into Walker's tanned Grecian nose and keep pushing until he got to his forehead. Give the guy a good reason for being glad he fixed teeth for a living.

What was wrong with Allie? Josh wondered again. How could she seriously consider leaving her career and friends, a city she loved and—yes, dammit—*him*, to go traipsing down to the deep South with a buffoon like Walker Hyphen Claremont-St. John? It didn't make sense.

Hadn't they had fun the past ten years? They'd been successful beyond their wildest dreams, if they didn't count the last two or three years. They'd known excitement and challenge and adventure. With the exception of that brief period after Cleveland, they'd had a comfortable, friendly relationship that suited him just fine.

Why did she have to mess everything up by dragging the Dentist into the picture? They'd been perfectly fine before he'd come along.

Only with the greatest of efforts was Josh able to clench his fists under the table and resist the urge to pummel the Dentist to a pulp. He hated the guy, Josh realized with a start. It'd been a long time since he'd hated anyone this much—probably not since he was seventeen and his old man had shown up out of the blue that long-ago Christmas Day.

In a way, what he felt now was the same thing he'd felt then. It was a primitive, animalistic surge of possessiveness, an instinctive, blinding rush of raw male aggression that made him want to stretch himself to his full six feet three inches, bare his teeth and roar at anyone who got too close. That one time, years ago, he'd been driven by a fierce protectiveness for what was his, and he'd been prepared to engage in a battle to the death to keep the attacker away.

He felt very much the same way now, and suddenly the thought seemed ridiculous. What kind of an opponent was the Dentist? Not much of one. Yet unbelievable as it seemed, that's just what he was: an opponent. Walker was trying to take Allie away. And just as he'd been prepared to protect his mother all those years ago, Josh was prepared now to do whatever he had to do to keep Allie out of the enemy's clutches.

"The Claremont-St. Johns are an old Charleston family," the Dentist was saying. "We're well respected in those parts, and anyone could tell you all about the family. I just want you to know that I wouldn't be offended if you wanted to check me out. Believe me, I understand how you must feel."

Not likely, Josh thought. Instead of checking Walker out, he felt more like punching him out.

In his place, Walker probably *would* conduct a civilized and discreet background check—or would he? There was a slight possessiveness in Walker's attitude toward Allie that didn't sit well with him. No, Josh didn't need to look up the venerable Claremont-St. Johns. He already knew the Dentist wasn't good enough for Allie. Besides, he'd decided that the only way she was moving to Charleston was over his dead body.

"I don't think that'll be necessary," Josh answered simply.

Walker took his words as a vote of approval and beamed. "Thanks. I knew we'd get along just fine. You know, I have three sisters," he said. "And between them and my mother, I learned a lot about treating women with respect. Allison will be safe with me. I promise you that."

Fat chance, Josh thought. He knew that, the second the Dentist got Allie to that house of his, she would be ripe pickings. A small and helpless victim. Any man who said he could live in the same house with Allie and keep his hands off her was a liar, Josh figured.

His hatred of the Dentist was joined by a swell of deep distrust.

"Well, that's just fine," Josh said, taking a long swig of wine to keep from gagging. "I'll be sure to tell her brother all about you next time I see him. Believe me, I won't neglect a detail. I can promise you that."

"Thanks, Josh," Walker said, smiling the white friendly smile that made Josh itch all over. "I appreciate that."

"No problem," Josh grunted.

With almost overwhelming relief, Josh saw Allie weave her way across the dining room, headed in their direction. She was stunning tonight, Josh admitted. Despite what he'd told her about her dress, it suited her perfectly.

Against the sparkling black sequins, the skin of her shoulders was a flawless milky white, and the round curves of her breasts above the low cut of her dress and the shadowed hollow of cleavage between them had made him twist and fidget in his chair all evening.

She came toward them now, the low lights of the chandeliers catching the deep red of her hair so that it glistened and shone. Yes, Josh thought, she was absolutely, breathtakingly beautiful. But then, he had always known she was. Hadn't he?

Of course he had.

Yet when, exactly, had her long slender legs become so tantalizing? When had the curve of her neck become the kind of curve a man wanted to put his mouth to? When had that quick turn of her head, once nothing more than an endearing, impetuous toss, become so seductive and alluring? When had she gone from giving off a playful, enthusiastic cheerfulness to exuding a mesmerizing, sultry femininity that made a man's blood run hot?

Suspiciously, Josh watched the Dentist and saw that the younger man noticed the same things about her. His blue eyes lit up like an eager puppy's as Allie took her seat at the table. If the waiter hadn't arrived with the bill just then, Josh might have gone back on all his good intentions and dragged Walker out of the restaurant by his lapels.

"This has been wonderful," Allie said to Josh, when he'd handed his credit card to the waiter. A smile of amusement lifted the corners of her full mouth.

For a moment Josh recalled with startling, overwhelming clarity what it was like to kiss that mouth, and he suddenly knew that nothing about Allie had really changed. He'd always known she was sensual—the most sensual woman he'd ever met. It was he who had forced himself to pretend he hadn't recognized that sensuality.

"In fact," she went on, her tone teasing, "it's been a *surprisingly* good time. Thank you, Josh."

A little flustered, Josh nodded jerkily. "Sure," he mumbled, forgetting he was supposed to sound impressive and articulate tonight.

"I guess we'd better be going," Walker said, pushing back his chair. "I've still got a flight to catch tonight, and I want to make sure Allison gets home safe and sound before I leave."

As the three of them rose—shaking hands, repeating thank-yous and you're-welcomes and we-must-do-this-agains—Josh could barely keep himself from staring intently at Allie. When she and the Dentist finally left him and walked away, he stood in a daze, gazing down at the rumpled tablecloth covered with bunched napkins, dirty coffee cups and wineglasses, and the remains of what had been an extraordinarily expensive dinner.

For some reason, the empty chairs and soiled table made him feel sad and lonely, reminding him of the last time he'd thrown a party. Everyone'd gone home with someone else and he was left in a suddenly quiet house to straighten up the worst of the mess alone.

With a slow, heavy tread, Josh made his way to the front of the restaurant. In the elegant foyer, he waited alone for the valet to retrieve his car, contemplating the long drive home to Long Island and dreading the thought of walking into his charming house by the salt marshes. It would be quiet in the house. A deep, depressing hush would fill the dark rooms, making them feel empty, despite the clutter of furniture and books.

Maybe, he thought as he pressed a tip into the valet's palm and slid behind the wheel of the Porsche, maybe he would just find a hotel room and stay in the city tonight.

"ALLIE? IT'S ME."

With a sleepy groan, Allie twisted the receiver so it lay more comfortably between the pillow and her ear. She tried to open her eyes, but they felt too heavy. "Wha? Who'izzit?"

"It's me. Josh."

Groggily, she managed to peel open one eye and squint at the bedside clock. Three-thirty-two. Good grief.

"Wha's wrong?" she mumbled almost incoherently. "Where're you, Josh?"

"Nothing's wrong. I just wanted to call and talk."

Holding a hand to her forehead, Allie tried to concentrate on his words through the sleepy fog that clouded her mind. "Huh?"

"So did your dentist friend get off okay?"

Shaking her head in confusion, Allie sat up and ran a hand through her hair, as the deep sleep she'd been enjoying finally dropped away, dissolving slowly like a morning mist in the sun.

"Are you all right, Josh? It's three-thirty in the morning. Is something wrong?"

"No, nothing's wrong."

"Are you drunk?"

There was a brief   nce before he grumbled, "No. Not yet, anyhow."

"Well, then, if nothing's wrong and you're not drunk, go back to bed. I'll talk to you in the morning."

Before she could hang up, however, Allie heard him ask, "So I take it Walker made his plane all right? It didn't get delayed or anything, huh?"

Realization dawned slowly, but it did dawn.

"Walker? Oh, I see." Allie's eyes narrowed in annoyance and she decided on impulse to lie to Josh and pay him back for waking her up. "If you're wondering if Walker is here in my bed right now, he most certainly is, and he's about as mad as I am that you woke us up. Goodbye, Josh."

Still, she didn't hang up. Instead, she listened to the cold silence that followed her words. When Josh finally asked, "Is he really there?" there was a deadly seriousness in his voice that brought her fully awake. The dangerous edge in his words startled her, wiping the flippant smile off her face as effectively as a slap.

"No, he's not," she said slowly, emphatically. "I was only teasing. Good heavens, Josh, what's wrong with you?"

"So you can talk, then?"

"Of course I can talk. Ask me if I want to, though. Go ahead, ask me. I mean, it is three-thirty in the morning."

"Do you want to talk?"

Trust Josh to take her literally, Allie thought, rolling her eyes. Preparing for the possibility of a long one, she settled back against the pillows and sighed. "All right. Let's talk. What's going on?"

"I don't know."

"Well, that's certainly a start. Where are you? In your study?"

"No, I was too tired to drive home."

"Oh. So, where are you, then?"

"At a hotel. Here in the city." He paused. "I'm sorry to wake you up, Allie. It was stupid. I just couldn't get to sleep."

"You can't get to sleep, but you were too tired to drive home?" Smoothing a wrinkle out of the pillowcase beneath her cheek, Allie frowned. "Josh, what's going on? You haven't been playing those big football pools again, have you?"

"Football?" Josh sounded startled. "Allie, it's May. There's no football until September. Anyway, what's that got to do with anything?"

"Well, baseball pools, then. Remember a few years ago when you got caught up in those pools, betting all that money on stupid sporting events? You used to have trouble sleeping then, too."

"Oh." Josh was quiet for a moment. "No, I haven't been gambling."

His voice sounded tired, and Allie's concern began to grow stronger. "Josh, what is it? You don't sound very well. Something's wrong, isn't it? You can tell me. You know that."

"Yeah, I know. But this is different."

"How so?"

For a man who was scarcely ever at a loss for words, Allie thought, Josh's end of the conversation was punctuated with a great many uneasy silences.

"I don't know. It's just different. I'm not exactly sure what's going on. I've got an idea, but... Well, don't get mad and hang up on me, all right?"

"Okay." Allie was completely awake now, and she looked at the ceiling, a worried furrow between her brows. "I promise."

"Really, I mean it. Sometimes you hang up, anyway."

"For heaven's sake, Josh," she said impatiently, "I said I promise. What *is* it?"

"All right. It's just that... Well, do you like this Walker guy? I mean, *really* like him?"

Taken back, Allie pulled the phone away from her ear, looked at it, then dragged her fingers through her hair again. "Well, yes," she said hesitantly. "Yes, I do like him."

Not the way I like you, though, she wanted to add. *Even if I happen to learn to love him someday, I'll never love him the way I love you.*

But she knew what kind of a reaction that would get. After watching Josh tiptoe around her for two solid years after that fiasco in Cleveland, she wasn't about to jeopardize their friendship again by saying something stupid like "I love you." She'd learned the hard way that Joshua Mercer had clearly defined boundaries for their relationship. Crossing those boundaries was the surest way to send him packing, emotionally and otherwise.

"Oh," Josh said. "So you really like him."

"That's not what this is all about, is it?" Allie asked. "I mean, I find it hard to believe that you're sleeplessly pacing the floor on account of my love life, Josh. So why don't you tell me what's bothering you?''

''I'm not pacing. I'm sitting here with a bottle of good whiskey.''

''Well, you know what I mean. Tell the truth, Josh. What's going on?''

''Nothing's going on. I just don't feel good about that guy, Allie. I honestly don't. You're my friend. Sometimes I think you're the best friend I've got, and I don't want to see you make a terrible mistake.''

''I thought you liked Walker. By the end of dinner you were downright polite, and you're hardly ever polite.''

''Thanks,'' he grumbled. ''I'm polite. I'm polite a lot. Besides, that's not the point. Of course I wasn't going to say anything right there at dinner. But that doesn't mean I liked him. In fact, I think you'd be making a big mistake by moving to Charleston. There's something fishy about that guy. I don't trust him.''

''You don't trust anyone, Josh. That's what made you such a great investigative reporter. You're suspicious of everyone.''

''Yeah, and I'm usually right.''

With a deep breath, Allie glanced up at the ceiling, trying very hard to be reasonable and sympathetic. It was tough, though, with someone who was so good at pulling scams as Josh was. If she knew anything about Joshua Mercer, this scam had to do with his Lena LaLorne story.

''Listen, Josh. I appreciate your concern. I really do. But this is my decision to make, and I've made it. I'm sorry you don't like Walker, because I do, and I'm sorry you think I'm making a mistake because I value your opinion. But the truth is, it's not any of your business. If I want to take a chance, I will. Maybe you're right. Maybe I'm making the biggest mistake of my life. But it *is* my life, and I have a right to screw it up if I want to.''

"How can you say it's none of my business? Allie, for over ten years my life has been your business, and yours has been mine.''

"Not in these kinds of matters, Josh. I've never once interfered in your romantic exploits, as brief and numerous as they've been. I've never tried to tell you how to run your love life, Josh. Not once.''

The silence on the other end of the phone stretched out for so long Allie finally prompted, "Josh?''

"Yeah. I'm here,'' he said, his voice quiet and deep. "Listen, I'm sorry. You're right. This is none of my business.''

"Apology accepted. Would you try to get some sleep now?''

"Sure.'' There was a rustling sound, as though he was moving the receiver from one ear to the other. "You know, I was thinking about what you said at dinner. About Tory and Val. You've got me a little worried.''

Allie smiled softly. She'd always respected the friendship between her brother and Josh, even while she'd been a little mystified about its nature. Based on some secret male bond forged in youth, it was as solid and enduring as a rock and more stable than most marriages.

"It'll be okay,'' she reassured. "Tory and Val love each other too much. Things'll work out, I'm sure.''

"Maybe." Josh sounded hesitant. "But I can't rest easy knowing Tory's in trouble. What do you think about my flying out with you? I was going out there, anyway, to start my research pretty soon."

Allie blinked in surprise, suddenly suspicious. "I'm not sure that's altogether necessary, Josh. I'm sure it's nothing..."

"Tory would do the same for me, Allie. I could make reservations for us on the morning flight to Seattle."

Allie frowned uncertainly. Why did the whole thing sound a little too pat? Just a tad too convenient?

"You know, Allie, if it *is* something important, Tory might find it easier to talk to me. Not that he couldn't talk to you," Josh added hastily, then explained in an embarrassed tone, "I just mean if it's a male thing, you know."

Suddenly feeling ridiculous for being so distrusting, Allie smiled. So that was it. Josh and his funny sense of modesty. She swore that sometimes he was trying to protect her from the "cruder" aspects of life. As if she was still a kid.

"Sure, Josh," she said, trying to keep the laughter out of her voice. "That sounds like a good idea. Tory'll be thrilled to see you."

"All right. I'll get us on the morning flight and be by at seven o'clock to pick you up."

"Seven." Allie briefly closed her eyes, trying not to think of her plans for sleeping in the next morning. "Fine. I'll be here."

"Good night, Allie."

As Allie replaced the receiver in the cradle, she thought about the sad, almost melancholy tone of Josh's voice as he'd said good-night. If she hadn't known better, she'd have thought he'd meant good-bye, instead.

THEY HAD SPREAD the photocopies of blurry newspaper photos and articles across their folding trays, and a stack of files teetered on the empty seat between Josh and the window. Allie sat in the aisle seat as usual because she hated takeoffs and landings. Now, she studied the fuzzy photo of a man and a woman on a beach, then picked up the yellowed glossy publicity photo of Lena LaLorne. With nothing much else to do on the long flight, she didn't think it would hurt to look over some of the documents and research Josh had brought with him. Besides, he'd asked her so nicely.

"There's really no way to tell," Allie said, gazing again at the newspaper photo. "The way the woman on the beach has her face turned from the camera, it could be anyone."

"Maybe," Josh conceded. "But don't forget, this is a copy of a news clipping. In the original photo their faces might have been clearer. In any case there have been enough of these photos to indicate a strong possibility that Lena and Sid Calentro were alive in the early fifties."

"I don't know, Josh. It could just be yellow journalism, like the tabloids print now. They're always publishing photos of people who are supposed to be Elvis or John Lennon. My guess is that's what these photos were. Taken by sensationalists trying to make a fast buck by snapping photos of perfectly ordinary couples in exotic places like Porta Verde, Buenos Aires and Algiers, then trying to pass them off as pictures of Lena and Calentro."

"But look at this." Josh handed her a torn sheet of legal paper, scrawled with several columns of numbers and place names. "This row is the dates of all the supposed photos of Lena and Calentro taken after their disappearance—at least, all the ones I've been able to turn up. This other row is the names of all the locations where the photos were taken. Do you see anything interesting about this data?"

Scanning the columns, Allie shook her head.

"Look," Josh said, taking the paper from her and drawing a heavy line with a pencil through several entries. "Cross out all the towns that aren't in South America. Cross out this date from a sighting in 1976 in Caracas, and what do we have?"

Allie bent over the sheet again. There were twelve entries left. "All the dates are between 1949 and 1954. All the towns are in South America."

"Right. Let's say—just speculation, mind you— that the sightings outside South America are false. And let's say that any photos after 1954 aren't real. Let's also pretend that the rest of the photos *are* accurate. That would mean that Lena and Calentro were in South America from 1949—the year after they disappeared—to 1954. These photos could be a sort of travelogue of where they were during those first five years."

Giving the sheet a closer inspection, Allie nodded thoughtfully. "It does seem suggestive that most of the photos were taken in South America within that five-year period."

"'Suggestive' is just the word I was thinking of." Josh smiled at her, then suddenly lifted a large hand and brushed a finger across her top lip. "You're wearing a cookie crumb."

For a brief moment Allie imagined that the touch of his rough finger was unusually gentle and that his hand lingered just a little longer than necessary on her cheek. Before she could reason away the impression, her heart gave a small, scurried skip. Instantly she chastised her unruly heart, firmly taking herself in hand. Her heart settled down quickly.

She hadn't always been so sensible. There'd been a time when she'd searched for signs of attraction from Josh, watching as alertly as a cat guarding a mouse hole, ready to pounce on the slightest movement. But those days, she reminded herself, were over and done with. After watching so intently for so long, she'd finally realized that there wasn't any mouse at home and that the only signs she'd ever seen from Josh were figments of her imagination, like the bright spots one sees after staring at something too long.

Now, she told herself sternly, was not the time to start all that nonsense again. With her decision to finally make long overdue changes in her life, she couldn't afford to start questioning and analyzing Josh's every word and gesture again.

Walker was a kind, generous man who appreciated everything about her and made no secret of it. She'd never had to wait breathlessly for a sign from him. She'd never be on tenterhooks with him, hoping for an indication that he cared for her. She'd made her choice—the right choice—and she was going to stick with it. Because, right choice or not, she simply couldn't bear the anguish of waiting for something with Josh that was never going to happen. She just couldn't bear to wait for that any longer.

"Ladies and gentlemen—" a disembodied voice floated through the cabin "—we'll be beginning our

descent into Sea-Tac International in just a few minutes. Please make sure your seat belts are securely
fastened and your seats are in the upright position. All
belongings should be safely stowed under your seat or
the seat in front of you, and your trays should be returned to their proper, locked positions."

Scooping up the photos and cramming them into a
file, Josh handed Allie half of the stack of files and
stuffed the other half under his seat.

"Almost there," he said. "It's going to be good to
see Tory and Val."

"Yes," Allie said, her voice a bit dull. "It's going
to be great."

The moment of danger was over, she told herself.
They were only friends, after all. She could hear it in
his voice.

Yet when Josh's hand closed over hers in the reassuring clasp that had become a ritual with them
whenever they flew together, Allie thought she might
burst into tears.

After ten years, she told herself with something very
much like self-ridicule, she *couldn't* still be waiting for
the mouse to appear. After only one faint stirring in
ten years, she knew with absolute certainty that Josh
felt nothing for her but friendship. Still, she reminded herself, her resolution to start over was still
new. After ten years of waiting, perhaps she had to
expect to feel that familiar disappointment once in a
while.

The only difference was that now she was ready to
fight it with everything she had.

IN A GRAY-WALLED windowless office in the center of
the J. Edgar Hoover Building in Washington, D.C.,

Senior Agent Gerald Fourier sighed at his secretary, who propped open his office door with a generous hip, waiting for his response.

Regretfully, Fourier glanced down at the paperwork that lay several inches thick across his desk. "Oh, all right. Send him in. But it better *be* urgent."

Martha grinned. "Right, boss." Over her shoulder she said, "You can come in now," and held the door open as a tall lanky man in his midthirties tried to negotiate past her considerable bulk. After a ridiculous battle of twisting and maneuvering, the man finally managed to squeeze around her and into the office. Her fun momentarily over, Martha smiled and winked at Fourier as she pulled the door closed behind her.

"Whew," Steve Johnson muttered, clearing off a chair. "Getting past her is like trying to get past Cerberus."

Fourier gave a small weary smile. "Cerberus? The dog guarding Hades?"

"You got it." Picking up the pile of papers on the visitor's chair and placing them on the floor, Johnson sat down and glanced around the untidy office, taking in Fourier's tired face. "Looks like hell in here to me, anyway."

"Budget time," Fourier explained, tapping a pen against the edge of his desk. With real interest, he asked, "How've you been, Steve? It's been a while."

Fourier knew he was one of the few people in the bureau who truly liked Steve Johnson. Other agents resented Johnson's single-minded dedication, misreading it as brownnosing, rather than the quirk of personality it really was—an oddly all-consuming preoccupation with justice. If Johnson had any faults, they were a tendency to follow too closely to the book and an irritating lack of imagination.

Settling in the uncomfortable, standard office-issue chair, Johnson shrugged. "I've been okay. Not too bad. You?"

"Buried under paperwork. What brings you to Washington? Last I heard you were climbing rungs in New York."

"Hmm. Word gets around. I've had a few successes lately," Johnson said modestly. "Anyway, got something I thought I'd better deliver personally."

For the first time Fourier laid down his pen. "Yeah? That sounds more interesting than budgets."

"It is. In fact, it's so interesting you probably won't believe it."

Thoroughly curious now, Fourier leaned back in his chair and crossed his arms behind his head. "Tell me."

"All right. This morning, I had a couple agents at La Guardia, watching for a kid named Ricky Macclay. Interstate car theft. Suspected. And who do you think my guys spot?"

Fourier didn't bother to reply.

"Victor Lazano and Web Scarpini. Getting on a plane for Seattle. With Luther Willis guarding the gangway."

Quickly Fourier scanned the extensive list he carried around in his head, pulled out the names like folders from a filing cabinet and merely nodded.

"Naturally my guys are curious. They pay attention. What are these three scumbags doing flying to Seattle? I didn't know they'd ever been outside Jersey. Turns out these three are following two people. A couple. They get on the same plane as the couple. Must have been some sort of mix-up, because Lazano and Scarpini almost missed the flight." Johnson paused, glanced around the office. "You wouldn't have any coffee, would you?"

With patience bred by years at the bureau, Fourier sat forward, buzzed Martha for coffee and leaned back again. Johnson fiddled with a loose arm on his chair and waited for his coffee. Only when Martha had brought in two cups and shut the door again did he finally continue.

"This is where it starts to get weird, Gerry. My men call in the names of this couple. One of them turns out to be Joshua Mercer. The other's his editor."

"Mercer?" Fourier flipped through names in his mental Rolodex. "Mercer, Mercer," he repeated, snapping his fingers as though he had a biography of the man at his fingertips. "That guy who did the book on the Trimaldi family? Don't tell me he's going after the Riazzis now."

Johnson smiled slowly, with deep satisfaction. "I wondered the same thing. Asked myself, 'Could this guy be that stupid?' So I started to check around. You aren't *ever* going to believe what I came up with."

Fourier considered himself to be one of the most tolerant, friendly men in the bureau, but even he was starting to grow impatient. "Just tell me, Steve. Then I can decide whether I believe it or not for myself."

"One of our undercover agents found out that he's working on a book about Sid Calentro."

For a moment Fourier wasn't sure he'd heard right. "Calentro?"

Johnson nodded. "Calentro."

"I don't get it."

"He's *looking* for Sid Calentro," Johnson said simply.

"What? Looking? That's crazy. The guy's dead," Fourier said, sitting up. "The Riazzis knocked him off forty years ago."

Johnson's smile widened. "That's what the bureau's always said. But I'll tell you, Gerry, the Riazzis have put their best goons on Mercer."

Fourier shook his head and shrugged. "Yeah?"

"There's only one reason I can think of why they'd be that interested in a guy like Mercer—Calentro's not dead at all. Apparently we were wrong. It happens sometimes."

For the first time in years Fourier felt truly stunned. Calentro? Sid Calentro alive? "That's impossible," he said with conviction.

Johnson shrugged. "It seems Joey Riazzi doesn't think so."

Fourier stared hard at him. "Damn." Swiveling in his chair, he stared absently at the far wall, thinking quickly. When he turned back, his face was grim. "Haywood's still heading the Seattle office. I'll give him a call."

"Better make it quick. Their plane's landing in—" Johnson looked at his watch "—less than an hour."

Fourier nodded.

"There's another thing, Gerry," Johnson said. "I want permission to fly out there. Temporary reassignment. I want to be in on this one."

Fourier studied the younger man. Without rancor, he suggested, "Another rung up, Steve?"

"Could be." Johnson set his coffee cup on the edge of Fourier's desk and got to his feet. "Let's hope so, anyway. So, do I have your okay?"

"Sure. You've done everything right so far. I can't think of anyone better to do the job. Just don't step too hard on Haywood's toes.'' Fourier paused. ''You know, Steve, if something comes of this, you'll be more than just a rung higher. I'll make sure of it.''

At the door Johnson paused. ''Thanks, but you know me better than that, Gerry. That's only part of it. If Calentro's still alive, I want to find him. I want to bring him in. And another thing, if he *is* alive and this Mercer guy's known about it all along, he'll wish he'd come to us with the information first. If Mercer has been withholding evidence, I'll nail him to the wall.'' Pulling open the door, Johnson glanced back and said, ''By the way, thanks for the coffee.''

When Johnson had gone, Fourier gazed absently for long moments at the mess on his desk, astonishment making him shake his head again. Sid Calentro still alive? After all these years?

''My God,'' he breathed softly, and reached for the phone.

CHAPTER FOUR

JOSH KNEW he was in potential hot water from the moment he pulled up outside Tory's house in the rental car—an expense Josh insisted on because he hated the dependency of being met at the airport and hauled off like so much cargo. Instead of looking down in the mouth like a properly harangued husband, Tory rushed across the wide suburban lawn, beaming and hollering, with Val right at his heels.

It was not, Josh thought, scowling and unfolding himself with difficulty from the compact car, exactly the kind of greeting calculated to convince Allie that Tory and Val were in trouble. Watching his two old friends with their arms around each other, practically bursting with contentment, Josh thought they'd never looked so happy.

He'd talk to Tory straight off, Josh decided, and put a quick end to that. Already he could see Allie frowning in confusion before her brother swooped in and scooped her up in a huge bear hug. She disappeared beneath a mountain of T-shirt, emerging a few seconds later with her hair tousled.

"You little brat," Tory said, chuckling. "You look prettier every time I see you."

Blond and petite, Val pushed past her hulk of a husband to embrace Allie. As always, Val was well-groomed, meticulously manicured, and adorable in a fashionable shirtdress. She held Allie at arm's length and smiled. "It's so good to see you. Your brother's been pacing the living room for the past hour, waiting for you two. You're doing your hair differently, aren't you? No bangs anymore. It looks wonderful. I always thought you'd look good with your hair up like that...."

Josh watched them uneasily, as Tory thumped him on the back.

"It's great to see you, Josh. Been too long." Tory's smile split his face. "How was the flight?"

With a warning glare, Josh gripped his friend's biceps and dragged him to the back of the car. "What the hell are you doing?" Josh muttered out of the side of his mouth as he unlocked the trunk. "You're supposed to be miserable, remember? Allie's here because you and Val are fighting."

Tory squinted. "Not anymore. Once Allie got here, everything was fixed, you said. Besides, how could I explain that to Val?"

"I don't know." Josh flipped open the trunk. "But just don't look *quite* so happy, okay? Try to act like a guy who's been through the wringer a few times."

Tory's grin widened. "Oh, Allie'll just think it's the afterglow from making up. But you wouldn't know about that, would you, old buddy? If I remember right, you've never stuck around long enough with one woman to get to the first fight, let alone the making up. Might be something you want to try sometime. It's not bad."

Unexpectedly Josh felt a twinge of anger. He knew Tory was only teasing, but his friend's words felt more like a jab. Annoyed, he yanked a suitcase from the trunk. "Just try to tone down the Ozzie-and-Harriet routine a little, would you? We don't want Allie to get suspicious— Oh, hi there, Val." Josh dropped the suitcase and accepted Val's hug, shooting Tory one last threatening look.

"You look exhausted, Josh." Val frowned in concern. "Haven't you been taking care of yourself? Allie, has he been living like an animal again?"

"If by that you mean have I been working hard, the answer is yes." Josh picked up the suitcase and let himself be propelled toward the house. "I have never in my life lived like an animal."

"That's not exactly true," Tory called as he and Allie followed them across the lawn. "Remember our three years in the fraternity?"

With affection, Josh smiled down at Val. "I stand corrected. But since college I've given up my wicked ways."

From behind him, Josh heard a snort and the murmur of Allie's voice. "Oh, yeah. Since when?"

IT WASN'T that he'd ever felt like a fifth wheel, Josh decided as he picked up his beer and adjusted the gas-barbecue grill for the tenth time. It was true that in college Val had always been around, but back then so had a lot of other people. Later Allie had usually accompanied them whenever Josh saw Tory and Val. No, he had never been made to feel like an outsider by Val and Tory, but there were times when he felt as though he was missing out on something, anyway.

It was the way they smiled at each other, Josh decided, as though they knew something no one else did. Like they had a secret between them, a secret he'd never understand. And Tory's words that afternoon had brought back that old feeling with an irritating rush.

Why not just admit it, Josh thought, poking roughly at a foil-wrapped potato. He was envious. He had always been envious. Josh gave the potato such a hard nudge that it shot off the grill and skittered onto the flagstone patio. Glancing around guiltily, he picked it up and tossed it back onto the grill, wincing when the hot foil burned his fingers.

"Damn!" he cursed, licking his fingertips.

Envying Tory was like envying Joe Frazier for being such a great boxer. No matter how much he wished it, no matter how hard he worked, he was never going to be as good. Some men were born with an ability, and some weren't. A man had to know his limitations. That was the trick to survival.

No matter how he felt about it, Josh told himself, he was never going to have what Tory had. The men in the Mercer family never did, and that was a fact he'd learned long ago. Not getting involved with a woman was a rule he lived by, like not hitting a guy when he was down or not taking a swing at a smaller man. All of them were nasty things to do, and someone was bound to get hurt by them.

"Are you almost ready for the steaks?" Val's voice sang out from the kitchen window.

Still sucking on his burned finger, Josh raised the long-handled barbecue fork. "Bring 'em on."

Maybe I just need a break, Josh thought. After three failed books, maybe everything was starting to get to him finally. It was the only explanation for his strange panic over Allie's threatened abdication and for the bewildering sense of emptiness he'd been feeling lately. This story about Lena LaLorne and Sid

Calentro just had to be a success. A success, he reassured himself, would surely put things right again.

Allie padded barefoot across the patio, balancing a platter of thick steaks. She'd changed from her suit jacket and miniskirt into a T-shirt that read So Many Men, So Little Time and a pair of jean shorts with the cuffs rolled up. Josh wasn't sure whether it was the T-shirt or the way her long, slender thighs looked in the shorts, but he turned sharply back to the grill, and his irritation grew even stronger.

"Here you go. Tory called from the stadium a while ago. He should be home in ten minutes. Val wants hers well-done." Swinging herself up onto the patio table, Allie crossed her ankles and watched him adjust the grill once again. "This is great, Josh. I'm really glad I came, even if it was for nothing. Val hasn't said a word about any trouble, so I guess they must have made up. Trust Tory to get all upset about a little fight. Probably because he and Val never do. Fight, I mean. I think it's cute, don't you?"

Josh realized he was clenching his teeth, and he forced himself to relax his jaw muscles.

"Don't you, Josh?"

He looked up. "What?"

"Don't you think it's cute?"

"What's cute?"

"Tory and Val. That they never fight, I mean. I think it's sweet that Tory got so upset—"

Flipping a steak onto the grill, Josh scowled. "What kind of a thing is that to wear, Allie?" he interrupted.

Startled, Allie blinked at him. "What are you talking about?"

"The T-shirt. What does that slogan even mean? It's disgusting. Do you want people to get the wrong idea about you?"

Allie stared at him, her green eyes wide. "It's just a T-shirt."

Glowering at her, Josh waved the barbecue fork like a conductor's baton to accent his words. "You come out here, flouncing around with that slogan across your...your breasts for all the world to see—"

This time Allie's mouth fell open, and she rushed in with, "Josh, you and Val are the only people here. I don't think you qualify as the 'whole world.' Besides I don't see why you're so upset—"

"All right then. For *me* to see."

As soon as the words were out of his mouth, Josh felt his face go a little red, and he looked away before Allie could see it. Good Lord, he thought. He really was going crazy. Angrily, he flung another steak across the hot grill.

"I give up," Allie said, her own voice angry. "I'm going back in the house."

Behind him, Josh heard her jump off the table.

"You're impossible tonight, Joshua Mercer. You've been walking around all afternoon just waiting to bite someone's head off. I don't know, maybe it's jet lag or something. But I'm not sticking around to become your next meal."

"Allie."

She paused on the flagstones, her back to him, and he knew she was debating whether to turn around or not.

"Look," Josh continued apologetically, "I'm sorry. I don't know what's wrong with me. Come back and talk to me while I grill these things."

Slowly Allie turned. Her green eyes were thoughtful, and he saw a worried frown on her face. With the patio light behind her, her auburn hair shone red-gold, and Josh could see the rise and fall of her breasts under the T-shirt. A hard knot formed in the pit of his stomach, and he recognized it as desire.

With a deep breath, he turned back to the grill, took a long swig of his beer and tried to suppress the ache the way he'd done so many times before. For some reason, it just seemed more difficult to ignore lately.

"I'm tired, Allie. And I'm feeling confused about things," he said honestly. "It's the book. You know what a bestseller could mean for me. I feel like everything's riding on my finding Lena LaLorne."

Returning to the patio table, Allie leaned back against it. "I know, Josh. You'll find her."

Josh stabbed absently at a sizzling steak. "But what if I don't?"

"Then you'll find another, even better story. You're Joshua Mercer. The bestselling crime novelist. You have talent and imagination, Josh. That's why you're so good at what you do. One book isn't going to make or break Joshua Mercer. He's made of tougher stuff than that."

"It's been three books, Allie. Not one. How many will it take before I'm no longer the best?"

The light touch of her hand on his shoulder made the knot in his stomach tighten. Closing his eyes, he swallowed hard.

"You'll always be the best, Josh. No one can take that away from you."

The knot twisted, and the ache burned deeper. Josh gazed up at the star-filled sky, then glanced down at Allie and asked the question he'd been wanting to ask ever since she'd told him she was leaving. He had to know if she'd lost her faith in him, just as he'd begun to lose confidence in himself.

"If my last three books hadn't been failures, would you be staying, Allie?"

Josh saw the surprise in her eyes, then the sadness, but she didn't look away.

"No," she said softly. "Those were good books, Josh. They really were. But even if they'd been financially successful, I couldn't stay any longer. It doesn't have anything to do with your books. It has to do with me and what I want out of life."

"But don't we have fun? Haven't you been happy?"

The smile she gave him was so soft and tender Josh could barely stop himself from reaching out, dragging her to him and covering her lips with his. What was happening to him? he thought a little wildly.

"Yes, I've been happy. It's just that what I want has changed. I want a family, Josh. I want a normal life and children and a husband."

At her words, the ache in him grew so raw that Josh knew it was more than just desire he was feeling. In a sudden flash of realization, he knew it had something to do with that damned vague emptiness.

Nodding abruptly once, he wiped the back of his hand across his upper lip and looked away. "All right. But you deserve the best, Allie. Just make sure you aren't settling for less."

"What the hell's smoking out there?" a low voice boomed from the house. "Good God, Josh. What are you trying to do? Burn the place down?" Bursting through the kitchen door, Tory bounded across the patio. "I could see the smoke from halfway down the block."

"Oh, no!" Allie laughed. "The steaks, Josh."

Wheeling, Josh stared in dismay, then snatched up a spatula and began to beat the flaming steaks. "Somebody bring some water! I'm all out of beer."

"SO, YOU WON AGAIN today," Allie stated matter-of-factly. She and Tory were sprawled lazily in lounge chairs in the backyard under the stars, sipping wine, while Josh helped Val clean up the kitchen. From where they sat, they could hear laughter and the clanging of pots through the open kitchen window.

"Yeah. The Texas Rangers have had a lot of injuries. They aren't doing so well this year." Tory raised his wineglass in a salute and grinned. "But *we* are."

Allie laughed. "I read in *Sports Illustrated* that you are, and I quote, one of the best catchers in the league."

Slowly Tory lowered his glass and his face grew serious.

Allie's laughter faded. "What's wrong, Tory?"

The big man shrugged, then sighed. "I'm thirty-seven, Allie."

"I know that. So what?"

"Did you read the rest of that article?"

Allie was silent, suddenly wishing she'd never brought up the subject.

Shaking his head, Tory smiled, but his smile wasn't completely genuine. "I read it. It said I was one of the best catchers *for my age*. I'm not complaining, mind you. I've been lucky. Most guys don't get to play as long as I have. But there's not too many more years left in these babies," he said, slapping his knees.

Allie watched him silently, unsure of what to say. She'd read that part, too, and the rest of the article.

Glancing over his shoulder at the kitchen window, Tory took a sip of his wine. "I'm quitting, Allie. I'm giving it up before they make me quit. Next year's my last."

"Tory—"

He held up a hand. "It's already decided. Thirty-eight is too old to be out there day after day breaking my back. I want to finish as a winner. I want people to remember Tory Shannon as a great catcher, not some crippled second-rate minor leaguer."

"Tory," Allie began, her voice full of emotion. "I don't know what to say. Baseball has been your life. For as long as I can remember, anyway."

"That's not going to stop. I've been thinking about going into the front office, maybe even managing or something if I don't have to be on the road too much." He patted her arm. "Don't look so worried. Every ball player has to face retirement. It's a fact of life. I'm actually looking forward to it."

Allie studied her brother. "You're really okay about this?"

Tory shrugged. "I don't know. It'll be something new. Anyway, I hope you and Josh can come out to the ballpark tomorrow. You might not get too many more chances to come to my games. Although, it's not as if you haven't seen enough already. How many games do you think you've been to?"

"Throughout my lifetime, I'd guess about a million." Allie smiled. "I screamed and cheered at all of them."

"I know. During a lot of them I could hear you. So tomorrow's on?"

"Naturally. We wouldn't miss it. But don't sit us in those VIP boxes a mile from the field again. I want to be right over the dugout."

Tory laughed. "I'll see what I can do."

Silence descended over the backyard, and Allie could hear Josh teasing Val about something and Val's laughing protest.

"Everything seems to be okay with you and Val," Allie finally said.

Stirring in his chair, Tory looked away and up at the stars. "Yeah. Everything's okay."

"I told you it would be, although naturally you wouldn't believe your little sister."

Tory cleared his throat in embarrassment, then took a sip of his wine, and Allie smiled. Her big brother never failed to amuse her. She was tempted to tease him about panicking over some silly fight with Val, then decided he looked too ashamed. Before she could change the subject, however, Tory did.

"So, uh, are you and Josh going to be working on his new book while you're out here?"

Allie shook her head. "No. I mean, Josh is, I think. But I won't be."

Tory looked interested. "Why not?"

Grinning, Allie raised her eyebrows. "I have some news of my own, big brother. I'm moving to Charleston, South Carolina. I met someone, and we ... Well, I don't know exactly what will happen, but we've decided to give it a try. Living together, I mean. Just a trial thing, you know."

Tory frowned. "This is sort of sudden, isn't it?"

"Well, yes. I suppose it is. I've known Walker— that's his name, Walker Claremont-St. John—for a few months. He's an orthodontist, Tory, and very nice. You'll like him.''

"Have you told Mom and Dad?''

Allie grimaced. "Not yet. I was hoping Walker and I would figure out what we were going to do—long range, I mean—before I told them.''

Tory studied her with concern. "I don't know, Allie. This doesn't seem like you. A few months isn't very long. You can't know the guy very well. Do you think it's wise?''

Wrinkling her nose, Allie frowned. "You sound like Josh. What is it with all the men in my life?''

"We're men, that's what. We understand how other men think. What's Josh's opinion?''

"The same as yours, I imagine,'' she said tartly. "It's okay for you men to go off and do something daring and unusual, but we women should stay at home by the hearth and quake at the thought of venturing out into the big bad world.''

"Now, Allie, I never said—''

"You didn't have to.'' Allie sniffed in annoyance. "Oh, never mind. Unless Walker proves he can hit a fastball and beat someone to a pulp inside a ring, you two aren't going to give him your stamp of approval.''

"That's not true. We'd just like to meet the guy before you go off with him, that's all.''

"Well, Josh met him.''

"And?''

Allie stared in frustration across the dark lawn. The most annoying part, she thought, was that no one seemed to give *her* judgment any credit.

"And what did Josh think, Allie?''

"Oh, I don't know," she said, irritated. "Why don't you ask him yourself?"

Before she could rise, Tory grabbed her arm. "Hey. Hey, cool down. Give me a break. I'm your big brother, remember? I just want what's best for you." He waited for her to settle back in her lounge chair. "Allie, I don't care if the guy swallows swords for a living as long as you're happy. All right?"

Allie nodded angrily once, then smiled. "All right. I'm sorry. It's just that I know what I'm doing and I want you to approve."

"Will you take a reserved judgment?"

"Sure." Allie grinned. "I just wish Josh was half as reasonable."

"Josh is never reasonable when it comes to his friends hitching up. Remember what a hard time he gave Val and me when we decided to get married?"

Closing her eyes, Allie giggled softly, remembering. "Yes. He was awful."

"He refused to be my best man until a few weeks before the wedding. I had to beg him every day for three months. Val's mom was about to kill him."

Allie's giggles turned to gurgling laughter. "Poor Josh. He was so miserable. I remember him standing beside you at the altar in that black tuxedo. He looked like the grim reaper."

"Yeah. It made for some real interesting wedding pictures," Tory said, laughing and wiping his eyes. "Good old Josh. At least some things in life remain constant. The sun always rises, and Josh will always be opposed to the state of matrimony."

Slowly Allie's laughter died, and she leaned her head back against the cushioned chair. Good old Josh.

Opposed to commitment of any type. He always had been.

But why? Allie wondered.

"What?" Tory asked.

Glancing at her brother, Allie realized she'd spoken aloud. Before thinking about it, she repeated, "Why? Why is he like that?"

Tory raised his hands in a gesture of helplessness. "Got me. I guess it probably has something to do with his father. Not that I know much about it. You know Josh. He never talks about that kind of stuff much."

"What happened with his father?"

Tory shrugged. "I don't know. I got the impression that the guy was a real jerk. Left Josh's mom or something, I think."

Allie waited, but Tory didn't continue. "Poor Josh," she finally said.

Tory snorted. "Poor Josh? I'll tell you, Allie, if some woman ever cared about Josh too much, it's not Josh I'd waste my time feeling sorry for. He'd make her life hell. We might be friends, but I saw him in action in college, and 'poor Josh' hasn't changed much since then."

Pensively Allie studied the sky above them, soft and dark as black velvet studded with glinting diamonds.

"No," she agreed quietly. "He hasn't changed much."

LOUNGING LIKE a grumpy grizzly, his back propped against the edge of the kitchen sink and his dark hair mussy from sleep, Josh froze in the act of raising his coffee mug to his mouth. It was his first cup of coffee that morning, Allie knew, and Josh was never really human until he'd had at least three.

She hoped this wasn't the beginning of a huge argument, although she knew wishing wasn't going to do any good.

"What do you mean you're flying home tomorrow morning?" Josh sputtered. "We just got here. You can't fly home already."

Allie dipped her spoon into a bowl of bran flakes, took a large mouthful and mumbled, "Yes, I can."

"What? What did you say?"

Swallowing, she laid down her spoon. "I said I'm flying home tomorrow, Josh." In a lower voice, she added, "Everything's fine here. There's no reason for me to stay. Not when I have so much to do back home."

"No reason?" Incredulously he stared at her. "You've come all this way, and you're not even curious about Lena LaLorne? After everything I showed you on the plane?"

"Of course I'm curious. But that doesn't change anything. I'm flying home tomorrow."

"Why? Why can't you stay a few more days? Just a couple of days, Allie." With his unshaven face and still-sleepy eyes, the smile he meant to be beguiling didn't quite come off. "I sure could use a little help, and since you're here—"

"No." Rising, Allie drank the last of her orange juice and headed for the sink with her bowl and glass. "Excuse me," she said, pushing Josh out of the way.

"I don't believe this," he said to the empty air in front of him. "She's here in Seattle with possibly the biggest story of the decade practically under her nose, and she's flying home."

"That's right," Allie said. "I'm flying home. Josh, this is your story. I offered to talk to Nancy about coming out here with you, and my offer is still open. But I'm not going to let you talk me into working on this book. I'm leaving Grauber, remember?"

"I remember." Taking a long sip of coffee, Josh studied her in frustration over the rim of his mug. "But a day or two, Allie. What difference could a day or two make?"

"No."

"Just go with me to check out this address. It won't even take an afternoon."

"No, I said."

"Children, children," Val teased as she shuffled into the kitchen. Even though Val was dressed only in her robe, Allie thought she detected a radiant glow around her sister-in-law. No one, Allie thought, had a right to look so cheerful in the morning. "Are you two fighting already? It's barely nine in the morning."

"Allie's flying home tomorrow," Josh stated bluntly.

Pausing by the open refrigerator door, Val looked at Allie in surprise. "What?"

"That was my reaction, too," Josh muttered.

"You're flying home tomorrow? But why, Allie? You just got here. Aren't you and Josh going to work on his new book?"

Allie sighed, deeply and audibly. "No, I'm not. I explained all that last night. Josh is on his own, and I'm going home to try to get ready for a whole new life."

"But, Allie," Val protested, "we hardly ever see you...."

"I know." Allie put her arm around Val's shoulders. "But I'll be back. Soon. I promise. Maybe I'll bring Walker with me next time."

"Terrific," Josh said under his breath but loud enough for them to hear. "That'll be something for all of us to look forward to."

Allie shot him a blistering look, then smiled at Val. "Besides, we have all day to spend together."

"I suppose you must have a lot to do," Val said. "Moving is never easy, I know. It's just that I was looking forward to going shopping with you and eating lunch at that new café I was telling you about—" With a chagrined smile, Val broke off. "I suppose the café will still be there next time you visit."

"We've got a date," Allie assured her. "Shopping and crepes. My favorite."

In disgust, Josh set his mug in the sink. "I'm going to get dressed," he growled.

As he stomped out of the kitchen, Val turned to her. "Bad mood, hmm?"

Allie grimaced. "That's putting it mildly. He's acting like a spoiled child who can't get his own way. You'd think I was ruining his career by leaving Grauber."

On the wall behind them the phone rang, and Val reached for it as she said, "Well, you two have worked together for a long time. It's probably upsetting for him to see you go. Hello?"

Val listened for a moment, then covered the receiver and widened her eyes at Allie, laughing. "Oh, my," she said in a fake Southern accent. "Bless me, honey child, but I do believe it's Rhett Butler on the phone for you."

With a stifled giggle, Allie grabbed for the phone.

"I'll just wait out here on the veranda for y'all," Val said as she moved to the screen door leading to the patio, "where I can look out over my beloved Tara."

With barely contained laughter, Allie raised the receiver. "Walker? How wonderful. I was going to call you this morning. I wanted to let you know I'm coming home tomorrow."

From the corner of her eye, Allie thought she saw a shadow move in the dining room just outside the kitchen door, and with a frown, she heard familiar heavy footsteps on the stairs a second later.

CHAPTER FIVE

BALANCED ON THE EDGE of her seat just above the dugout, Allie pulled at the brim of her baseball cap to shade her eyes and smacked her fist into the mitt she wore on her left hand.

"Come on, Gilchrist," she urged. "You can do it."

Beside her, Val sat in dark sunglasses, surreptitiously reading an article on French fashions in a women's magazine and only watching the game when her husband was up to bat or behind the plate catching.

Allie had always thought it odd that Tory had fallen for a woman as delicate and ladylike as Val. Although, in a family whose lives revolved so much around Tory and baseball, Val had been a breath of fresh air. Suddenly Allie had acquired a "sister," someone to discuss makeup, go shopping and giggle about men with. Although Allie's own concern with clothes and hair generally stopped with a trip or two to the mall twice a year, she appreciated Val's knowledge and had made good use of it on a number of occasions. What Allie liked best about her sister-in-law, however, was the sensitivity and gentleness Val had engendered in Tory shortly after they'd met.

She and Josh had often joked that Val and Tory were like two pieces to a puzzle. Neither of them seemed quite complete without the other, but together, they made a great couple.

"Come on, Gilchrist! Don't let him strike you out!" Josh shouted, jumping to his feet beside Allie. "Swing, dammit!"

"Josh," Allie said, tugging at his arm. "Sit down. That lady behind you can't see."

"What?" Josh asked distractedly as he lowered himself to the seat. "What did you say— Oh, damn!" Up again, he threw a punch at an imaginary opponent.

"Josh," Allie insisted, pulling at him.

Looking as though he was in the depths of despair, Josh fell into the seat and pulled at his baseball cap. "That's it. The inning's over. Why'd they ever trade Everett for Gilchrist? The guy hasn't swung at a pitch all season."

Without looking up from her magazine, Val murmured absently, "It's only May, Josh. He had a .280 average last year." She turned a page.

For a moment Allie and Josh gaped at one other, then began to laugh. When Val gave them a suspicious look, they only laughed harder.

"Hot dogs! Hot dogs! Get 'em while they're hot!" a vendor shouted across the crowd.

"Oh, Josh," Allie said, "tell him to wait."

Josh rolled his eyes. "Allie, you've already had a hot dog, a bag of popcorn, a soft pretzel and a snow cone."

"That was hours ago. Quick, grab him."

Josh shook his head, but stood up and reached into his pocket for his wallet. "You're going to be sick," was all he said.

Poking up the brim of her cap, Allie watched the hot-dog vendor spot Josh, give him a thumb's up and bend down to rest his case of hot dogs in the aisle. In that second, previously hidden behind the vendor, Allie saw two men in dark suits standing in the next section. Across the rows of spectators, the tallest one was staring straight at her with a cold, dispassionate gaze.

With a shiver of unexplainable fear, Allie returned his stare, unable to look away. The man had eyes like blue ice, and he was watching her pointedly.

The next moment the vendor stood up, blocking the two men from view again, and passed a hot dog down the row of spectators. Shaken, Allie managed to get to her feet to peer around him, but the two men had disappeared.

"Josh," she whispered nervously.

"Thanks," Josh was saying to the man beside him as he took the hot dog. "Here you go, Allie. I hope you don't get a horrible stomachache from all the junk you're eating. Although I don't know why I'm worried. You could eat a case of Twinkies and never flinch."

"Josh," Allie began again, ignoring the hot dog he held out to her.

Something in her voice made him pause, and Josh frowned. "What's wrong?"

Uneasily Allie tilted her head in the direction where the men had been standing. "Over there. There were two men over there."

Whirling, Josh scanned the crowd, instantly alert. "Where?" he asked. "Who are you talking about?"

"In the next section. They were in suits. Two of them."

Turning back to her, Josh studied her, then took her arm and helped her into her seat. "You're as white as a sheet, Allie. I told you not to eat all that stuff." Reaching across Allie, he handed the hot dog to Val. "Here, Val. Get rid of that."

Startled, Val looked up from her magazine. "What's wrong?"

"Oh, nothing. Allie just ate too much junk again. You want to walk around?" he asked, his voice concerned, despite his words.

Vehemently, Allie shook her head. "I'm telling you, Josh," she said quietly so Val couldn't hear. "There were two scary-looking men over there, and they were watching us."

"They were probably just staring because you and Val are so gorgeous. Don't worry, I'm here. I won't let any perverts get close."

"It's not funny, Josh. They weren't perverts. Perverts don't wear dark suits and ties."

"Oh, really? That's strange. I thought they came in all sizes and shapes."

"Not at the ballpark, they don't. How many people do you know who dress in a suit for a baseball game?"

Suddenly still, Josh gazed at her thoughtfully, a muscle in his jaw working. His dark eyes were disturbingly and abruptly hard. "Two of them, huh?" he finally asked.

"Yes. Two."

"Did they look like—" Josh paused, his face blank "—like feds?"

Allie shook her head. "I don't know. I don't think so. They looked meaner than that, and their suits were better."

Josh nodded wordlessly, which only increased Allie's alarm. She hated it when Josh became still and quiet like this—like a leopard, slinking soundlessly through the jungle, just waiting to pounce.

"I'm going to go look around," he said.

"Josh, no." Allie grabbed his arm and glanced anxiously at Val, who was still deeply absorbed in her magazine. "They're gone now. They know I saw them. You won't find them. I know you won't."

For another moment Josh watched her, as though debating whether or not to heed her words. Finally he leaned back in his seat. "All right. But I think I'd better go check out that address this afternoon."

"Oh, Josh," Allie hissed. "I don't think that's such a good idea. Not now."

A small, not entirely pleasant smile formed on Josh's lips. "I think it's a terrific idea, *especially* now."

Damn! Allie wanted to shout. Why did this always happen? No matter how hard she fought, Joshua Mercer always seemed to win in the end.

Falling heavily back into her seat, Allie stared blindly at the dusty baseball diamond before them. If she was smart, she'd go back to Tory's, pack her bags and catch the first flight to New York tonight—not wait until tomorrow. If she was smart, she'd head straight for Walker and safety and not give Josh another thought.

But that would never happen, she knew. If she left now, she'd be wondering and worrying about Josh the whole time—and those two men in dark suits. Maybe she was just getting alarmed about nothing. Chances were, they were just two businessmen taking an afternoon off from work. Some businessmen worked on Saturday, didn't they?

But what if it was something more ominous than that? What if Josh had, once more, opened his mouth to the wrong person?

Damn Josh, she thought. Josh *and* his stupid books. He was doing it to her again.

"All right," she said from between clenched teeth. "But I'm coming with you."

Josh raised his eyebrows in surprise.

"If those two men are anything like what we think they might be," she went on, "you don't think I'm going to let you go alone, do you? You'll get yourself killed one of these days, Joshua Mercer."

Recovering quickly, Josh shrugged. "Whatever you say, Allie."

Fuming, Allie crossed her arms over her breasts and slumped down in her seat.

"Well," she heard him say. He sighed deeply under his breath. "So much for discretion."

Not bothering to hide the annoyance in her voice, Allie muttered, "You can say that again."

Two HOURS LATER, when Josh pulled the rented compact up to the curb outside the Blue Moon Motel, he took pleasure in the skeptical look on Allie's face. The aging seedy motel looked like it had been the scene of countless secret trysts and shady deals.

"*This* is the address you got? I don't think so, Josh. Lena LaLorne wouldn't be living in a place like this."

"She's not," Josh answered, reaching into the back seat for the leather backpack that held his notebooks and tape recorder. He winked at her. "I had another idea."

The startled look on Allie's face pleased Josh even more. He was only teasing her, but it was nice to know she was susceptible to that kind of teasing. In fact, it made him feel sort of warm inside.

"Don't look so shocked, Allie. We aren't staying. We're ditching the car."

"Oh," Allie said a little too casually. "I knew that."

"Uh-huh." Stepping out of the car, Josh resisted the temptation to glance up and down the street to see if they were being observed. He really didn't have to look. He had a strong eerie sensation down his spine that told him they were. While that feeling might have made other men edgy, Josh relished it. It confirmed everything he was hoping for. It meant someone else thought he was on the right track, too.

"This place is perfect," Josh said cheerfully as he held Allie's door for her. "Don't look around. We can leave the car in plain sight, and while any interested parties are waiting vigilantly, we will have snuck out by the pool and be long gone."

"How in the world did you know this motel was—" Allie broke off and held up her hand. "Never mind," she said quickly. "I don't want to know."

With a disdainful toss of her head, she marched courageously across the sidewalk and pushed open the glass front door of the motel like a crusader wading into battle with the heathen hordes.

In the hall outside room 37 a few minutes later, Josh fumbled with the keys. The carpet beneath his feet was old and faded and the walls were painted an unappealing gray-green, but the room itself was spotlessly clean. It smelled like disinfectant.

Nervously Allie went to the small window that overlooked the back courtyard and empty pool.

"What do we do now?" she asked.

"Wait. Someone's dropping off another car behind the motel. I told him to leave the keys in it."

"Someone? A friend?"

"You don't want to know."

Flicking back the curtain, she looked out. "There's no car out there."

"I know. That's why we're waiting."

Setting his pack on the floor, Josh sat on the edge of the bed, tested the mattress by bouncing a few times, then lay back.

"Josh?"

He was staring at the ceiling, which was crisscrossed with jagged cracks. "Hmm?"

"You know I'm still going home tomorrow, don't you?"

He didn't answer. That large crack, he thought, running down the middle toward the corner of the ceiling, looked a lot like a giant duck.

"I'm only here this afternoon to make sure you don't do something stupid. You understand that, don't you?"

Still Josh didn't answer her.

"In fact," she said, sitting down with a squeak in a chair under the window, "I think it would be a good idea if you came back with me to New York. Regardless of whether Lena LaLorne is at that address or not. I didn't like the looks of those guys at the ballpark."

At his continued silence, she said sharply, "Josh?"

Maybe not a duck, Josh thought, still looking at the ceiling. Maybe a Colt .45.

"What do you see in him? In Walker, I mean," Josh finally asked, his voice low and quiet.

He heard her sharp intake of breath.

"After all these years why did you settle on this guy?" he went on. "I'm just curious, that's all. What's so special about him?"

When she remained silent, he turned his head and looked over at her. She was sitting in an armchair with worn brown fabric rubbed shiny with age, her face turned to the window.

"He must be something pretty special," he prompted, wondering if she, too, could hear the thin note of petulance in his voice that he couldn't quite cover up.

"Well..." she finally said slowly, "maybe because he wants so many of the same things I do."

Suddenly, violently, Josh wished he hadn't asked. He already knew what it was about the Dentist that attracted her. He knew exactly what it was. That squeaky clean, spotlessly white life, that aura of normality and stability—those were the things, he sensed instinctively, that had drawn her to the man. Hadn't she been talking night and day about wanting a husband? A father for the children she wanted to have? Who better than someone like the Dentist? He would give her the life she was used to. He moved at ease in the world she had grown up in and now wanted again.

Walker Claremont-St. John wouldn't disappoint her. He wouldn't mess things up. He wouldn't desert her or fail her. The Dentist was probably the best man for her, Josh thought. And he hated him for that.

Like a movie suddenly flickering to life on the dingy ceiling above him, Josh's memory stirred, and an image appeared. Once again he was eighteen and following Tory across the threshold into the bright, clean, shining kitchen of that rose- and ivy-covered house on Magnolia Street. The whole house had been filled with sunlight and smelled of lemon polish, and he had felt as out of place as if he had stepped into the middle of an episode of "My Three Sons."

He'd been terrified, more terrified than he'd ever felt on the darkest, meanest street of the neighborhood he'd grown up in. Like a large, hulking black dog—a mangy stray Tory had brought home with him—he'd stood in the center of that sunny kitchen, afraid to move, afraid to walk because he might leave scuff marks, afraid to touch anything and leave dirty fingerprints.

The Shannons, with their reddish blond hair and light eyes, fair complexions and neatly laundered clothes, had tried their best. But all that weekend in their cheerful, fairy-tale house, he'd felt like a clumsy, gauche, dark beast. A monster who'd crawled up from the sewers of South Chicago. That weekend he'd learned that poverty and neglect, dirt and desperation, weren't just things a person lived in. They were something a person was. That kind of poverty and all that it entailed clung to a person's skin like a foul smell and got under his nails so that he could never wash it away.

He'd done his damnedest. Over the years he'd forced himself to learn, to mimic the other young men in his fraternity, to watch and listen, to act the way they did, to insinuate himself into polite society and to forge a place for himself among them, those golden people who, he'd thought as a child, had existed only on TV. Yet he'd never felt completely at ease.

Over the years he'd fooled a lot of people, but he'd never really been able to fool himself. So he found himself, again and again, returning to the streets. The grimy underworld, the foul, dirt-encrusted underbelly of society where crime was more common than compassion and the rules were brutal and hard, but tangible and easily understood—that was the world he knew best. Funny, but in the end, he'd used that sad world, written about it, and by explaining and understanding it, tried to buy himself a place in another world—one that was as far from the streets as possible and where he had never felt completely comfortable.

There were still times, usually late at night, when it came back to haunt him. Mostly he would recall the smells—the stink of vomit and urine in stairwells, of stale cigarette smoke hanging heavy in the air, of age-old grease and unwashed sweat—and the sounds of sirens in the streets, the wail of babies, the furious, defeated shouts of couples tearing out each other's souls for what life had condemned them to. In a blinding moment he would hear and see and smell it all again and know the truth. He had never really escaped.

Despite the lovely Tudor house and the money, despite the success and the women, he was still the young eighteen-year-old standing in the center of the Shannons' kitchen, facing in terror a slender young girl with shining red hair pulled back in a ponytail, her face scrubbed fresh and glowing and her skin smelling like powder. He was still the young man who saw her take in his heavy, black leather jacket, faded blue jeans, steel-toed boots and long scruffy hair. He would always be the boy who saw the quick flicker of alarm in her wide green eyes and her uncertain glance at her brother in search of reassurance. And he would never be able to outgrow, outdistance or outwit the painful twist of humiliation and despair that one glimmer of fear had caused him.

"Josh?"

With a start, Josh heard Allie call his name. He could hear her moving restlessly by the window, the sound of her slow breathing audible in the quiet room. Through the smell of disinfectant, he thought he caught a whiff of the clean coconut scent of her shampoo. He closed his eyes, not answering, and for just a moment remembered that other hotel room, the one in Cleveland....

That night she had smelled so good in his arms, warm and fresh like early spring sunshine on new leaves. He thought he'd never touched anything as soft and smooth as her skin.

That night he told himself he wanted her all his life, even before he'd seen her standing in that kitchen. She was everything he ever needed, the salvation he longed for, his one chance to escape the darkness. He'd held her in his arms, and when she'd moved against him...

Beside him the bed creaked and Allie touched his knee. "I think the car is here," she said.

For a moment—too long a moment—Josh kept his eyes closed tightly. He could feel the warmth of her body close to his. So close he had only to reach up and touch her, pull her to him and hold her once again.

Would she whimper and moan as she had that night, calling his name over and over in a breathless rush that thrilled him to his very soul? Or would she haul off and slap him for what he'd done and—God help him—what he wanted to do again now?

"Josh?" Allie said softly. "Are you asleep?"

He had no right to her, Josh reminded himself sternly. He didn't deserve a woman like Allie. He thought he'd squashed all remaining vestiges of desire and longing for her. So why, he moaned inwardly, why was he doing this to himself?

Clearing his throat, Josh opened his eyes. "What? Oh, yeah. Yeah. I must have dozed off."

"The car's here." She studied him closely, concern shadowing her eyes. "Unless people are in the habit of leaving cherry-red Maseratis in the alley behind the Blue Moon Motel."

Running his hand roughly through his hair, Josh sat up. "Yeah. I mean, that's the car. Are you ready?"

Allie stared at him doubtfully. "Sure. Why not? I wasn't doing much, anyway." She frowned. "Josh, are you all right?"

"Of course I'm all right." Josh snatched his pack from the floor, avoiding her eyes. "Why wouldn't I be?"

Raising her hands in defense, Allie shook her head. "No reason. I guess you're just being your usual grouchy self."

Without replying, Josh headed for the door and peered down the empty hall. He tried to concentrate on what he was doing, on what needed to be done, but he could still feel the hot rush of desire coursing through his veins, doing things to his body he'd prefer Allie not see.

Just one fleeting memory, he complained silently, and the old unsatisfied longing was chewing at his guts again. It was enough to drive a man to violence.

Grouchy, she'd called him. Well, why not? He had a right to be grouchy.

"Come on, then," he said. "While the coast is clear."

"I'm right behind you," she replied, laying a hand on his back.

Her touch nearly sent him rocketing down the hall. "Jesus, Allie. Don't do that."

"Do what?"

"That. Just don't." He glared at her, then looked down the hall again. "Come on. Let's go for it."

He could hear her at his heels as they quickly made their way to the exit at the end of the dimly lit hall. Before pushing open the door, Josh surveyed the bare courtyard around the empty pool.

"Okay, let's go," he said. Once in the car he fired up the engine and finally gave her a smile. "I hope those guys brought plenty of sandwiches with them. They're going to get mighty hungry waiting for us to come out of that motel."

"If they know anything about you," Allie said sweetly, "I'm sure they'll have come well prepared."

Startled, Josh shot her a disbelieving glance. She couldn't have meant what he suspected she meant, could she? No, of course not. Not Allie. But he thought he detected the ghost of a smile on her lips before she turned her face to the window.

"HELLO. MY NAME is Frank Houser," Josh said pleasantly to the young woman holding open the screen door with her foot. A toddler with solemn eyes peered around the woman's legs at Allie. "We're from Mutual Alliance Insurance. Here, let me give you my card…" Josh was fumbling in the pocket of his leather jacket when the woman interrupted him.

"I'm sorry. We already have insurance. If you'd like to come back some evening, though, my husband—"

"Oh, no. No." Josh laughed airily. "We're not selling insurance. We're trying to locate a policy-holder who lives at this address. A Mrs.... Mrs...." Josh stopped, squinting up at the sky as though the name was on the tip of his tongue.

"Rita, do you recall the name offhand?" he asked Allie.

Allie smiled stiffly and merely shook her head.

"Well, there you go," Josh said, clasping his hands in front of him humbly. "I guess I'll have to go back to the office, after all. You see, it's on the other side of town, and we thought we'd be able to take care of this little matter while we were nearby. It's been busy lately, and the boss hasn't been too happy with me, you know. I'll try to explain to him, though. Sorry to bother you."

Somewhere in the redbrick, comfortably middle-class house, a baby began to cry. The young woman glanced anxiously over her shoulder.

"Well, maybe I can help you. What's this about?"

Josh inclined his head. "That's very kind of you. If you're sure it's no bother..."

"No. No bother." The cries grew louder. "How can I help?"

"Well, we're trying to locate an elderly woman, a Mrs.... Well, there you go again. In simple terms, she's owed a small disbursement—nothing signifi-cant, mind you, but you know how the elderly can use every penny these days—and this is the last address we have for her. She has to sign some documents, you see."

"Oh. You must mean the woman who owned the house before us."

"Who owned the house before you?" Josh repeated, looking slightly stricken.

"Yes. I know she was elderly, but I don't know her name. The house was empty when we bought it, and the bank handled the sale for the previous owner." At the expression of regret on Josh's face, the woman looked worried. "I'm sorry. I wish I could help you, but..."

"We understand," Josh said politely. "Thank you, anyway, for your time."

By now the cries had escalated to angry wails.

"Sorry," the young mother said again as she shut the door.

Silently Josh and Allie made their way down the sidewalk to the street. Josh's disappointment was so strong Allie could feel it emanating from him in waves.

"Josh, I'm sorry. It was a long shot, though. You knew that."

He nodded wordlessly and stopped by the car to lean despondently on the hood.

"At least you know an elderly woman used to live here," Allie said brightly.

"Yeah." Josh gazed dispiritedly at the redbrick house. "I guess it was too much to hope for, that she'd still be here. We'll have to talk to the neighbors. Which side of the street do you—"

He broke off as the front door of the house suddenly flew open again.

"Hey!" the young woman called. Pushing the toddler firmly back into the house, she came down the steps toward them. "Wait. I remembered something."

The sudden hopeful look on Josh's face made Allie inwardly cringe. *Lady,* she wanted to say, *this had better be good.*

Stopping by the car, the young woman handed Josh a small stack of what looked like thin glossy magazines, then smiled at Allie.

"We get these catalogs in the mail every once in a while. They're addressed to someone named Ellen Driscott." She looked a little embarrassed. "I probably should have given them back to the postman, but I figured they weren't too different from junk mail. Do you think that was wrong?"

"No," Josh said reassuringly. "I'm sure they're exactly the same as junk mail. Besides, we wouldn't want to tie up our postal system any more than it already is, would we?"

The woman gave him a funny look as though she wasn't sure whether or not he was pulling her leg. *Good luck figuring that one out,* Allie thought.

"Anyway, maybe this is the woman you're looking for."

"Thank you," Josh said with complete sincerity. "I really appreciate this. My boss'll be happy, and you've made our job a hundred times easier."

"Oh." The young woman looked pleased. "Well, that's good. You're welcome."

As Josh pulled the car onto the freeway ten minutes later, Allie fingered the pages of the catalogs, murmuring, "Ellen Driscott. Ellen Driscott. Ellen. Elena. Ellen. Elena." She looked over at Josh. "Do you suppose Lena's a diminutive of Elena?"

"I don't *suppose* so," Josh said, pulling around a truck. "I *know* so."

ALLIE PUSHED a broccoli spear around her plate, sipped from the small china cup of tea and stole another look at Josh. Huddled close together at the back of an enormous vinyl-covered booth, they had a clear view of the front door of the Chinese restaurant, but were themselves hidden in shadow, away from any prying eyes.

Beside her, Josh scribbled furiously in a notebook, his own plate of mu shu pork pushed to the side. He kept pulling at a lock of hair so that it fell over his forehead, and his rugged face was set in an appealing look of concentration.

In silence Allie nibbled a water chestnut and watched him. His firm mouth was fixed, and she noticed a small unshaven patch of black whiskers under his square jaw that had escaped his razor that morning. She'd bought him an electric razor one year for his birthday, but although he'd thanked her at the time, he'd continued to show up with little cuts on his chin and an occasional dab of shaving cream on his earlobe. Josh had always been resistant to change.

Biting his lip, he looked across the restaurant in deep thought, then licked the tip of his stubby pencil and began to scrawl on the page again. He'd pushed up the sleeves of his faded denim shirt, and his muscular forearms rested on the white tablecloth, encircling his notebook protectively.

Unexpectedly Allie felt an almost irresistible urge to reach out and trace the strong line of his jaw, run her fingers through his tousled hair and brush a fingertip along the thick muscles of his arm. Stunned by the intensity of her desire to touch him, she looked away, then impatiently stabbed a bamboo shoot.

Josh was an attractive man. It was perfectly natural for a healthy woman like herself to feel desire for an attractive man. There was nothing wrong with that. It didn't mean a thing.

Just because he made her feel light-headed and a little weak in the knees at times was nothing to panic about. Before, perhaps, it would have been cause for alarm. Before, perhaps, she would have ridiculously prayed for him to notice her attraction to him and feel the same, but now she was too wise for that. She had her life under control.

She had a wonderful new life waiting for her, and she wasn't going to let herself forget it, no matter how much raw sexuality Joshua Mercer exuded.

"Feel better?"

Startled, Allie's head snapped up guiltily. "What?"

Josh's mouth curved into a smile. "You said you just had to have Chinese food or perish. Although after everything you consumed at the ballpark, I can't imagine where you have room to put it. I was wondering if you felt better now that you've gotten your fix of soy sauce."

"Better?" Allie stared at him blankly. "Oh. Yes. Much better."

He was watching her, smiling in amusement as though he'd been able to read her thoughts of a moment ago, and she twisted uncomfortably in the booth.

"How's the Vegetable Delight?" he asked.

"Fine. Not enough bok choy, but otherwise fine."

"Good."

Wordlessly Josh continued to smile at her, his eyes dark and intent. She saw his Adam's apple move, and the corded muscles of his neck were taut and strained. Still he watched her without speaking.

Around them the restaurant seemed to grow quiet and fade, receding as the silence between them stretched out. Then, as though in a slow-motion dream, Allie heard a rustle of denim. Breathlessly she saw Josh move nearer to her. With a sense of long-awaited anticipation, she saw him lean closer to her until she could feel the warmth of his breath and smell the faint muskiness of his cologne. Her heart skipped a beat, paused, then skittered in panic as he lifted his hand. Holding her breath, she closed her eyes, raising her face ever so slightly.

Josh's rough fingers gently brushed the side of her face, her cheek, the tip of her ear, and she nearly moaned. Then suddenly he pushed himself away from her.

"Your hair's coming loose," he said kindly. "You almost dragged that strand through your Veggie Delight."

In openmouthed bewilderment, Allie stared at him dumbly.

"I don't care what Val says," he continued, turning back to his notebook. "I like your hair better down. It's too pretty to hide in that tight little coil. Besides, it never stays up very long."

Allie gaped at him, stunned and uncomprehending. Her hair?

A sudden wave of embarrassment and self-reproach washed over her. Her hair. What a fool! What a silly fool she was. Josh only meant to brush back her hair. He wasn't going to kiss her. He never was.

"Hey, where are you going?"

Scrambling, Allie scooted out of the booth. "To the ladies' room," she snapped.

Josh looked wounded, then shrugged. "Sorry I asked," he grumbled, and went back to his notes.

In the rest room Allie leaned both arms on the counter and glared at her reflection in the mirror. Her face was flushed, her eyes were suspiciously shiny, and her hair was indeed falling around her face.

"You idiot," she told herself sternly. "Get ahold of yourself."

Oh, what was wrong with her? She'd nearly made a complete fool of herself. Hadn't she told herself a million times? Hadn't she just reminded herself, as she'd done over and over again, that Josh wasn't interested in her? He wasn't attracted to her one little bit.

One night, just one long-ago night, he'd gotten drunk and taken her to bed, and it must have been absolutely awful for him, because he'd never mentioned that night again.

Straightening her back and raising her chin, Allie looked hard at the woman in the mirror.

"He doesn't find you attractive," she said firmly. "Don't forget it again."

Clearing her throat, Allie gave a determined toss of her head, smoothed her hair and bravely marched back into the restaurant. When she reached the table, Josh looked up apprehensively as though he expected her to clobber him. When she reached for her purse without sitting down, he frowned.

"What are you doing?"

"I'm going back to Tory's, and you're going to drive me there."

Josh squinted at her. "But I thought you agreed to go to the library with me."

"I've changed my mind," she said simply, her voice stubborn. "I want to spend some time with Tory and Val before I leave tomorrow morning."

Josh shook his head in bafflement, but rose and dropped some money on the table. "I don't get it," he said, following her across the restaurant. "Why, all of a sudden, did you—"

Wheeling abruptly, Allie gave him a fierce look. "Don't," she nearly shouted in exasperation. "I don't want to argue about it. Everything is a battle with you, Josh. Everything. We argue about every little detail. You always have to get your own way. Can't you give it a rest?"

Raising his hands as though to fend her off, Josh took a step backward. "All right. I just asked a simple question. Jeez, bite my head off."

Without waiting for him, Allie stalked to the front door and outside into the parking lot.

In the car they drove in uneasy silence. Josh sat expressionlessly behind the wheel, never glancing at her, apparently judging it safer to keep his mouth shut. With every passing mile Allie grew calmer and felt more terrible about yelling at him.

It wasn't Josh she was angry with. It was herself. She had no right to take it out on him just because she'd nearly made a fool of herself. Certainly it wasn't his fault. It wasn't his fault that he wasn't attracted to her, that she'd wasted ten years of her life waiting for him to notice her. She thought she'd gotten over that. She thought she'd come to terms with it.

She was just nervous and jumpy, that was all. She was making a big change in her life, the biggest change she'd ever made. After years of wishing, of being unsatisfied, of wanting more, she'd finally made up her mind to turn her back on her old life and start over. It felt a little like teetering on the edge of a precipice, trying to talk herself into stepping off and into the black, yawning chasm.

Frowning, Allie thought about that. She wasn't sure that was how a major change was supposed to feel, but how would she know? She'd never tried to make one before. Maybe regret and longing and reluctance were natural feelings when a person ended one life to begin another.

Unconsciously Josh sighed softly beside her, and Allie snuck a quick peek at him. Resting his head against the seat, he drove with one hand, a crestfallen expression on his handsome face.

Allie felt a pang of guilt. She'd been unreasonable. He was her friend, and she'd shouted at him. Not only was she a fool, she was a spiteful fool.

"I suppose," she began stiffly, "that you're dying to find out if Ellen Driscott is still in Seattle."

At the sound of her voice, Josh sat up and glanced at her uncertainly, unsure of how to react to such a skimpy olive branch. Apparently he chose nonchalance. He shrugged. "Yes. I guess so."

Nodding once, Allie looked away at the rapidly darkening sky outside the window. When she turned back, Josh seemed to be engrossed in his driving, but she knew he was alert and waiting for her next move.

"Well, since it's on the way to Tory's, I guess we could stop by the library first," she said, relenting. "If you still want to."

Josh's lips twitched as though he was trying to suppress a smile. "Sure. I guess we could."

"We can't stay long," Allie hastened to add. "But a few minutes wouldn't hurt, I suppose."

Josh turned to her, and the smile he was trying to hide finally escaped. "Thanks," he said simply.

"Don't mention it."

Feeling a hundred times better, Allie exhaled deeply and leaned back in her seat as the little sports car sped down the highway.

CHAPTER SIX

FROM WHERE HE SAT at the microfilm machine, Josh could see Allie conversing with the plump blond woman behind the reference desk. A second later the woman rose to go off in search of the reels of microfilm Josh had told Allie to request. Impatiently Allie tapped her foot, then turned to gaze in his direction. Quickly, before she could catch him watching her, Josh pretended to be absorbed in the newspaper page on the screen before him.

He'd already had one close call this afternoon. No reason to make Allie any warier of him than she already was. For the hundredth time, Josh berated himself for pulling such a stupid move back at the restaurant.

Ever since they'd left the motel earlier that afternoon, he'd felt as if he was walking on eggshells. In the close confines of the little car, he'd been so aware of Allie he could scarcely breathe. No matter how hard he tried to block it out, he felt the warmth of her femininity all around him—the sweet, fragrant, womanly smell of her, the stir of her breath, the soft curves of her body under her white fisherman's sweater and the tantalizing fullness of her lips when she smiled at him.

At the restaurant he'd felt her watching him, studying him from beneath her lashes when she thought he wasn't looking. For one insane moment he'd flattered himself that her eyes were inviting him to do what his body had been demanding he do all day, and he'd nearly kissed her.

Damned scoundrel, he cursed himself now.

Just in the nick of time, he'd brushed a soft wisp of auburn hair from her cheek and fallen back in the booth, shaken by the close call. When she'd stormed out of the restaurant a few minutes later, he was certain she'd known.

Sick with regret, he'd followed her to the car, sure she was about to tell him their friendship was over. In the rush of relief he felt once he realized she wasn't about to do that, all he could think of was how lucky he'd been. But now, sitting in the quiet library, he felt again the bitter twist of self-reproach.

He'd always known Allie was a special woman. Even if she hadn't been Tory Shannon's little sister, Josh still would have known she was off limits to him. Not all women were like her—the ones who didn't mind brief affairs. But there were others—women he'd only dreamed about, women who *loved,* women who deserved fidelity and commitment—and those women were prohibited to him. Like innocent lambs, they were better off protected from wolves like him. He'd always known that Allie was one of those.

Recently, however, he'd been finding it harder and harder to resist his attraction to her. Little by little, he could feel himself coming closer to committing the same terrible mistake he'd made four years ago in Cleveland. So far only his conscience had kept him from trampling again on that forbidden ground. But lately the control he'd wielded seemed in danger of slipping.

Today he'd almost kissed Allie. But that wasn't the worst of it. The worst of it was that, this evening, he still wanted to.

Things were starting to fall apart, but at least he thought he knew the reason why. Allie was just a good friend, he assured himself. She might be beautiful, intelligent and more fun than any woman he'd ever known. He might even describe her as his *best* friend, but she was still only a friend. The problem was that he'd just been working too hard, driven by worry over his career and Allie's threatened move. Lately he'd been neglecting his social life, and the strain was beginning to show. That was all.

When he got back to Tory's, he'd look through his address book. Surely he'd still have the phone numbers of a few women in Seattle. He'd call one up and take her out. They'd have dinner, a few laughs, then a little fun later. He'd feel better afterward. He'd stop thinking about Allie day and night.

"Josh?" Allie bent over him, her eyes concerned. "Josh?"

With a start, he realized she'd been calling his name, and he shook his head to clear it.

"Here are the issues you asked for. They don't have this year on microfilm yet, but I don't think we'll need it. Do you?"

Josh took the spools of film from her. "No, probably not. This should be fine. Thanks."

"Sure." Allie studied him, her expression uncertain. "Well, if you're all set here, I thought maybe I'd go look in the phone books."

Josh paused in the act of rewinding the roll he was through with. "Phone books?"

"Maybe I can find a listing for Ellen Driscott." Allie waved deprecatingly at his stacks of microfilm. "Seems simpler than searching through all those years of newspapers."

Josh smiled in amusement and threaded a strip of film into the machine. "Allie," he said patiently. "I don't think Ellen Driscott's going to be in the phone book."

"Why not? Lots of people are."

"Yes, but they aren't hiding from the Mafia, the FBI and the entire American media, either."

"Well, I'm going to check them, anyway." Making a face at him, Allie turned. "Sometimes you just make things too complicated, Joshua Mercer," he heard her say before she flounced away.

No, he didn't, Josh silently told the machine. Most of the time, he didn't have to. Life made things complicated enough without his help.

IN THE MIDDLE of the vast reference room, Allie sat at a long wooden table, a huge stack of Washington state telephone books at her elbow. The cavernous room was nearly empty, and every cough, every scrape of a chair leg and every footstep seemed to echo hollowly, magnified in the silence.

Allie wearily closed the Auburn City telephone book and reached for the next on the pile. As she began to flip through the pages, her attention was soon distracted. Again.

Once more she replayed the scene in the Chinese restaurant, analyzing every word and gesture. No matter how many times she went over it, she couldn't shake the feeling she was missing something. It was ridiculous, she told herself once more. Josh had *not* been about to kiss her. She knew he hadn't.

And yet . . .

Oh, why couldn't she stop this? Torturing herself this way was not going to accomplish anything. After ten years Josh hadn't suddenly changed overnight. She had simply imagined it—and nearly made a fool of herself in the process.

Thank God she was going back to New York tomorrow. Being around Josh twenty-four hours a day was making her crazy. Now she was imagining he'd wanted to kiss her. What next? Hearing voices? Seeing little spacemen?

"Allie."

Tomorrow she would board that plane, return home and begin her journey to a new, *sensible* life with Walker. Tomorrow it would all be over.

"Psst. Allie."

Mystified, Allie glanced around at the empty tables closest to her, then shrugged and opened the telephone book to the *Ds.*

"Allie," a voice hissed. "For God's sake."

She looked up again. Good grief, she really was going crazy. She'd only been joking about hearing voices, but—

"Allie. Over here," she heard from somewhere behind her.

Nervously wetting her lips with the tip of her tongue, she slowly turned in her seat and stared at the shelves of books behind her.

"Come here," the voice said.

Getting to her feet apprehensively and holding the telephone book against herself like a shield, she tiptoed toward the shelves. She'd barely reached them when a powerful arm snaked out and dragged her through a tiny opening in the shelving and into the aisle beyond.

"Josh!" Allie gasped. "What in the world—"

"Shush. I don't have time to explain. Do you have your purse with you?"

His face was set and expressionless, but the way his eyes glittered alarmed her.

"No, it's on the table. What's going on, Josh? What's the matter?"

Without answering, he glanced up and down the aisle, still holding her arm so tightly she could barely keep from wincing.

"I want you to go back to the table—casually, mind you—and get your purse. Then I want you to *slowly* walk back here to me. Got that?"

Allie gaped at him.

"Go on, Allie. We don't have much time."

Her alarm turned to fear. "Josh, you'd better tell me what's going on—now. What's happening?"

His expression hardened, and for a moment she thought he might not answer her again. "Remember those two guys you saw at the ballpark?"

An icy dread crept through her, and Allie shivered. "Yes," she said in a hushed, frightened voice.

"Well, I think they're here."

"Oh, no. Oh, Josh. They followed us?"

"I don't know, but it looks that way. Now, will you just do what I ask? There's no more time to discuss this."

She stared at him. "What are we going to do?"

"Allie, please—"

"No, Josh. I want to know what we're going to do."

He shook his head in frustration. "We're going to hightail it out of here. If we just stay calm and hurry like hell, we can probably get out without them seeing us."

"What?"

"Don't argue with me, Allie. Just do what I say."

Before Allie could protest, a quiet creak in the next aisle made her heart stop. Her eyes widened as she stared at Josh. A second later they heard another creak, like someone walking stealthily in new leather shoes, farther down the aisle.

Soundlessly Josh pulled Allie into the opening between the shelves, glancing warily behind him. With his strong arms wrapped around her and the telephone book she still held, Josh pressed her back against his chest. Lowering his head, he whispered softly in her ear, "When he leaves, do exactly what I said."

Allie silently shook her head, bumping his chin and feeling her hair get stuck in his whiskers. Raising a hand, Josh smoothed her hair down.

"I'm not asking you," he hissed fiercely. "I'm telling you."

Again she vehemently shook her head and felt Josh's arms tighten angrily.

Suddenly they heard the creak of leather again in the reference room on the other side of the shelves. Pulling her roughly back behind the shelves, Josh gave a quiet warning. "Ssshh."

Cautiously, moving inch by inch, they peered together around the shelf. A man stood in the center of the reference room, looking over the nearly empty tables. Allie frowned.

"Josh," she whispered. "That's not one of them."

Josh stared at her. "What?"

"Look at him. He's wearing a light blue suit—not a very good fit, either—and a trench coat. Besides, he has blond hair and a crew cut. I'd swear the other men I saw were both da͞ ͞ired. I've never seen this man before."

"But he's obviously searching for something."

"Maybe he's looking for a book."

Josh shot her a look of annoyance. "Allie, that guy's—"

"Hush," she said. "Look."

A second man, taller and also dressed in a trench coat, joined the first. They seemed to discuss something intently, then walked together toward the front of the library.

"They're FBI," Josh said confidently. "I've seen enough of their field agents to spot one a mile away. They must have been following us all day."

"I'm telling you, Josh, the two men at the ballpark didn't look anything like these guys. The other two weren't FBI agents, I'd bet my life on it."

Josh grimaced. "Don't say things like that. Not now, anyway."

"Josh, let's get out of here."

"That's precisely what I had in mind."

"No, I mean *out of here*. Go back to Tory's, pack and catch the first plane home."

"Allie, we can't."

"What?" Whirling in surprise, she faced him with anxious eyes, which slowly narrowed. "Oh, yes, we can. I am."

Josh froze, his face obstinate. "Oh, no, you aren't."

"Oh, yes, I am," she stated belligerently. "And you're coming with me, right back to New York."

A vein in Josh's neck pulsed visibly, and his lips tightened. Patiently he explained, "Allie, I don't know where we're going, but I can tell you right now that it's not back to Tory's. Not with these jokers tailing us. Think about it a minute. There's probably a dozen more of them waiting at the house right now. And at the airport, too."

Allie felt her mouth go dry at his words, the fight in her receding like the sea at low tide. "Oh, my goodness!" she gasped as realization dawned. "Do you think those were FBI agents we slipped away from at the motel?"

"I wouldn't doubt it."

Stricken, Allie stared blankly ahead.

"We're fugitives," she finally exclaimed with growing dismay. "The FBI is after us again." Suddenly she turned on him. "Joshua Mercer, I'm going to kill you. This time, I'm really going to kill you."

"Not now, Allie. Kill me when we get someplace safe."

ALLIE DECIDED it was probably the wildest ride she'd ever had in a car, which was quite a statement after ten years of driving with Josh. If she'd known how Josh intended to throw the feds off their scent, she might have tried harder to convince him they should turn themselves in.

"We'd better stop at a car wash." Josh steered the car cautiously down a side street. "Don't want to attract too much attention."

Still too stunned to speak, Allie merely nodded. A bushy branch, stuck in the passenger side mirror, banged against the window, startling her. She tried to look out but could barely see through the mud-splattered windshield.

"Sorry about that hedge. Guess you were right," he commented calmly. "I could have sworn that opening was wide enough."

Swallowing hard, Allie tried to steady her pounding heart. She didn't know which had frightened her more, the gray Ford that had followed them out of the library parking lot or the high-speed ride through back alleys, deserted lots, a construction site and what had appeared to be a small aqueduct.

It wasn't until she glanced down that she realized she was still gripping the telephone book with white-knuckled fingers. Frowning in confusion, Allie stared at the book, then widened her eyes. Good grief, not only was she a fugitive, but she'd also stolen library material.

"There's a gas station with a car wash over there," Josh said, turning the wheel. "Might as well fill up the tank while we're at it. Then we can figure out what we're going to..." He paused. "What's wrong?"

Allie held up the thin book. "I think I just stole this. I'm a thief."

With a snort of derision, Josh reached for the book and threw it into the back seat as he turned the car into the gas station. "Calm down. It's just a telephone book. You can send the library a donation when you get home." Turning off the engine, he opened his door. "Do you want anything? It looks like they've got a snack bar."

"No, thanks," she replied frostily. "I'm not very hungry."

Before shutting his door, Josh gave her a teasing look of astonishment. "I never thought I'd live to see the day. Not even a bag of chips?"

In angry silence, Allie stared at the mud-streaked windshield.

Josh hesitated at her grim expression. "Look, Allie," he began, a note of apology in his voice. "I'm sorry I dragged you into another—"

"Don't. Don't say it, Josh. I don't want to hear it. Not now."

For a moment longer he gazed at her, then gave a curt nod and slammed the car door. She watched Josh stroll into the station, pause in front of the counter to talk to the attendant, then return to the car and reach for a gas pump.

Allie tapped her foot with impatience, seething. How could he? He knew perfectly well she wanted to go back to New York tomorrow morning. She'd made her intentions absolutely crystal clear. Yet here she was, stuck on the other side of the country with Josh, running from the FBI and God only knew who else.

If she hadn't known how much more difficult his job was going to be with the FBI breathing down his neck, she'd have thought Josh had planned the whole thing. That would be just like him. He was a stubborn, pigheaded lout who always had to have his own way.

Through the windshield, Allie watched as Josh pulled branches from the front hood and the bumpers. Childishly she stuck her tongue out at his back, then turned away with a sigh, catching a glimpse of the telephone book in the back seat. Reaching back, she snatched it up and began to flip savagely through the pages, muttering under her breath.

"All right, let's drive through the car wash and decide what we're going to do next." Josh settled in the seat beside her. "I think we should find another library and see if we can't track down Ellen Driscott."

Still staring at the page, her anger momentarily forgotten, Allie murmured in disbelief, "We don't have to."

"What?"

"I said, we don't have to." She pushed the telephone book at him. "We found her."

Incredulous, Josh stared at the page and the name Allie marked with her fingernail. "My God."

"And you scoffed at me for looking through the telephone books. Don't *you* feel stupid now?"

"Ellen Driscott," he read in disbelief. "Where is this? What telephone book is this?"

"Birmingham," Allie told him. "I'd only gotten to the *Bs.*"

"Birmingham. My God, you're a wonder, Allie. You're a genius. Birmingham." He paused. "Where the hell's Birmingham?"

Opening the glove compartment, Allie pulled out several maps, found one for Washington state and shook it out. Josh took one side, and they spread the map across the dash.

"I don't see it," Allie complained after a moment.

"What a minute," Josh said in an excited rush. "Here it is. Birmingham. I'd say it was about 120 miles north of Seattle. Almost on the Canadian border."

In silence they gazed at one another. She knew what he was thinking without him having to say a word.

"You want me to go up there with you," she stated flatly.

He didn't reply.

"What are my other choices?" she asked.

Josh's gaze was open and direct, but she could see the tension around his mouth. "You don't have to go," he said. "I'm going up there one way or another, but you don't have to come with me if you don't want to. You can get out of this car right now and go back to Tory's. Or go to the airport. Anywhere. Of course the feds'll pick you up immediately. They'll question you, and you'll have to tell them the truth. Everything." He paused. "You're not in any trouble. They'd let you go. But only after you tell them everything they want to know."

It was emotional blackmail, Allie thought in frustration. She knew how much this story meant to him, and Josh knew she knew. If she told the FBI everything, she'd be destroying any hope for his book. The FBI would be all over Lena LaLorne within the hour, and Josh would miss his chance to talk to her. They'd never let him near her.

Allie stared out the window, her brow furrowed. Just once, she thought, she should turn the tables on Josh and get out of the car. Tell the FBI everything and fly home to New York. That was exactly what she should do. Hadn't she promised herself she was going to make a clean break? A fresh start?

She sighed and turned back to him. "Once you talk to her, can I go back to Tory's?"

His relief was palpable. "The very next instant."

"You swear?"

Josh grinned and started the engine. "Scout's honor."

It wasn't until they were on the freeway headed north that Allie remembered Josh had never been a Boy Scout.

WHEN THEY FINALLY REACHED 113 Wisteria Street in Birmingham, it was eight-thirty, and the neat gabled house set back from the street was nearly in darkness. A lone light shone dimly from a side window, weakly illuminating the carefully trimmed bushes beneath it.

Allie and Josh sat in the car in the relative darkness between two street lamps and watched the house. Then Josh took a deep breath, stirring beside her. He reached behind them for his backpack.

"This is it," he said, his voice tense but excited. "Let's go meet a living legend."

However, after several long minutes of knocking and waiting, then listening to a slow fumbling at numerous locks and chains, they watched as the front door cracked open to reveal an elderly woman who looked like anything but a legend, living or otherwise. In a shapeless yellow housedress and worn slippers, her white hair half-hidden under the type of bonnet Allie's grandmother used to wear over her curlers at night, the woman squinted out at them suspiciously, obviously ready to slam the door in their faces at the slightest provocation.

Mutely she blinked at them from behind huge glasses with thick lenses that enlarged and distorted her eyes, giving her a startling resemblance to a goldfish in a bowl. She carried a three-pronged walking cane and was badly stooped, her back crippled by what Allie guessed was advanced osteoporosis. Allie tried in vain to see even the slightest similarity between this woman and the Lena LaLorne of the movies. There was none.

"Miss Driscott," Josh began gently, "my name is Joshua Mercer. This is Allie Shannon. We're sorry to bother you, but we were wondering if we could have a few minutes of your time."

The woman continued to consider them silently for a moment or two. "What do you want?" she finally demanded, her voice slow and cracked as though it had gone unused for a long while. "Who are you?"

"I'm a writer, Miss Driscott." Josh glanced at Allie but didn't explain her presence. "We've come a long way. From New York. We'd like to talk to you about Lena LaLorne."

Allie watched closely for the slightest flicker of recognition, but the woman's face never altered from its wary suspicion.

"Could we talk to you about Lena and Sid?" Josh asked.

"You must have the wrong house, young man." The woman began to shut the door. In a querulous voice, almost a whine, she said, "I'm watching my program. On the television. You have the wrong house."

"I realize it's been a long time," Josh insisted. "I know you must be frightened and don't want to talk about—"

"I don't know what you're saying," the elderly woman's voice rose a nervous fraction. "I'm watching my program."

"Josh," Allie said, laying a warning hand on his arm.

Josh took a deep breath. "I'll be staying at the Birmingham Arms Hotel, Miss Driscott. Room 345. If you want to talk about Lena, please give me a call."

"I don't even know who you are," the woman muttered as she pushed the door closed.

For a few moments Allie and Josh stood on the front stoop, listening as the thud of the cane and the shuffle of slippers faded away. Wordlessly they turned together and walked back to the car.

Only when they were once more seated in its warm closeness did Allie venture, "Josh, do you think we could have made a mistake?"

Josh stared across the street at the house. In the light from the street lamps, she could see puzzlement in his steady gaze.

"No," he finally replied. "I don't think we have."

"What makes you so sure?"

"I didn't hear a television."

Allie thought about that. "Maybe she turned it down when she answered the door."

"Maybe. And maybe she just wanted to get rid of us."

STRETCHED OUT on the bed in her room at the Birmingham Arms Hotel, Allie stared at the ceiling. In the adjoining room, she could hear Josh moving around—the rustle of papers, the squeak of bedsprings, the shout of laughter when he'd called Tory to tell him what was happening and the sound of water in the bathroom sink, all distinguishable through the thin wall separating their rooms.

She thought again about the call she'd made to Walker and the uneasy hesitation in his voice after she'd told him she would be detained in Seattle for a few extra days. She pondered her half-conscious failure to tell him where she was and her strange unwillingness to be more specific about her return date.

"Your brother's troubles turned out to be more difficult, then?" Walker had asked.

"No." She'd drawn out the word reluctantly. "Everything's fine with Tory and Val. They've made up."

"I see," he'd said, although she wasn't sure what it was he saw. "I guess I'll cancel my plans to meet up with you in New York tomorrow, then."

"Yes. You probably should."

The rest of the conversation he'd talked about an operation he'd helped out on, the repairs he was making on the yacht and the dinner he was arranging for her to meet his mother and sisters the following week. She'd barely stifled a noisy yawn during a discourse on whether he needed his golf clubs regripped, catching herself with a scowl.

Weren't these the things that interested her, too? Well, maybe not at the moment, but they were what she'd been looking forward to filling her life with. Wasn't that why she'd found Walker appealing in the first place? His interests were so wonderfully ordinary.

Yet she couldn't deny she felt little disappointment about missing a date with him. And with that realization came another, equally disconcerting—she'd barely thought of Walker all day. In fact, she'd almost forgotten about him.

She should have been furious at Josh for keeping her here on the West Coast when she had so much to do back home, but she wasn't. She wasn't upset at all. She'd gotten caught up in his theories and enthusiasm about Lena LaLorne.

It seemed like old times with the two of them together, picking through facts, reviewing information, trying to put the pieces of the story together and arguing over possibilities. That feeling, she knew—that comfortable feeling of camaraderie and shared preoccupation—was dangerous. So dangerous she wouldn't let herself think about it. She hadn't wanted to come to Seattle with him, and she certainly hadn't wanted to make this trip to northern Washington. But she couldn't pretend she wasn't enjoying herself just the tiniest bit.

With a quick rap on the connecting door, Josh pushed it open and took a few steps into her room. His dark hair was mussed from running his hands through it, and he stared down at his notebook with a frown, chewing thoughtfully on the end of a pencil.

"But why did she move?" he asked intently, as though they'd been having a conversation all along.

Propped against the pillows of her bed with her ankles crossed, Allie raised an eyebrow speculatively. "I beg your pardon?"

"Why did she move?" Lost in thought, Josh looked up from his notebook and slowly focused on her. "Why did she move from Seattle to Birmingham?"

Allie shrugged. "I don't know. Maybe she likes small towns. I guess you'll just have to ask her when you go back tomorrow. If she'll talk to you."

"The Polk Register said Ellen Driscott owned the house in Seattle for fifteen years. She's an elderly woman. After fifteen years she'd have felt settled there. Comfortable. Probably unwilling to pull up roots. What happened two years ago that made her suddenly decide to move? And to a smaller house in a much less affluent neighborhood than her previous one?"

"Maybe she ran out of money. It could be anything, Josh. I don't mean to burst your bubble, but aren't you getting a little ahead of yourself? We don't even know if this woman *is* Lena LaLorne."

"I know. I know it's her."

Allie sighed. "Well, whether it is or not, we're never going to find out if we starve to death. I'm dying of hunger. I thought we were going to try to hunt down some dinner."

Snapping shut his notebook, Josh gave her a brilliant smile. "You're always starving. God knows how you stay so thin."

"I have high metabolism, and it demands to be fueled at regular intervals."

"Fueled is a good word for it. I saw a burger place down the street if you don't mind—"

"Umm. That sounds wonderful. With a huge basket of fries."

Josh shook his head. "One of these days, Allie, the surgeon general is going to put your face on a warning poster. 'This woman scoffed at fats, sugars and cholesterol.'"

"Look who's talking," she retorted, sliding off the bed. "You lived on scotch, coffee and granola bars all last winter."

"Yes, but *those* are good for you."

AFTER DINNER they went back to Josh's room and studied the files he'd brought with them. Josh had bribed the waitress at the Burly Burger into making them a pot of coffee, probably sweet-talking her in the bargain, Allie thought, because he'd also come away with two thick pottery mugs, as well as the glass coffeepot itself.

At two in the morning Allie finally rose from her place in the middle of the mess of papers and photos and stretched her tired muscles.

"I'm turning in. If I look at those photos one more time or drink one more cup of coffee, I'll throw up."

"Hmm," Josh murmured absently, his eyes on the newspaper article he held. "Pleasant thought." Still reading, he pulled his leather pack closer and thrust his hand inside, pulling out a wrinkled blue shirt. "Here," he said, throwing it in her general direction.

"What's this?" Allie held the large cotton garment delicately with two fingertips.

Josh finally looked up from his article. "Huh?"

"This. What is it?"

"A shirt." He saw the look on her face. "It's clean, Allie. I'm not asking you to do my laundry. You can borrow it if you want something to sleep in."

"Oh." She looked at the shirt. "Thanks."

"Don't mention it. Right off my back, Allie. Anytime. Right off my back."

"I'll remember that."

Stepping cautiously over the mess, Allie paused at the open door and turned to look at the room. The floor was covered in a jumbled disarray of notebooks and files, spread fanlike around the man who leaned back against the bed. His blue denim shirt was open at the throat, his sleeves were rolled up, and his thick black hair was standing on end.

Sitting like that with his legs stretched out before him, so dark and so big he seemed to dwarf every piece of furniture in the room, Allie was reminded of the big brown bears at the zoo.

A soft smile of affection touched her lips, and a sweet, sharp pang of tenderness twisted her heart.

Joshua Mercer was absolutely and completely the wrong person for her to care about. He drank, he swore, he fought, he was irresponsible and unpredictable, and he went through women the way he went through running shoes. He didn't want what she wanted, and he wasn't attracted to her. But God help her, she loved him more deeply than she'd ever loved anyone in her life.

"'Night," Allie said softly. Without waiting for his reply, she shut the connecting door behind her.

CHAPTER SEVEN

WHEN ALLIE WALKED into her room, the red message light on the phone was winking, and with surprise, she called the front desk.

"A Mr. Walker Claremont-St. John called. At eleven-thirty-two. No message other than that he called."

"Oh." Taken back, Allie bit her lip. "He...he didn't say to return his call?"

"No, ma'am."

Allie felt her stomach lurch. "Thank you."

Walker had phoned her at the hotel.

Unsteadily she replaced the receiver in its cradle. He must have called Tory's house, wanting to speak to her again that night. He must have gotten the phone number of the hotel from her brother because *she* hadn't given it to him. She hadn't told him where she was. Not that she was being deceitful...exactly.

Lowering herself to the edge of the bed, Allie held Josh's blue shirt in numb hands and stared darkly at a spot on the opposite wall. Then why? she asked herself. If she wasn't trying to deceive him, why hadn't she told Walker where she was? She'd allowed him to assume she was still in Seattle at her brother's house. She'd never told him she was in a hotel in Birmingham, Washington, with her old pal Joshua Mercer.

But Walker must know that now, as well. Despite what Josh thought about him, Walker wasn't stupid. If Tory hadn't already told him she was with Josh, he'd have guessed.

But guessed what? Allie asked herself with sudden anger born of guilt. There was nothing for Walker to guess about. Nothing at all. There was nothing, absolutely nothing between her and Josh. Not one little...

Raising the blue shirt, Allie buried her face in it to stifle the sob that rose unexpectedly from her throat. Like the one card holding up the stack of cards, she felt her self-control give way with that sob. In a rush of overwhelming despair, the tears welled from her eyes and she struggled to silence her sobs.

It was no use trying to fool herself. She knew why she hadn't told Walker where she was. She'd been lying to herself. She'd been lying to Walker. There *was* something between her and Josh, the most important thing of all.

In a blinding rush of realization, Allie knew she would never move to Charleston. She couldn't do it to Walker. She couldn't do it to herself.

It was no use. Oh, she wanted to move to Charleston. Part of her wanted that life so badly she ached. A home, children, hanging curtains, family picnics, pot roasts, dirty diapers, college funds, little sticky fingers clutching at her hair—oh, she wanted it all! The yearning was so deep it was like a gnawing hunger, and it was so close, just within her grasp. Yet she knew now with absolute certainty she would turn away from it. It wasn't going to be hers, after all.

For between her and Josh was something she and Walker would never have—her love. She loved Josh.

She'd always loved him, and no matter how far she ran from him and the utter hopelessness of the situation, she knew she would continue to love him for the rest of her life.

How could she have ever thought of marrying one man when she knew she loved another? She couldn't do that to Walker. The guilt she now felt was real. The regret was justified. She was alone in a hotel with the man she loved—regardless of the fact that he didn't love her back. Although nothing would ever happen between her and Josh, she'd as good as lied to Walker, and even if he hadn't found out, she still knew. She knew she'd lied to him about everything because she'd lied about everything to herself.

Josh had been right. Things didn't work that way. She wanted the life-style and forgot about the life. Someday Walker would realize what she'd done, and he would grow to hate her. She would grow to hate herself.

Dear God, she cried silently, Josh's shirt pressed against her face, what was she going to do? She knew now that her dreams of living in Charleston had gone up in smoke. She'd lost her dreams about a husband and a family. Those dreams would never be hers because she knew she could never have *any* relationship with anyone but Josh. And he didn't love her.

As she sobbed, she began to realize she wasn't weeping from guilt for what she'd almost done to Walker. Her tears were for herself, for all the years of longing for a man she could never have—and for all the long years of fruitless waiting she knew she would face in the future. It was impossible. The years stretched before her, bleak, loveless and empty, and there was nothing she could do about it.

Overcome by grief, Allie didn't hear the connecting door open. She never noticed Josh until he was standing a few feet away, staring at her with a look of devastation and dismay on his face.

"Allie? Are you . . . are you crying?"

Huddled on the edge of the bed, his shirt covering her face but not quite muffling the sobs that tore from her throat, Allie turned away, trying to hide from him.

"Allie?" he asked again. "What's wrong?"

She only shook her head, twisting on the bed so her back was to him. Her slender shoulders heaved with her stifled cries.

Hesitantly Josh took another step, his heart twisting. He reached out a hand to her, but she shrank from him.

"Please, Allie. Talk to me. What's going on? Please," he begged.

Raising one hand to brush him away, she shook her head again. "No," she gasped, then hiccuped. "No. I don't . . . I don't want to talk about . . . about it."

In an agony of indecision, Josh stood with his hands at his sides and stared down at her. Finally he sank to his knees, wrapped his arms around her and held on even when she pushed and hit at his shoulders.

"It's okay," he murmured, knowing he was lying. "It's okay. I'm here, Allie. It's going to be all right."

After a long while her sobs grew quieter, and when she pushed away from him, he let her go. Almost angrily she wiped her face with the shirt he'd given her.

"Walker called," she finally said.

Josh watched her, feeling as though his insides had just been torn out. "Oh," was all he could manage.

He wanted to hold her again, but his heart was too heavy. Instead, he knelt beside her until his knees began to ache and his back was breaking.

They didn't speak again until she thanked him in an embarrassed voice and told him she was going to sleep. They hadn't needed to say anything more. Reluctantly he rose and made his way to the connecting door, holding on to the frame for support as he somehow stumbled to his own bed in a state of stunned, shocked horror.

He hadn't imagined she would react like that. He'd planned it, but he'd never thought.

He *never* thought, Josh accused himself, the words screaming silently through his brain. He never thought about anyone. He only thought about what he wanted. Isn't that what Allie had accused him of that very afternoon?

When he'd called Tory that evening and asked him to leave a message with the Dentist telling him where Allie could be reached, he'd thought he was being clever. So goddamned clever. The Dentist would find out they were together at a hotel and naturally think the worst. What man wouldn't? Even if Allie found out about the call, he could say he was only trying to be thoughtful. He could claim he'd never considered that the stupid jerk might think . . .

But he'd never imagined she would cry. He'd never dreamed Allie would cry like that, each sob slashing at him like a whipcord of guilt. He'd never felt such pain, standing there helplessly in the face of her sorrow, unable to assuage her and knowing that he—*he*—had done this to her.

My God! Josh mouthed silently, sitting on his bed and holding his head. He was a bastard. He'd felt only pleasure and pride when Tory warned him about "pulling Allie's strings." He was so good at it. Time after time, year after year, he'd been so good at swaying people, at fixing things—fixing things *his* way. He was so very, very clever.

Like steel bristles scouring his soul, Josh made himself look back on everything he'd done lately. He'd engineered everything. He'd plotted and schemed and twisted everything to suit himself. He was a manipulative bastard, he told himself with loathing.

Suddenly he admitted with startling truthfulness what he'd known all along. He wanted Allie. He'd always wanted her, but he'd always known he could never have her—so he'd be damned if anyone else would, either.

How many adoring men had he chased from her life in the past ten years? Too many to count.

Pressing the heels of his hands against his ears, Josh squeezed hard, trying to shut out the sounds of her sobs, which still echoed in his mind. Not this time, he told himself. This time he would put things right. It didn't matter anymore whether he liked the guy or not. It didn't matter anymore that it twisted his gut to think of Allie with that grinning fool. The only thing that mattered was that Walker was the man Allie wanted. He'd seen that all too clearly tonight.

By God, he'd get on the very next plane. Damn his story! He'd go to Charleston, and he'd tell the Dentist everything. He'd tell him how he'd manipulated the whole trip. He'd confess how he'd planned for the Dentist to call the hotel and find them together. He'd swear that nothing had happened between them. It would take every ounce of strength he had. It would be the hardest, the most difficult thing he'd ever done in his life. It would tear his heart out to do it. But he'd go. He'd beg and plead if he had to, but he'd make that stupid idiot see the truth and take Allie back.

Because, he finally admitted for the first time in his life, because he loved her.

"ALLIE?" Josh called again, and again received no answer.

In the feeble shaft of morning light seeping through the drawn curtains of the hotel room, Josh could see Allie's rumpled bed. From the doorway he stared at the tangled pile of blankets, and for one horrible moment he thought that the bed was empty, that she'd guessed what he'd done and run away from him in the night.

Then the blankets stirred, and a rush of relief that made him dizzy swept through him.

"Allie?"

One hand appeared above the blankets, pulled them farther over her head. "Go away."

"It's morning," he said inanely.

"Don't care. Go away."

Josh stood at a loss in the doorway, his heart aching. "We were going over to see Lena. Miss Driscott. Remember?"

"No." Her voice was hoarse and thick.

She must have cried all night, Josh thought. He felt like wailing himself. "Allie, please—"

"Go without me," she said, more strongly this time.

Twisting under the blankets she pulled herself up to lean against the headboard. Her auburn hair was a wild tangle that spilled over her shoulders. Her eyes were shadowed, and her face pinched and pale. Although she clutched the blanket to her, he could see she was wearing his blue shirt, and his heart gave another lurch.

"I don't feel very good," she added. "I'm just going to stay here in bed."

She certainly didn't look well. Josh doubted he'd ever seen Allie look so pale and drawn. He couldn't remember her *ever* being ill before. But she wasn't really ill now, either, he reminded himself. She was heartbroken over Walker, and it was all his fault.

"At least have some breakfast," he said. "I'll go get you something from the—"

"No. I'm not hungry."

"Allie, I know you're upset, but you've got to take care of—"

Smoothing the bunched blanket that lay around her, Allie shut her eyes. "I'm not moving to Charleston."

At her words, Josh reached out a hand for the door frame. Even though he'd expected them, he was overwhelmed by dread at what he knew he had to do. He felt a little sick himself.

"Allie," Josh began, pausing to swallow because his throat had gone so dry, "if he thinks that something happened between us, if he's angry about that, I'll call him. I'll go to Charleston and tell him the truth."

If anything, her face grew even paler. "What?"

Oh, God, Josh wanted to moan, *don't make me have to tell her everything. Don't make me have to confess everything I've done to her.*

"I know you love him. I hadn't realized that before. He'll understand," Josh said, his voice beseeching. "I'll make him understand. I'll tell him that—"

With a quick frantic movement that startled him into silence, Allie covered her ears.

"Stop it, Josh. I'm not going to see Walker any-more. So just stop it. I don't want to talk about it. God, I just don't want to talk about it."

His breath was trapped in his lungs. He was being smothered with guilt. What had he done to her? He hated knowing she could be this grief-stricken over another man. But mostly he simply couldn't stand to see her so upset.

"Allie, please, listen to me," he begged.

"No! No, I won't. Just go away, Josh. I don't need you to run interference for me. I don't want you to explain anything to anyone." She gave a small bitter laugh. "I don't believe this. After the way you went on and on about him, I thought you'd be pleased."

"I know I wasn't very nice about the whole thing. I still don't like the guy much. But, Allie, if you—"

She couldn't stand it anymore, Allie suddenly thought. She couldn't bear to hear the man she loved trying to convince her to stay with another man. It was tearing her heart into small, bloody pieces.

Grabbing for the nearest pillow, she hurled it furiously at Josh, stopping his horrible words and making him duck. With quick instinctive reflex, he caught the pillow in the air, held it and stared at her in confusion.

"Shut up, Josh!" she shouted. "Just shut up and leave me alone."

Josh's mouth opened, but no words came out. His brown eyes were filled with compassion for her, and she almost wanted to laugh again. He thought she loved Walker. He felt sorry for her.

How sorry would he feel if he knew the truth? If she told him right now that she loved him, that that was the reason she was going to break it off with Walker, she knew exactly what would happen. The sympathetic light in his eyes would turn to nervous dismay. His gaze would slide away in embarrassed pity. His face would grow troubled, and he would withdraw from her, shut her out, distance himself from her just as he had in Cleveland four years ago.

She didn't think she could handle that right now. She sensed that would be the last straw, the thing that sent her right over the edge.

"I'll be okay," she said stiffly, steadying her breath. "I just need some time alone."

"I want to help."

He stood in the doorway, clutching a corner of the pillow she'd thrown at him so that it dangled at his side. His dark handsome face—scarred and lined and strong with the inner strength that had taken him so far, made him so much—was sad. Sad for her.

"I know you do," she said gently. "Thank you. But believe me, it's better this way."

Josh stared at her with indecision. At last he closed his eyes, appearing to take her words as some final, immutable defeat. His broad powerful chest seemed to shrink a bit, and his wide muscular shoulders sagged.

Without another word, he dropped the pillow onto the desk beside the door and turned to go, with his head bowed like a boxer leaving the ring in disgrace to the sounds of boos and ridiculing hisses.

ALL THE WAY to the little house on Wisteria Street, Josh gripped the steering wheel so tightly that the jagged scars across his knuckles stood out starkly white, reminders of every blow he'd ever dealt to another man's body. But he'd thrown other punches in his life, he reminded himself—horrible blows, not directed at the body. And he hadn't only thrown them at men.

Across the street from the little clapboard house, Josh sat hunched in the driver's seat and stared blindly at his hands, still wrapped around the wheel.

All night long in the Birmingham Arms Hotel, he'd lain awake, tortured and burning with guilt and something more—something like terrifying self-knowledge. As though Allie's tears had washed away a fog from his own eyes, he could see himself clearly for the first time. The realization of what he'd done to her cut him to his soul, and from the cut oozed years of memories and regret.

Senseless remorse, he told himself now. Senseless, because it was too late.

He had always had his way, he realized, no matter whom he had to hurt to get it. That Christmas Day twenty years ago, he'd learned he had the physical and mental ability to change the world the way he wanted it. Of course, he always told himself that what he did was for the good of others. He'd only used his strength to protect the ones he loved.

Now he knew that was a lie. He wondered if he'd ever really believed it himself.

That long-ago Christmas morning, the front door of their tiny cold apartment had banged open and his father—no, the man who'd sired him—came bounding into the room, his tall lithe body clad only in jeans and a faded T-shirt so the maze of tattoos on his sinewy arms stood out against his pale skin. His gaunt face, aged by drink, fast living and hard times, bore a smile of sly expectation.

He'd thought they'd be glad to see him.

Josh remembered turning to where his mother sat on the couch beside his aunt Dorothy. Frozen, he'd stared at his mother, saw the startled widening of her eyes, read the quick flash of fear that swept across her features, and then—

Then she'd smiled.

He'd known as surely as he'd known his own name that she was going to take the bastard back. She always took him back. For a month, sometimes even two or three, the kitchen would be filled with the raucous laughter of his father's friends, ashtrays overflowing with cigarette butts and bottles everywhere. For a while there would be arguments and tears, shouts and blows, the police at the door in the middle of the night, the bruises his mother hid under long-sleeved shirts, the strap marks he tried to hide from his friends at school, and the shame. God, the shame. The humiliation of it all.

His father had flung his arms up, his feet splayed wide in the center of the worn, faded carpet, now growing filthy with the wet black snow that he'd tracked in.

"Give us a kiss, Helen," he'd bawled. "Got released three months early 'cause the warden was feeling the holiday spirit. How d'ya like that?"

Hesitantly, smoothing her tattered robe with one hand and patting her head of badly dyed tight curls with the other, his mother had risen to her feet, a weak, uncertain smile playing on her lips.

But Josh had beat her to it. He'd sprung to his feet, his hands clenched at his sides. In the two years since his father's most recent incarceration, he'd grown up. At seventeen, he was already over six feet and filling out fast. His mother said he was going to be bigger even than his grandfather, whom everyone had called Big Bob Brendan.

At his quick movement he heard his mother pause behind him. His father eyed him warily. Something on Josh's face must have warned the man, because the smile began to fade from his face.

"You got bigger, boy," he said, his voice still sickeningly honeyed with false friendliness. "Growed up since I seen you last."

"What do you want here?" Josh snarled.

His father narrowed his eyes, his face hardening. "That ain't no way for a boy to talk to his daddy. It's Christmas, boy."

"You aren't welcome here. Not on Christmas or any other day. Not anymore."

He said the last two words with such viciousness he heard his mother gasp behind him, "Josh!"

Straightening himself, his little black eyes glittering and growing smaller, his father took a step toward him. "Helen, you let this boy talk to his daddy like that? You been without a man in the house too long, boy. You need me to teach you a lesson on behaving proper to your elders—"

Josh hadn't let him finish. He'd bent his knees in a well-balanced crouch and raised his fists, just as he'd learned in the ring. He threw only one punch, but he put everything—all his strength and all the years of humiliation, cowering and hatred—into that single blow. He was a good boxer, a fast learner, and the punch was expertly placed.

He felt the rip of flesh across his knuckles as he made contact with his father's teeth and saw his father stagger back against the wall, reaching for the door to steady himself as blood trickled down the corner of his mouth.

With a frantic keening, more like a wounded dog than a human being, his mother bounded forward.

"Josh, no!" she cried.

Behind him, Aunt Dorothy was whining, muttering verses like chants. "The eye that mocketh at his father, and despiseth to obey his mother..."

His mother was wailing, plucking at the sleeve of his shirt, and he brushed her off.

"Get out!" he spat at his father, who was still holding on to the door, not so much in weakness as in surprise at the black hatred and terrible wrath on Josh's face. "Get out of here and never come back. Do you hear me? Or I'll kill you. I swear to God, if you ever bother us again, I'll kill you."

His father left, and he never did come back. Josh vowed that day, when his mother had rushed sobbing from the room to throw herself across her bed, that he would be the one to take care of her from then on. He would protect her. He would provide for her. He would take care of her, and he had.

He'd taken care of her from college where he'd gone on a wrestling scholarship four months later. He'd taken care of her from Detroit where he'd gotten his first newspaper job, sending her checks every month and flying in one weekend to settle her and Aunt Dorothy in a safer apartment. He'd taken care of her from New York, arranging an apartment for her in a retirement community in Arizona after Aunt Dorothy passed away—an apartment she would never live in.

In the end he'd even taken care of her after she swallowed those pills and quietly, anonymously, faded out of the world, leaving behind only a short note explaining how sorry she was, apologizing for being too lonely to want to live any longer and hoping the funeral wouldn't cost him too much.

He had thought he'd known what was best for her. He always thought he knew. But he'd been playing God, without the advantage of omniscience. He'd chased his mother's husband from her life because it was better for her, he'd always told himself.

Now he realized that the person it had really been better for was himself.

IT TOOK HER FOREVER to answer his insistent knocking.

"Miss Driscott, I only have a few questions," Josh said. "Please, won't you let me in for a couple of minutes?"

The old woman studied him from behind her glasses, her blue eyes huge and cloudy behind the lenses and her lips puckered in disapproval. When she unbent enough to ask, "Where's the pretty girl you had with you yesterday?" Josh took it as a sign he was making progress.

"She wasn't feeling well this morning," he said, hoping to gain her sympathy. "She had to stay at the hotel. If you feel better talking to me with her around, I'm sure she'd—"

Shoving open the door with a leg of her cane, the old woman scowled at him. "Come on," she grumbled ungraciously. "I can see you're determined. No sense in getting the girl out of bed if she's ill."

The hallway she led him down was bare. No rugs lay on the wooden floor, no pictures brightened the walls. The living room was little better. Except for a sofa, a blue armchair set just to the side of a blank television set and a scarred table holding a reading light, the room was empty. There were no knickknacks, no photographs, no mementos culled from a lifetime of living. She'd done nothing to make the place seem homey. The furniture was good quality, he saw, but threadbare and worn. The whole room had a temporary feeling, as though she'd just moved in or was about to move out.

When she indicated the sofa with a nod of her head and shuffled to the armchair, he waited for her to sit down, then followed suit. Her enormous watery eyes watched him, not missing that small act of politeness.

"What is it you're so desperate to talk to me about?" she asked pointedly, her old voice quivering.

Sitting forward, Josh placed his hands on his knees. "I want to know about Lena LaLorne."

Silently and without expression, the woman scrutinized him for several long moments, then suddenly she laughed, a high, rasping sound like a cackle.

"She was a movie star," she said. "Back in, oh, the forties." She gave him a look that told him how stupid she thought he was. "Anyone could tell you that."

"But I want to hear it from you, Lena."

The woman stopped laughing. Pressing her lips tightly together, she turned to look out the window behind the television set. He saw her hand fiddle absently with the handle of her cane.

"Lena LaLorne is dead," she said, pronouncing each word clearly and precisely.

"I don't think so," Josh said gently. "I think you know she's alive."

When she didn't respond he added, "You're Lena, aren't you?"

She maintained her silence, wrapping it around her like a protective shawl as she continued to stare out the window. After several minutes Josh was about to speak again when, with a start, he saw a solitary tear trace down the papery skin of her cheek.

"Miss LaLorne?" he asked softly.

She turned toward him, her eyes distorted and wavering behind the thick lenses. "She's dead."

There was something in the two words, something in the way she said them, some final, unquestionable, despairing certainty, that shook him. She wasn't talking about some obscure movie star. She wasn't speaking metaphorically.

"What happened?" he asked finally, breathlessly.

"She died. Of pneumonia. Old age. Call it what you want. The doctors did. But I knew what she really died of. A broken heart." Her hand went to the sleeve of the cardigan she wore over her dress, and she fumbled with a handkerchief she'd tucked into the sleeve. "I buried her in the Baptist cemetery here in Birmingham two years ago next month."

Sudden understanding of the situation hit Josh. "You were with her a long time, weren't you, Elsa?"

She stared at him, almost in terror, then she nodded. "Yes. Yes, I was with her a long time." Finally freeing the handkerchief, she brought it to her face and pressed it to her cheeks. "You're not a writer. You're the police," she said flatly. "Lena always said that they would come."

"No, Elsa. I'm not the police. I really am a writer."

She gazed at him, wariness and uncertainty crossing her face.

"I only want to talk to you," Josh continued soothingly. "I want to know what happened. That's all. I'll never tell anyone where you are, if that's what you want. No one will bother you."

She still looked skeptical.

"After Lena died," he began, hoping a simple question might prod her into talking to him, "you took the name she'd been using, didn't you? Her real name, before she went to Hollywood, was Ellen Groviski. The Driscotts were on her mother's side. She'd been calling herself Ellen Driscott all these years, and when she died, you started using that name."

"You seem to know a lot about her."

"Only what the rest of the world knows. At least, right now. I want to know more, but I need your help for that, Elsa."

Sighing, she looked away from him. "I buried her as Frances Webberly. That was the name I'd been using all those years. I had to pretend I was Ellen Driscott. You see, it was the only way I would have access to the money that . . . he'd arranged."

"Sid Calentro," Josh said.

"That's why I had to move. No one knows me here as anything other than Ellen Driscott." She paused. "Though no one really knew us anywhere we went."

"What happened?" Josh asked, tamping down his rising excitement. "What happened to Sid?"

"We lived in that house for fifteen years," she said with longing, as though he hadn't spoken. "We liked it. It was a pretty house. Before that, we'd only rented houses. In Oklahoma City. In New Orleans. In San Francisco." She gave a small private smile, remembering. "That was one of my favorites. We loved San Francisco."

Josh tried a different tactic. "How long was it just the two of you—you and Lena?"

"Since 1955." She saw his startled movement. "Oh, yes. That long. Forty years." As though she couldn't quite believe it herself, she repeated, "Forty years."

"What happened to Sid?" Josh prompted.

"We separated. The three of us. We had to. *They* almost found us. Almost stumbled on us in Buenos Aires. We changed identities, changed everything so that no one could ever trace us. Then we crossed back into the States. It was supposed to be safer for us."

"And where did he go?"

The old woman turned away again, abruptly.

"Elsa? Where did Sid go?"

"I don't know. We never saw him again."

It seemed that somehow, in some way, he'd crossed a forbidden line. Just when he thought she was beginning to open up, she shut down. Puzzled and frustrated, he tried everything he could think of to coax her into further reminiscing, but she dodged his questions, gave evasive answers, sinking deeper and deeper into her chair with stubborn taciturnity.

"May I come by again?" he asked at last. "Tomorrow, maybe?"

She refused to answer.

"I'll bring the girl with me, if you like. Can we talk some more tomorrow?"

Her face was impassive, her lips clamped tightly together.

Finally Josh simply rose to his feet and crossed the room, pausing at the doorway. Looking back at her, at her silent desolation, it suddenly occurred to him why he'd been so good as a reporter and an interviewer all these years.

He'd used any means he could—bullying, threatening, subterfuge, badgering and even deceit—to wrench stories from people. He'd done it in the name of justice and truth, but he'd never considered what it did to them. He couldn't think about that. He couldn't care about them, not in that way—only as players in a story he was determined to piece together and reveal.

He'd taken what he needed from his subjects and never cared because, he'd told himself, he had to be objective. He had to maintain his distance from them to make them tell their stories at all.

Although he saw the truth in that reasoning, it suddenly didn't seem very important. Just once, he wanted to try another way.

"Are you going to be okay?" he asked in a worried voice.

Elsa didn't reply.

"All right." He sighed, still reluctant to leave her. "If you need anything, Elsa, anything at all, you know where you can reach me. The Birmingham Arms Hotel. Room 345. I'm afraid I had to register under the name of Brown because . . ."

He paused. She wasn't listening to him, he realized. Why was he going on and on like this?

"Listen. Elsa. If you need me, you only have to call."

When he left the small bare living room, she was still sitting in the blue armchair, as silent as the sphinx, staring out the window.

SPECIAL AGENT Steve Johnson fixed his icy gaze on the man hovering near his desk in a large room in the FBI's Seattle office. Several men at nearby desks, he noticed, paused in the middle of what they were doing to listen.

The agent shook his head silently at Johnson's question.

"Damn." Johnson closed his eyes, breathing deeply in anger. "What the hell have you been doing, Zimmerman? How hard is it to find two people in a city this size?"

Zimmerman chewed nervously at the inside of his cheek. "We tried to trace the car, but it wasn't rented. By now they could be anywhere."

"They're here," Johnson snarled with complete conviction. "They're in Seattle. I know they're here."

Zimmerman shrugged. "Sorry."

"Sorry? *Sorry?* Sorry that neither of you two bozos thought to get a damned license-plate number? I oughtta—"

"What's the problem here, Steve?"

On the other side of the desk, a tall dignified man in his late forties paused, glancing from Johnson to Zimmerman and back again.

"Your men lost them," Johnson said with contempt. "At the goddamned library. And now they just don't know where in the world they're going to begin looking for them." Scorn dripped from his words like water melting off an icicle.

"All right, Zimmerman," Carl Haywood said dismissively. "That'll be all for now."

When Zimmerman walked away, heading rapidly toward the back of the room and safety, Haywood looked pointedly at the surrounding desks and the men still watching them. A dozen pairs of eyes were quickly downcast.

"Steve, if I could talk to you in my office...?"

"Did you get the tap on the brother's phone?" Johnson asked, not rising from his desk.

"I'm working on it."

"Working on it," Johnson sputtered, looking down at his desk. He knew better than to shout at Haywood. "It's been two days."

"I know that, Steve," Haywood answered. His voice was calm and controlled, but a note of exasperation and anger warred just below the surface. Johnson was good, Haywood knew. He just wished the guy wasn't such a bastard. "It's not easy in a case like this. Mercer and his friend haven't done anything illegal. You don't even *suspect* them of any illegal activities. Being tailed by the Mafia and expressing an interest in old movie stars isn't a crime in this country. At least, not as far as I know."

A note of sarcasm had crept into Haywood's own voice. It seemed to be the order of the day. He wondered how long it would be before tempers really started to flare over this case.

"I need that tap," Johnson said between clenched teeth. "These two aren't just innocent bystanders, Carl. We *know* they have important information on Sid Calentro."

From several desks away, a voice murmured, "Sure, and I just saw old Sid coming out of the john." Muffled laughter greeted the comment.

Infuriated, Johnson sprang to his feet, feeling tried beyond all reasonable limits. Why hadn't Gerry given him more authority out here?

"You think it's funny," he growled at the room of FBI agents. The laughter died. "You think it's a big goddamned joke. Well, I'll tell you how much of a joke it's going to be if Joey Riazzi's men get to this couple first. You'll be out there looking for *pieces* of them." Turning back to Haywood, Johnson gritted his teeth. "Washington isn't going to be too happy if a nationally renowned writer and his editor turn up facedown in Puget Sound. They're going to like it even less when they find out we've been on the case the whole time and screwed it up."

The skin around Haywood's mouth turned white, and his blue eyes went steely cold. Still, his voice was calm and level. "I'll get the wiretap, and my men will find Mercer and the woman for you."

Turning on his heel, Haywood made as though to walk away, but turned back suddenly and thrust his face close to Johnson's. For a brief second the anger simmering in him boiled over. "I promised Gerry Fourier I would help you any way I could, Steve. But I never said I'd let you bully my men and insult me while you did it. So lay off."

Dropping back into his chair, Johnson heard the older man march away. With barely repressed fury, he yanked open a desk drawer in frustration, then just as suddenly slammed it shut with all his might. The sound cracked through the large room like a rifle shot.

CHAPTER EIGHT

JOSH SAT on the edge of the bed in Allie's empty hotel room for nearly two hours, paralyzed with despair and racked by guilt.

She'd left him. Of course, he'd known she would. He'd known Allie would figure out what he'd done. He'd known she would hate him, run as far from him as she could.

When he'd returned from his interview, he'd thrown open the connecting door between their rooms, wild with excitement and the need to share everything he'd learned with her. Instead, he'd been greeted by an empty room. The curtains were still pulled shut, the bed was unmade, and Allie was gone.

God, Josh moaned, lowering his head to his hands. If there was something he could do, if there was anything he could say to her to put things right, if he could just think clearly enough to figure out what to—

When the door to the room flew open, Josh slowly raised his head without caring who it was. *Let them shoot me,* he thought. *Let them lock me up. I don't care.*

Beaming widely and struggling to push her way through the door with two armfuls of boxes and bags of every shape, Allie said breathlessly, "For heaven's sake, Josh, help me. My arms are falling off."

Disbelieving, Josh could only stare at her.

"What's wrong with you?" she squealed. "Help me! I think I'm stuck in the doorway."

Slowly he got to his feet.

"Josh!" Several colorful shiny sacks slithered from her grasp and landed on the floor. Less encumbered now, she pushed easily through the door, stepped over them and into the room, walked lightly past him and dumped the rest of the bags on the bed before turning to him with her hands on her hips. "A lot of help you are. Thanks."

"Allie?"

"The least you could have done was..." Pausing, she studied him. "What's wrong, Josh? You look awful."

Josh raked his hand through his hair, took a deep breath and closed his eyes. He knew he should ask her where she'd been, but he couldn't seem to get past the fact that she hadn't—thank God, she hadn't—left him.

"What's wrong?" she repeated, laying a hand on his forearm.

Josh shook his head and gave a short laugh. "God, Allie, where have you been? I've been sitting here for two hours..."

"I took a taxi to the mall," she said, her voice fraught with worry.

"The mall? You said you were sick. You said you couldn't get out of bed."

"I perked up," she said simply. "What happened? Didn't she want to talk to you? Did something else happen? Oh, no!" Her hand flew up to cover her mouth. "The FBI."

"No, no," he said quickly. "I was just... just concerned about you, that's all. You didn't leave a note."

"Yes, I did." Whirling, she searched the bedside table. "It was right here. I put it—" bending over, she scooped a small scrap of paper off the floor between the bed and the table. "—right here."

Josh took the paper and stared at it. He felt a rush of chagrin, followed by sudden ire. "This is what you left me? Allie, you could have been dead! The FBI could have been holding you somewhere. And you leave me this? A postage stamp is bigger than this."

"Sorry." She turned away calmly and started to unpack the bags.

"Sorry," Josh repeated to the empty air. "She's sorry."

"Here. What do you think?" Holding up a dark green flannel shirt, she pressed it under his chin and considered. "Oh, yes. I like that. That's definitely your color, Josh. And look at these. I know you prefer blue jeans, but I couldn't resist these khakis. Do you think they'll fit?"

Outclassed, he resignedly accepted the pants.

"I got you two more shirts, just in case," she was saying as she thrust those at him, too. "And of course—" meekly, he took the plastic package of briefs and another of socks "—toothbrush, razor, shaving cream." She piled them on top, stood back and smiled at him. "You're all set."

Holding the stack of clothes and packages awkwardly against his chest, Josh gave her a docile look. "I take it I'm dismissed now."

"I get the shower first."

"Of course."

"Try on the pants."

"Right away."

As he walked through the connecting door, he heard her call, "Don't forget to take the tags off."

Grinning like an idiot, he waved a hand and pulled the door shut behind him.

LATER THAT AFTERNOON, Allie propped her chin on her hand, her elbow resting on the table in the Burly Burger, and nibbled on a bread stick.

"Well, I think it's perfectly clear," she said, waving the bread stick at Josh.

"You do?"

"Sure. It's obvious." She bit off the end of the stick. "She's in love with him."

"What?" Josh grinned in disbelief and picked up his club sandwich. "That's ridiculous, Allie. You've seen Elsa. She's not exactly the romantic type."

"How do you know? Besides, she might have been. At one time." Gesturing at his plate with the bread stick, she asked, "Are you going to eat those fries?"

"Help yourself."

When she'd scooped up a handful, running them through the catsup on his plate, Josh asked, "If you're so hungry, why didn't you order more than just a salad?"

"I'm feeling fat. Shopping always does that to me. I thought I'd better diet."

"Diet? Allie, you're thin as a rail, though only God knows how."

"You think I'm too thin?" she asked, suddenly worried. She paused, holding a french fry near her lips.

"No. I didn't say that. That's not what I . . ." With a hopeless shrug, Josh took a huge bite of his sandwich and chewed furiously. "Why would you say Elsa was in love with Sid Calentro?"

"Because she doesn't want to talk about him. She talked about Lena, but she avoided your questions about Sid. She was probably in love with him for years, but he was Lena's man. Remember, she referred to Sid Calentro as 'he.'"

"So? How does that prove she was in love with him?"

"It doesn't *prove* anything. But that's my bet. Women do that all the time, talk about their ex-loves in the third person. *He* did this, the slimy so-and-so. *He* did that."

"That doesn't sound like love to me. That sounds like they can't stand the guys."

"Of course they can't. That's how you know they're still in love." At his bewildered look, Allie tried to explain as patiently as possible. "If you didn't love the guy, you wouldn't care. It wouldn't bother you to say his name. Thus, if you can't say his name, you must still care."

Josh still looked befuddled. "That's how women think?"

"Sure." Trust Josh, Allie thought, to not know a little thing like that. It was funny actually. Everyone always thought of Joshua Mercer as such a ladies' man, yet in a lot of ways, he didn't have a clue about women.

He definitely didn't know much about her. For instance, he had no idea how much effort it cost her to sit across the table like this and smile and chat with him as though her heart wasn't filled with despair. He didn't realize how much she longed to slide over to his side of the booth, wrap her arms around him and press her cheek against his chest to smell the warm masculine scent of him and to feel the hard muscles under his shirt shift and move as she settled closer to him.

He simply hadn't the slightest notion.

For hours that morning she had cowered under the covers, too heartsick to face the day, too miserable to face the rest of her life. She'd buried her face in her pillow, feeling sorry for herself and wishing she could crawl under a rock and never come out.

But finally she'd begun to tire of self-pity. It wasn't going to do her any good, she knew, and besides, it was getting boring.

So what if she'd just lost her chance at a normal life? So what if she'd quit her job, sublet her apartment and hadn't a clue about what she would do for a living, or where she would live. So what if the only man she had ever really loved—the only man she would ever love—hadn't the faintest idea of how she felt and, what's more, didn't want to know? Lying in bed all day and moaning over the disaster she'd managed to make of her life wasn't going to make anything better. All she'd get were bedsores.

She still had no idea what she was going to do, but she was going to deal with it rationally. Take one day at a time. If she could concentrate on what needed to be done that particular minute and not let herself consider the long, cold bleakness of her future, she'd keep herself busy, and maybe someday something would occur to her.

With that thought, she'd pulled herself out of bed and gotten dressed. Eventually she'd come up with the idea of taking a taxi to a nearby mall to purchase all the things they'd left sitting in their suitcases at Tory's. She was being useful, she told herself, and the truth was, she did start to feel a little better. Enough, at any rate, to keep the worst of her despair squashed into a corner of her soul where she wasn't constantly reminded of it.

"By the way," Josh asked her, finishing the last bite of his sandwich, "I forgot to ask how you paid for all that stuff you bought. You didn't use a credit card, did you?"

Allie made a face at him. "Do I look that stupid? Of course not. I know they might be watching our accounts. I wrote checks."

At Josh's horrified look, she laughed.

"I'm only joking, Josh. Jeez, have a little faith, would you? I paid for everything with cash."

Sighing, he laid down his napkin. "If this takes a while, we could have problems with our cash flow, you know. How much do you have left?"

Allie considered. "About three hundred, I guess."

"That's about all I have, too. Maybe a little more. That should tide us over for a week if we're careful."

"You mean, no candlelit dinners in intimate French restaurants?"

The look he gave her was strangely startled. Almost as though he was embarrassed, Josh glanced away and raised his hand to the waitress for the check.

"Uh, yeah," he said. "Exactly."

"I'll probably live." Allie studied him, wondering what she'd said to make him look like that.

"The thing to do now," he went on briskly after the waitress handed him the bill, "is to decide our next move. I say we stay put for a while and keep going back to talk to Elsa until we're sure we've gotten everything out of her we're going to." He paused, frowned, then asked her, "What do you think?"

Allie widened her eyes at him. Josh was asking her opinion? That was a new one. Usually he simply decided exactly what he wanted to do and just bulldozed through until he'd done it. She frowned suspiciously. Something was up. She could tell that much. She wondered what he was pulling now.

"Sure. That sounds like a good plan to me."

"Good." Standing up, he shoved his wallet into the back pocket of his pants. "So, what do you want to do now?"

Flabbergasted, Allie squinted at him. "Huh?"

"What do you want to do?"

"Josh, are you all right?"

"Yeah. I'm fine. Why?"

"Because you're being—I don't know—like considerate or something. You actually asked me what I wanted to do."

"So?"

"So, usually you just tell me. What's wrong with you?"

"Nothing's wrong," Josh said, irritated. "I'm just . . . I'm just trying to . . . to . . ."

"Be considerate?"

He looked uneasy. "Yeah."

"Oh, boy. Something really *is* wrong."

"Very funny, Allie. That's very funny."

Rising from the table, Allie followed him to the front of the Burly Burger. Above the door a little bell tinkled when he pushed it open and stepped out onto the sidewalk.

"You really want to know what I want to do?" she asked as they walked along the town's main street.

Glancing down at her, Josh smiled, and her heart did a wild flip-flop.

"Yes, I really want to know."

"All right," she said. "I'll tell you."

"NO, JOSH, DON'T force it." Annoyed, Allie brushed his fingers away. "It doesn't go there, and forcing it won't make it fit."

Side by side, they were sprawled on their stomachs on the floor of Allie's hotel room studying the skeleton outline of a giant jigsaw puzzle. Puzzle pieces littered the floor around them.

"You know, I think I've heard that line before," Josh said.

She gave him a swat. "I'll bet you have. Look, that's the sky," she explained patiently, pointing toward the puzzle. "You're trying to fit a piece of the barn in the sky."

"I think it looks nice there."

Trying to suppress a grin, Allie rolled over onto her side and shook her head. "You're impossible. You're hopeless. You'll never be a jigsaw puzzler."

"Should I be concerned?"

"Devastated. When you're retired, you'll have to take up crochet or needlepoint."

The grin she'd been fighting broke through, and Josh felt his breath catch at that sweet, perky, teasing smile of hers. The smile he knew so well. Her green eyes sparkled, and her hair fell around her shoulders in soft, shining waves of russet.

Unable to help himself, he raised a finger and brushed back a strand of her hair, letting his finger linger for as long as he dared on the softness of her cheek. Despite his guilt, he couldn't deny that he was glad—so damned glad—that Allie was beside him now.

He wanted to tell her what he'd discovered last night. He wanted to shout to the world that he loved her, had always loved her. But he bit back the words. She was in love with another man, he reminded himself. Even if she wasn't, even if by some unforeseen miracle she welcomed his love, he would never allow himself to give it to her. He couldn't.

In the end, no matter how much he despised the man, Josh knew he was his father's son.

He realized he'd let his hand rest too long against the silkiness of her cheek. Her smile was fading, and her face began to drain of color. Hastily he snatched his hand back as though he'd been burned.

"So," he said quickly to cover his unsteadiness, "what are you going to do when we get back to New York?"

She was watching him silently, her green eyes no longer sparkling but clouded and haunted.

"Will you talk to Jack Gates about getting your old job back?"

From under his brow, Josh saw her swallow with difficulty, saw her lower her head, then absently pick up a puzzle piece with her fingertips.

"I don't know."

Instantly he realized what he'd done. "I'm sorry, Allie. I'm an idiot. I didn't mean to bring it all—"

"That's all right." She glanced up at him, her face somber. "It's all right, Josh. Really, it is."

"Have you..." He paused. "Have you talked to Walker?"

Pretending to study the puzzle, she shook her head. "I wrote a letter to him this morning." She gave a small unhappy laugh. "Not the best way of handling it, I know. But I just couldn't—"

"Allie," he began, unsure about how to comfort her.

"Josh," she said at the same time. It was only one word, only his name, but the way she said it froze him.

She was gazing at him with such intensity he couldn't look away. She was telling him so much with that look. There were a million messages in her eyes, and he couldn't read one of them. He *wouldn't*.

"Josh," she said again, her voice a small whisper. "Hold me, Josh. Just once. Hold me, please."

His mind went numb. His breath caught. His heart stopped. For a long moment he could only stare at her, while his soul wrestled with a lifetime of emotions—joy, fear, longing and despair. He nearly reached over and pulled her to him. He almost toppled over the edge and into the darkness he longed for.

At the last minute he pushed himself back from the precipice. Rolling onto his back and away from her, he covered his eyes with his forearm, shielding his face from her, and ground his teeth.

He wanted to. God, he wanted to hold her. He wanted to do much more than just hold her. But he wouldn't do that to her. He'd hurt her enough already.

"I can't," he groaned.

Allie gave a small, pained gasp. "Oh," she breathed, a tiny note of humiliation.

Then suddenly she was scrambling to her feet beside him, puzzle pieces flying. She slipped and started to stumble to her feet again, scurrying like a small animal gone wild with fright. Josh reached for her.

"Allie," he said, gripping her arms and wanting to explain, wanting to wipe the look of hurt from her face.

She pushed at his arms, trying to shake him off, and he heard her give a single sob.

"No. Let me go!"

"Allie," he commanded, and then he was pulling her toward him.

Even as his mind shrilled *no!* he was dragging her against him, wrapping his arms around her small form, tangling his fingers in her silky hair and smothering her mouth with his. It took only one taste of her lips, and he knew the fight was over. He couldn't stop. He couldn't help himself now.

Her lips were full and ripe, and he plundered them, all restraint breaking loose at the first touch of his mouth on hers. Years of longing and desire crested and swelled, crashing over the dam of self-control he'd carefully built up. In the end, all thought and reason were nothing next to the thundering rush of passion that burst free in his veins, sweeping away his every constraint like twigs in a raging flood.

In one quick second, years of denial were suddenly forgotten. He couldn't think. He didn't want to think. He only knew that he was holding her. Tasting her. Allie.

He felt her fragile body under his hands, and with the moan of a man who's finally beaten, he crushed her against him and sought her mouth again and again. Her lips parted, inviting, and she returned his kisses with a fierce, hungry passion that mirrored his own. Like starved beggars, they clutched and grasped, drinking each other in, devouring each other's kisses, yet never getting enough.

Toppling onto the floor, scattering the puzzle pieces, Josh slid his hands down the curve of her back, not knowing if he could stand the exquisite joy of touching her, of feeling her body against his own. After so long, he thought wildly. After so very, very long. Grasping her hips, he pulled her against him, nestling her tight to him, and groaned aloud.

She was fumbling frantically with his shirt, pulling ineffectively at the buttons. Then suddenly her hands stopped, and he heard her give a small laugh.

"Oh, Josh. You left the tags on."

His breath was coming too fast. His blood was boiling, searing in his veins. Rising to his knees, he growled, "Oh, hell," and pulled his shirt over his head without unbuttoning it.

She watched him, her eyes fixed on his bare chest. He saw her green eyes widen. He saw the flicker of uneasiness across her face. Then she, too, knelt and yanked off her own sweater.

"Oh, no, you don't," he cried. Reaching for the waistband of his pants, he fumbled to take them off.

She was on her feet, struggling with the zipper on her jeans, rushing to peel them off and beat him.

With his pants around his knees, Josh got tangled up. He tried to kick his shoes off but instead, began to topple over.

"Josh!" Allie screeched in laughing panic, just as he righted himself.

Her jeans slid down her slender legs to a pile on the floor. "I won! I won!" she shouted with glee, before he stifled her gloating cries with his mouth.

For a brief moment the realization of what he was doing hit Josh like a thunderclap, almost sending him reeling. But he knew it was too late now. Perhaps it had always been too late. Perhaps it had always been inevitable.

Sweeping her up and into his arms, Josh held her against him gently for a moment, his eyes filled with wonder. Allie clung to him and felt his hot flesh against her cool skin, wanting to cry with the utter glory of it.

When he cleared the bed of covers with a sweep of his arm and laid her down, she watched him strip his briefs off and lie beside her. A sudden, almost instinctive wave of apprehension mixed with longing swept through her, and her breath caught.

Every ripple and ridge of muscle under his smooth warm skin, the hollow at the base of his throat, the dark curling hair on his chest that narrowed to a thin trail to his groin, every line and curve of his powerful body was like a homecoming to her. Four years ago she'd tried to memorize him with her fingers, her eyes, her mouth, as though unconsciously sensing the wasteland of emptiness that stretched ahead of her. Now, after far too long away, she was home again.

Reaching for him, her memory stirred. The clean male scent of his skin, the roughness of his chest hair under her fingers, the slick smoothness of his powerful shoulders, the heavy solidness of his muscular thighs, the wide expanse of his chest that cushioned her cheek—in a rush of remembrance, she filled her senses with him and sighed with pleasure and relief.

His large scarred hands slipped the bra from her shoulders. With unbelievable gentleness, his rough fingers danced down the soft skin under her arm, and he cupped her breast in the palm of his hand and inhaled sharply.

Josh's dark eyes were nearly black, watching her, drinking her in, then he lowered his head and found her lips. His kiss was soft yet insistent, as though he was struggling to hold himself back, afraid of crushing her under the weight of his need.

But Allie knew that need. She'd read it in his eyes, and she'd felt her body answer with a violent, overwhelming desire of its own. She ached for him. She hungered for him. Every inch of her body yearned for him, down to her very depths. She didn't want him to hold back.

Raising her hands to his shoulders, she pulled him closer still. Tasting his lips, she answered his kisses with eagerness. Arching her back, she pressed her breasts against his heated skin and suddenly was rewarded. She felt his control slip a little under her urging.

"Allie," Josh moaned. "God, Allie. I don't want to—"

"But I do," she gasped breathlessly. "I've waited so long, Josh. Don't make me wait anymore."

Clutching his shoulders, she moved under him, feeling his weight settle more heavily on her, feeling his kisses grow more urgent.

"If you don't slow down," he said, his breath coming in quick pants against her mouth, "if you don't stop pushing me, you little vixen, I'm going to go over the edge."

"Go, Josh," she pleaded. "Take me with you."

Lifting her hips, she pressed herself against his thigh, heard his throaty groan as he dropped his guard and felt the quickening in his body that she knew he'd never be able to stop now.

"Allie," he moaned again, and reaching down, he slid her panties down her legs, cupped her hip in his hand and moved her under him.

Cradling him between her thighs, she could feel his erection, large and hard against her hip. She clung to his shoulders, trying to move her body nearer, sending him another step closer to the edge. With one hand on her bare hip, he stopped her. When she felt his fingers touch the darkness between her legs, she gasped, and her body shuddered with a responding rush of pleasure.

His eyes were black and feverish, but they were smiling. "I'm not pushed as easily as I used to be," he teased, as his fingers did things to her that made her dizzy and caused her breath to come in frantic pants.

Her body was on fire, Allie thought. Icy, burning fire that burned faster and faster, flaring up, raging, blazing—

Then suddenly she was shattering into a hundred thousand tiny fragments, grasping his shoulders, crying out his name, holding on to him as though she might be torn away, swirling and spinning into the blackness.

She was still whimpering his name when she felt him push against her, felt her body resist him, then suddenly relent. The first thrust brought her back to earth with a gasp of alarm. Then gradually her body took him in and somehow accommodated him.

"My God, Allie. Allie," he groaned. One hand tangled in her hair as he covered her lips with frenzied kisses, the other cupped her bottom and pulled her even closer to him.

She felt the fire in her begin to spark and flare again, racing through her in a headlong, fiery rush. With each powerful plunge, he fueled the flames until she felt that she would surely disintegrate in a white-hot blaze.

At the last moment, just as the fire broke free and exploded deep within her, she heard his voice calling her name and his ragged cry of release. This time when she shattered and was swept away, it was with him. __

CHAPTER NINE

JOSH SAT on the edge of the bed, gazing at the telephone receiver in his hand. Finally he glanced behind him at Allie's sleeping form, then quietly replaced the receiver and turned again to study her.

She was sleeping on her side, her auburn hair spread across the pillow in shimmering streams like an ocean sunset. One hand was tucked under her cheek, and her dark lashes lay softly against her skin. She was, he told himself again, breathtakingly beautiful.

Last night she had given herself to him with such abandon and desire, over and over again. Yet he had never quite satisfied his need for her. He couldn't seem to get enough of her—of the smell, the taste, the feel of her. When she smiled at him, the whole world brightened and became a place of wonder and delight.

He loved her. He knew that without a shadow of a doubt. There was no use in trying to reason through that fact. It was written indelibly on his soul, and no amount of wishing could erase it. He loved her, and it was going to be his cross to bear for the rest of his life.

He'd stumbled and fallen again. He'd done last night what he'd sworn he'd never do again. He'd taken her in his arms, and once he was there, no just God could have expected him to step away. It simply would not have been humanly possible.

She had wanted him, too. Her response to him had been too complete, too absolute for him to think anything else. Yet her advances had also been reckless. He understood that what she'd done had been done in a moment of weakness and vulnerability. Her heart was broken, and she was on the rebound. He had realized that, knowing full well that he should walk away, but he couldn't. Instead, he'd taken advantage of her emotional state. Somehow, he thought, it was even worse than getting her drunk.

He didn't know how he would make it up to her this time. Once, yes. One mistake could be forgiven. One time could be overlooked, and a friendship could be salvaged and rebuilt. But twice? She'd hate him. She'd hate his guts.

Because Allie wasn't the type of woman to have a one-night stand. He'd always known that. What they'd shared last night, he knew with absolute certainty, she would view as a beginning. A promise. The start of something long-lasting and permanent.

He had no right, he chastised himself now. He had no damned right to offer her something he didn't have to give.

What did he know about commitment? What did he know about permanency? What did he know about loving and cherishing and protecting a woman? He'd never experienced those things, and the one time he'd tried . . .

The one time he tried, he forced himself to conclude, he'd failed so miserably she'd taken her own life.

Goddamn him, Josh thought, bowing his head, pulling at a lock of hair and clenching his teeth. If he thought he'd felt guilty yesterday, then today life itself was going to be a living hell.

Allie would never understand. Rising to his feet, he let his gaze wander over her, lingering on her face, her breasts and the sweet   ntle curve of her hip under the white sheet. He loved her desperately, he thought in sudden agony, but he had nothing worthwhile to give her, and she would never understand that.

Very quietly, his heart black with anguish, Josh gathered his clothes off the floor and silently left her room.

ALLIE YAWNED, stretched slowly and opened her eyes. Her muscles hurt in ways they hadn't hurt for a long while, and with sudden memory, she smiled drowsily and turned in the bed to—

Sitting upright, Allie stared at the empty place beside her. In alarm, she scanned the room, hoping to see him. But the room was deserted. With her heart in her throat, she scooted off the bed and ran for the connecting door, flinging it open, then jerking to a shocked halt.

The door of Josh's room was just closing, and without thinking, she called his name.

"Josh, wait!"

The door stopped a few inches from the door frame, and with anguished, disbelieving eyes, Allie stood frozen at the edge of his room, watching. After several long moments, the door swung open again and Josh looked across the room at her, his face hard and unsmiling. He didn't speak, and she let the silence grow until she couldn't stand it anymore.

"Where are you going?" she finally asked in a faint voice.

He looked away.

"Josh, where are you going?"

He cleared his throat, avoiding her eyes. "I have to... have to go see Elsa. She called. This morning."

"Why didn't you wake me?"

His discomfort was evident in his every gesture, even in the stiffness of his stance. He wiped the back of his hand across his upper lip, staring with fascination at something in the hall outside his room.

"I, uh, thought you might want to sleep."

Dazed, unable to comprehend that the nightmare was actually happening again, Allie took several steps into the room, her bare breasts rising and falling with each strangled breath.

"You're lying," she accused. "You're lying to me, Josh. You were leaving me. You were leaving me again."

Josh jerked as though he'd been hit in the face, winced and closed his eyes. A muscle in his jaw twitched with tension.

"I have to go, Allie. Elsa's expecting—"

"No!" she cried, rushing forward and slamming the door shut before he could walk out. Panting, sick with hurt, she stood with her back against the door, blocking it.

Josh stepped away from her, looking across the room, refusing to meet her eyes. She saw the muscles in his neck cord as he grit his teeth.

"No, Josh. Not this time. This time I'm not going to let you just walk away."

"Allie—"

"No. I want to know why. Why? Why are you doing this? Why are you leaving like this?"

"It's no good, Allie. That's all. It's just no good."

Devastated, she stared at him. "No good?" she repeated.

"It can't work. Now, let me—"

"No!" Spreading her arms wide across the door, she stood her ground. "I threw myself at you last night. I understand that. But I thought you... You enjoyed it, Josh. You enjoyed it, too." Her voice quivered, and she paused. Uncertainly she asked, "Didn't you?"

"For God's sake!" Clenching his hands before him, Josh walked farther away from her, wheeling so his back was to her and stiffening his shoulders as though in pain. He wouldn't look at her. He wouldn't even let her see his face.

"Josh, please. Please. I just don't understand."

"There's nothing to understand, Allie. It happened. I didn't mean it to. I didn't want it to. But it did. I'm sorry. I wish it hadn't happened, but I can't take it back."

Stricken, Allie felt the blood drain from her face. Slowly she dropped her arms, crushed. "You're sorry it happened?"

"More sorry than I can say."

She wondered briefly if she was going to faint. Her legs grew weak, and she couldn't seem to catch her breath, as though she'd been punched in the stomach.

"I guess you better go now," she finally managed, her voice a thin, dead monotone.

"Allie..."

Unheeding, she walked back to her room, her arms folded across her breasts. Hot tears stung her eyes, but ruthlessly she suppressed them. She wasn't going to cry. Not this time. She wasn't going to cry ever again.

She heard him at the connecting door, hesitant and wary. He didn't come into her room, but stood watching her from the doorway. Finally he said, "I'll be back in an hour or so."

Slipping under the sheets on her bed, the sheets between which they had lain and made love just a few hours ago, she nodded wordlessly.

"Don't answer the door to anyone but me."

She didn't bother to even nod.

"Allie," he began, "I do care about you. More than you'll ever know. I hate myself for this. Do you understand? If I could make it right . . ." He left the sentence incomplete, but his meaning was abundantly clear. He couldn't.

"You could stay with me," she tried one last time.

For a long, terrible moment of anticipation, he only stood silently in the door, as though struggling, fighting a war within himself. Finally he shook his head.

"No," he said, his voice grim. "You don't know what you're asking."

She squeezed her eyes shut, willing the tears away, forcing the hurt not to rise in her throat like bitter bile and fighting to keep from shouting. She lost the last battle.

"Then *tell* me!" she cried. "Tell me what I'm asking!"

Only silence answered her. When she opened her eyes, she saw the empty doorway. He was gone.

"I'VE THOUGHT about this all night," Elsa said, once Josh had settled in the spot on the sofa he'd occupied the day before. "I've wondered and worried about what *he* would want."

She looked out the window briefly. "About what she would want," the old woman added. "Maybe I'm making a mistake, but at my age, mistakes don't matter very much."

Expectantly Josh waited. He'd flicked on his tape recorder, and it was busy turning in the darkness of his leather backpack, recording every word.

"We moved around so much," Elsa began again, "because we were looking for him. She never gave up hope, you know. She never stopped dreaming that one day they would be together again. She loved him so very much, you see."

As though overcome, Elsa turned her face to the window again, gradually getting herself under control.

"After the three of you separated in Buenos Aires, did you have any idea where he'd gone?" Josh asked.

She shook her head. "No. None. He thought it would be safer, you see. He'd set up the accounts in such a way that no one could trace Lena and me. But he'd done such a good job that he would never be able to find us that way, either. We were supposed to meet in Philadelphia the following year, but he never showed up. After that, we had no way of knowing where he was. Neither had he any hope of finding us. That meeting in Philadelphia was our only chance of connecting." She looked across at Josh, as though she'd almost forgotten he was there. "Would you like some tea? I think I'll make some."

"Yes, thank you," Josh replied, watching as she rose with difficulty from the blue armchair and shuffled from the room. "This is it," he whispered to the recorder in the backpack beside him. Then after a second's thought, he added, "This is it, Allie."

When Elsa finally returned a while later and they were seated at last with cups of tea in hand, she asked, "Did I tell you we moved around quite a bit?"

Josh shook his head. "I don't think so," he lied. "Why did you do that?"

"She was determined she would find him one day. I don't think she ever considered that he might be dead. That wasn't a possibility to her. She always said she would know if he was gone." Elsa sipped her tea. "And I believed her. Their love was that strong."

"Did she have a plan for finding him?"

"Oh, my, yes. Better than that. She spent an enormous amount of money on private detectives. That's one of the reasons so little was left at her death. She'd gone through a fortune searching for him." She sighed. "But he'd done such a good job. He'd wanted to protect her, and he'd just about erased any evidence that we'd ever been alive after 1949."

Josh picked up on the qualification. "Just about?"

"Um. Yes. There were little things—rumors, stories. It was hard to tell which of them were just that—gossip and falsehoods—and which might be the truth. Of course, she had to follow up on all of them. She was driven."

"Did she ever come close to finding him?"

"Once or twice. We visited a house in New Orleans where she said he'd been. She was certain of it. She said she could feel him in the air, in the woodwork, in the walls. Maybe it was just wishful thinking, but she believed it." Elsa leaned forward, set her cup on the floor beside her and sat back with painful slowness. "That's why we'd come to Washington. She'd heard that he might be hiding somewhere in the Northwest. Of course, she never found him."

Josh studied the tea in his cup, then finally looked across the room at the elderly woman who'd born so many secrets for so many years.

"Do you think he's still alive?"

Elsa shrugged. "He might be. It's possible. If he is, I think he's somewhere not too far off. Maybe in Canada. The last report she received before she died mentioned an island off British Columbia. She was awfully excited about that report. Maybe she was right to be. At any rate, *she* certainly believed he was alive. She believed it right up to the moment she died." Elsa gazed pensively at some unseen point in front of her. "It would be a pity if it turned out that final report was the right one, the one she'd been waiting for all her life. It would make it all so much worse, somehow, don't you think? I mean, if she'd come so close to finding him, only to die before she'd had a chance to see him one last time."

"Could there have been another reason they never found each other?" Josh asked. "Maybe he didn't want to. Maybe he'd met someone else, settled somewhere and didn't want to find her."

Straightening, Elsa slowly turned to him, and even behind the thick lenses of her glasses, he could see her eyes flare with anger.

"No. That's not a possibility. There's not a chance of that at all. You didn't know them, young man. You never saw what they were like together. You could feel the passion. You could see the sparks. It was more than love. There was a bond between them that even death itself could not sever." She eyed him coldly, then suddenly leaned back in her chair, spent. "It was much more than love. It was like what's between you and that young girl you keep promising to bring back and never do.''

Josh choked on a swallow of tea, and Elsa gave him a sharp glance, studying him shrewdly. Suddenly she threw her hands up and cackled loudly with unrestrained glee.

"Oh, I see," she crooned. "Yes, indeed. I see. Well, there's a fool born every minute, isn't there?''

JOSH WAS JUST pulling the red sports car onto the main street of town when he saw them. Less than three blocks away, a long dark sedan idled beside the curb outside a hardware store. Two men stood on the sidewalk, looking around them at the quiet street. One of them was blond, but both wore black suits—stylish and well cut, just as Allie had described. He couldn't be sure, but he thought he saw a third man seated in the back of the car.

The second he saw them, Josh's mouth went dry and his heart thudded. The next moment he swung the car off the street and into the parking lot beside a bank, pulling quickly into a parking space.

Thank God, he gasped silently. Thank God, they were in a small town. In a larger city he probably would have gone sailing happily past them and met directly with an untimely and painful death. But in sleepy little Birmingham, the two suited men and their sleek black car stuck out like a sore thumb.

Josh gripped the wheel with shaking hands, feeling perspiration dampen his armpits. He had to get Allie, he thought. He had to find her and get her out of here now.

Throwing open the car door, Josh was already running before he'd pocketed the keys. Leaping over a low wall separating the parking lot from the alley behind, he dashed down the cracked pavement past garbage cans and beat-up cars. At the hotel, he skirted the entrance, found the back door and bounded up the three flights of stairs to their rooms.

"Allie!" he called, throwing open the door.

Sitting up in bed with a head of tousled hair and red-rimmed eyes, she gazed at him in surprise. She was wearing his blue shirt again, he noticed with a small ache.

"Get up," he ordered. "Get up and get dressed."

"What?" Allie blinked at him. "What's going on?"

"Come on," he almost shouted. "We've got to get out of here. Those men you saw at the ballpark have finally caught up with us."

"Oh, no!" Wide-eyed, she clutched the blanket to her. "When? Where? Where are they?"

"A few blocks away. I hope. I think they're deciding where to start looking for us, and something tells me they'll pick the hotel first."

Her face grew even paler, if that was possible. "What are we going to do?"

"Well, we're not going to sit here and wait for them, I can tell you that much. Get out of bed and get dressed." Snatching up the jeans she'd worn yesterday and discarded on the floor, he threw them at her. "Here, put these on."

Obediently she slid from the bed, pulled on the jeans and tucked in his shirt. "Where are my shoes?" she asked, looking at the disarray around her. "I can't find my shoes."

"Forget your shoes, Allie. Just come on."

She turned on him. "Forget my shoes? Are you crazy? I'm not going anywhere without my things. I just bought us all new stuff."

"Allie—"

"No!" she cried, stomping her foot. "I will not go anywhere with you ever again without at least a clean change of underwear and a toothbrush. I won't, and that's that, Joshua Mercer."

"Oh, for God's sake!" he shouted back. It wasn't any use, though, he could tell. She'd gotten that look in her eyes that said she'd die before she gave in—which was precisely what was going to happen to her, he thought in frustration, if he didn't get them out of there in the next few minutes.

Angrily shaking a pillowcase free of its pillow, he started to bundle whatever was at hand into it. "Dammit, Allie, sometimes..." He let the threat trail off.

She was scurrying back from the bathroom, clothes and toiletries piled in her arms, and she crammed those into the pillowcase with the other things he'd found.

"My shoes!" she cried, diving under the bed.

Josh shook his head. "I hope you realize that this is what happens when you live like a slob."

"Me?" she cried, indignant, hopping on one foot as she pulled a shoe on the other. "Look who's talking."

"Would you please just come on now? I mean it, Allie. Quit fooling around." Josh yanked open the door and peered down the hall.

"All right. I'm ready," she said.

He looked over his shoulder to see her standing directly behind him. Her hair was wild and tangled, the wrinkled blue shirt was half-pulled out of the waist of her jeans, and her face was still streaked with dried tears.

"You look like an orphan," he said.

Resentfully she glared at him. "That's what I get for spending time with the likes of you," she retorted, and strode off down the hall before he could stop her.

"SO WHERE ARE WE GOING?" Allie asked after Josh had shoved her into the passenger seat of the sports car, slammed her door and jumped in behind the wheel.

"To find a phone first. We've got to warn Elsa."

"Elsa!" Allie gasped. She'd almost forgotten the old woman. "Do you think—"

"They have to get to us before they can find her," Josh said. "At least, I hope so."

When he turned the car onto the street, Allie glanced in the rearview mirror. A long black car was parked beside the curb a few blocks down.

"They're still there," she said. "Should we be glad or not?"

"I just hope it takes them a while to discover we were at the hotel. Even a few extra minutes might make all the difference."

Several streets down, Josh pulled the car up close to a telephone booth, thumbed through the local directory and dialed the number. It seemed to Allie that she watched him for ages as he listened to the ringing on the other end, his forehead dotted with perspiration. Then he hung up and dialed again.

"Come on, Josh," Allie finally called, her nerves raw and fright making her voice a little shrill. "Don't waste any more time. Let's just drive straight to her house.''

Josh's expression was bleak as he listened a moment longer, but finally he nodded and returned to the car.

''If something's happened to her...'' he began ominously. ''She's a sweet old thing, Allie. It's my fault she might be in danger.''

''We'll find her,'' Allie reassured him. ''She'll be fine.''

Yet when they pulled up outside 113 Wisteria Street and banged on the front door, there was no answer. Furiously Josh pounded on the door with one hand, keeping a finger of his other hand pressed on the doorbell.

Surely, Allie thought, the racket they were making would wake up even the soundest sleeper.

''She's not here, Josh.''

Stubbornly Josh pounded on the door again and rattled the knob. ''It always takes her forever to answer the door,'' he said. ''She'll answer. She's got to answer.''

Allie felt a rush of sympathy for him, not a feeling she'd expected to have so soon after this morning. Placing a hand on his arm, she urged, ''Josh, she's not here. She'd have answered by now.''

''I can't, Allie.'' He looked wild with distress. ''I can't just leave her—''

''Yoo-hoo!'' a voice called from the next house.

Allie peered around the evergreen bush beside her. A petite, elderly, white-haired woman smiled and waved at them from the stoop next door.

''Excuse me! Are you looking for Miss Driscott?''

Josh pushed back from the door, his face anxious yet suddenly hopeful. "Yes, we are. Do you know where she is?"

"No, but I saw her leave in a taxi not fifteen minutes ago."

"Do you have any idea where she went?" Allie asked.

"Not a smidgen of one. But I wouldn't wait around for her if I were you. She had an awful lot of suitcases with her. Maybe she was going on one of those cruises. My daughter went on one last summer. Let me see, which one was it? Not the Royal— Oh, dear. I've forgotten again. She took a lot of luggage with her, too."

"Well, thank you," Josh said, leading Allie down the walk.

"Do you want me to tell her you were here?" the woman asked, but they were already in the car, slamming the doors.

"Where do you think Elsa was off to?" Allie asked, turning in the seat. "Did she say anything to you this morning about going on a trip?"

"Nothing." Josh frowned. "She didn't say a thing."

"Maybe it was a spur-of-the-moment thing."

Josh started the car but made no move to pull away from the curb. "I suppose so, but she couldn't have been called away, could she? Who would call her? And if it was her own idea, why did she suddenly choose to go away now? Why didn't she mention it?" Josh gazed at Allie intently. Then as though he'd made a decision, he lifted his backpack from the seat behind them, fished out the tape recorder and handed it to her. "Listen to this, Allie. Tell me what you think. It's the interview I had with Elsa this morning."

He turned the wheel of the car and pulled into the street.

With her finger on the play button, Allie paused. "Where are you going?"

"I'll show you in a moment. Just listen to that."

"But what about our friends in the black suits?" she asked as he turned the car down the next street. "Shouldn't we be heading for the nearest freeway?"

"We will. But I have to do something first. It'll only take a minute." He saw her anxious glance. "It's important. It won't take long. Listen to the tape while I find this place."

Obediently Allie began the recording. Elsa's voice, cracked and faded with age, instantly filled the car, almost startling her. She listened as Josh drove, feeling herself being drawn up in the old woman's memories. She was so enthralled that she continued to listen when he got out of the car at a small service station, apparently to ask directions.

"You can skip that part," Josh said, getting back into the car. "It took her forever to make tea. Fast forward it a bit."

After a moment the old woman's voice came on again, her words weaving a picture of Lena's years of unsuccessful searching for her missing lover. Allie sighed. When Josh finally stopped the car outside a small church, she continued to listen, watching as he silently got out of the car, shut the door and walked alone past the small, white-painted Baptist church to the adjoining cemetery.

As Elsa's words drifted around her, Allie watched Josh wander among the graves, searching the headstones. The old woman's tale of love and longing touched a chord in her—one of empathy. Lena had loved and waited for so many years, and Allie felt for her. She, too, knew what it meant to wait and love in vain.

This morning she'd felt hollow and numb inside, as though she'd died. But she wasn't dead. The fear of being found by the black-suited man with the icy blue eyes had cut through her lethargy, stinging her awake. It was her fear of death that told her she was still alive.

Alive. Bruised and battered though she might be, she was still alive. Lena hadn't given up, she told herself now. Lena had never stopped hoping.

Then she heard Elsa's last comment about her and Josh and the high-pitched laugh that followed his silence. She sat for a moment in the car, then turned the recorder off and reached for the door.

Josh had positioned himself in front of a grave bearing the name Frances Webberly when she came to join him, stopping a few feet behind him. Over his shoulder, she could see the name chiseled in the pink marble, the letters still sharp and clear, not yet aged by time.

Allie stared at Josh's back, at the black leather jacket stretched across his wide shoulders and his head of thick black hair. His words this morning had ripped her joy to shreds. His rejection of what they'd shared last night had cut her to the quick, and a part of her hated him for that. But it wasn't over yet, she told herself. No matter what he said, no matter how ruthlessly he shoved her away, she wasn't giving up just yet.

As she watched him silently study the grave, his head bowed, Allie thought again about Lena and what

the woman had gone through for forty years. Maybe
she had been a fool to wait for Sid Calentro. Maybe
she could have—should have—cast away her dreams,
forgotten about him and made a new life for herself.
But how, Allie asked herself, could Lena have stopped
loving him? Wasn't that what it was all about? She'd
not been able to stop loving him.

Allie felt compassion and sorrow well in her for the
woman who had loved so faithfully for so long and
whose search had been so futile despite her un-
quenchable hope. To love that unquestioningly and
without reward for forty years was a tragedy, Allie
thought. Yet it was a sort of triumph, too. It was, she
reflected, Lena LaLorne's final and greatest tribute.

Before her, Josh turned slowly, almost wearily, and
Allie saw with surprise that his face was grief-stricken,
his eyes dark with pain. He stopped abruptly when he
saw her, startled, then tried to hide his sadness from
her. He wasn't completely successful.

"I had to see," he explained. "I wanted to see for
myself that she was here."

Allie nodded. "I understand. It's terrible, isn't it,
Josh? I feel so awful for her. After all those years of
loving Sid, only to die without ever seeing him again.
Only to be buried anonymously in a strange place un-
der a name that wasn't even hers." She bit her lip.
"We should find him, Josh."

"What?" Josh had turned back to look once more
at the headstone.

"Let's find him, Josh. Let's find him for her. For
Lena. She believed he was in British Columbia. Let's
go to those islands, Josh, and let's find him." Allie
paused. "All she really had was hope, didn't she? If
we can find him, it would make it all so much better.

All her hoping wouldn't have been for nothing. She deserves at least that much, don't you think?''

Slowly Josh nodded. "We'll find him, Allie. We'll find him for her." With troubled eyes, he scanned the cemetery around them. He shivered. "Let's go now."

Allie gave him a searching look. His face looked drawn and strained. He saw her expression and gave her a weak smile.

"I haven't been to a cemetery since my mother died," he said by way of explanation. He'd meant the words to sound light, but a sudden crack in his voice gave him away.

"You haven't?"

"No. I . . ." He stared across the tombstones. "I couldn't seem to make myself."

Allie knew his mother had died the year before he'd brought his first manuscript to her, although she'd had to learn about it from Tory, who hadn't even known, himself, until months after the woman had passed away. At the time Allie had thought it odd that Josh hadn't told any of his friends about his mother's death. He hadn't asked any of them to be there with him, and as far as she knew, he'd buried his mother alone. Once again she wondered what had made him so determined to bear his loss in solitude.

"I don't blame you," she said now. "It's hard enough to lose someone. Sometimes coming to these places, being reminded of it, doesn't help."

He was listening to her intently, a look of relief in his eyes. "Yes. That's it."

"When my grandmother died," Allie continued, "I didn't want to go with Grandpa to the cemetery. I didn't want to see her grave. It wasn't that I didn't want to admit she'd died, but I liked thinking about her baking cookies in the kitchen. Every time I had to go with him, it got harder to remember her that way. Finally I told Mom, and she understood. She told Grandpa I had clarinet lessons on Saturdays and would have to skip our visits to Grandma. Unfortunately Mom's a stickler about honesty. I hated the clarinet.''

Josh gave her a sad smile. ''That's what makes you so special, Allie. You didn't want to forget.'' His eyes scanned the rows of graves once last time, then he took her arm. ''Some people,'' he said as he led her back to the car, ''don't want to remember.''

CHAPTER TEN

THE TRIP across the Canadian border to Vancouver was much more subdued than the trip from Seattle to Birmingham. For the whole ride, Allie and Josh were quiet, lost in their own thoughts. After the first fifty miles, Josh no longer checked the rearview mirror every few minutes for a black sedan, but he still didn't relax. He sat rigid behind the wheel, a muscle in his jaw tensely jumping.

Allie rested her forehead against the side window and watched the passing scenery without taking it in. The silence between them was dreadful, but she didn't know how to break through it. Josh's words this morning were like the bricks of a wall—each one had built the barrier between them higher and higher, until it was almost impossible to scale.

When they entered the outskirts of Vancouver and headed into the city, she glanced at Josh, wishing she knew a magic word to say to bridge the frigid distance he'd put between them. It was just like Cleveland, only worse, she thought. This time, she knew he felt something for her. She was absolutely certain of it, and that only made his coolness seem more final.

For four years she'd told herself that, if only he wanted her, if only he cared about her the way she cared for him, everything would be all right. Well, he *had* wanted her. And he *did* care for her. Yet despite that, everything was not all right.

Everything, in fact, was miserably, horribly wrong, and she had no idea how to put it right. Even if she'd known what to say and where to begin, she wasn't sure she dared to bring up the subject just then.

What if he answered her? What if he told her what was wrong, and it was something awful and wounding? She was managing now, but just barely. She wasn't sure she could withstand another blow so soon after the one he'd dealt this morning.

"We'll get a couple of rooms, then find you some lunch," Josh said.

The sound of his voice after such a long silence made Allie sit up.

"I'm not hungry," she said. "If you want to start working right away on—"

"You haven't eaten all day. You need to eat." His words were matter-of-fact.

Allie shrugged. "What I'd really like is a shower."

He turned to her and gave a strained smile. "I think that could be arranged."

"Wonderful. That would be great." With a sigh, Allie turned back to the window. She clasped her hands tightly together in her lap and closed her eyes.

She hated this—hated the careful, polite tone of their voices, the strained and impersonal comments they made to one another. All she wanted to do was take him by the shoulders and shake him, shout at him, force him to lay aside whatever it was that made him push her away. Instead, they were tiptoeing around one another, saying please and thank you as though they'd only just met.

Perhaps, the thought suggested itself slyly, perhaps he just didn't love her. A sharp stab of pain accompanied the thought, and it was with a tight throat that Allie saw Josh pull into the circular drive that swept around a fountain to the front door of a large hotel.

"Josh..." Allie began. The Royal Windsor was in the center of Vancouver and familiar to them both. Several years before, they had stayed there for a weekend when Josh had grumpily agreed to a promotional tour. The service was excellent and the rooms lush and comfortable, she knew, but at a price. "Are you sure—"

"It's all right," he said. "I'll pay the deposit in cash and put the rest on my credit card when we leave. We'll be leaving here with the story, Allie. I just know it."

She bit her lip uncertainly.

"This hasn't been an easy trip for you," he added. "I'd like to make it up to you if I can."

She didn't want him to make it up to her—not in this way, at any rate. Yet neither did she want to make things even worse by refusing his attempt at reconciliation, as inadequate as it was. When the doorman scurried over to open her door, she merely smiled wanly at Josh and stepped out of the car.

ALLIE HAD SHOWERED, dressed in jeans and a shirt of dark green silk, and was thumbing through the local newspaper when Josh finally returned from his errands. She heard the sound of the key in the room beside hers, listened to the slam of the door, then sighed at his tentative knock on the connecting door.

"You look...refreshed," he said, dropping a white sack onto the bed beside her.

Refreshed, Allie thought with irritation. How wonderful. Not gorgeous or beautiful or tempting, but refreshed. It was what people said to a doddering old aunt after she'd had a little nap.

"You didn't order room service like I suggested, did you?" he asked, slumping into a chair and opening another white sack.

"No."

"That's what I thought. So eat up. Hamburger and fries. Your favorite. Oh, and—" he reached into another sack and handed her a paper cup "—milk shake. I thought I'd better make sure you got your daily dose of junk food."

Allie looked at the hamburger without appetite. Unwrapping it, she made herself take a small bite.

"What are those?" she asked, indicating the three books and the small stack of maps he'd dumped at the foot of her bed.

"I wanted some maps of the area. One of the islands along the coast in particular. Take a look at that top one."

Laying the hamburger aside, Allie reached for the map and shook it out. She studied the jumbled clusters of islands in silence, her face registering growing dismay. Looking up at him, she groaned, "There are hundreds of them. Josh, what are we going to do?"

"Put our heads together." He finished off his burger and rose to sit beside her on the bed.

"We can't check every single one of these islands out." Allie waved her hand across the map. "That could take months. Longer, maybe."

"No, we can't. You're right about that. We're going to have to find someone who already knows about them."

"What about the coast guard? Do Canadians have a coast guard?"

"I was thinking more of someone who works the islands. A fisherman, say, or someone who leads fishing expeditions."

From where she was leaning against the headboard of the bed, Allie peered over the map. She saw Josh smile.

"You know of someone, don't you?"

"Maybe." He looked pleased with himself. "I was talking to a guy in the bookstore. He said his uncle has a lodge farther north up the coast. Takes fishing parties out sometimes for a week at a time. He knows the islands pretty well."

"How far north?" Allie asked skeptically.

"Only a few hours."

Reading his mind, she asked, "Does it have to be right now?"

Josh shrugged. "Why not? I can't think of anything we have to do that's more pressing, can you?"

Yes, she wanted to say. She could think of something much more pressing—like working out whatever had come between them. She couldn't go through another two years of stiff formality with him. It would drive her crazy. It already was driving her crazy.

"Come on, Allie," he coaxed. "It'll be fun."

"YOU SAY you're looking for some old geezer who used to know a movie star, eh? Sure you've come to the right place, son? We're a little north of Hollywood, you know."

"It was a long time ago," Josh explained. "Are any of the islands along the coast privately owned?"

"Sure, lots of them," Bert Noonan agreed without looking up from the engine he was tinkering with. Dressed in khakis and a plaid flannel shirt, his short, stocky frame looked sturdy and capable of more strength than most men his age possessed. In his late sixties, he had a face deeply etched with lines, weathered by the sun and sea.

Allie and Josh stood on the wooden pier, watching the older man select a wrench, wipe it on his shirtfront and bend over the engine of the large speedboat. Behind them a wide, tree-shaded lawn led up to a low log-and-timber lodge with a generous front porch. A group of middle-aged men in fishing hats and vests sat on the porch, drinking beer and rechecking their gear. Once or twice, Bert glanced anxiously across the lawn in their direction.

"Got to take those jokers out today," he explained, jerking his head in the direction of the lodge. "From Cincinnati. It's getting kind of late. Damned engine stalled on me a yard from the pier. Hope they don't mind night fishing."

"I can see you're busy," Josh began, "and we don't want to bother you—"

"No bother. Hell, they probably won't know the difference. They might even think you're *supposed* to fish at night."

"About the private islands," Josh prompted. "Have you ever noticed anything strange about any of the people who own them?"

"Strange?" Bert looked up from the engine and wiped his hands on a grease-streaked blue cloth. A wide smile split his face, and he gave a great burst of laughter. "Strange? Son, you don't live all on your lonesome on an island up here unless you're a little off your rocker to begin with.''

"What about someone who's excessively concerned about privacy?''

Bert scratched the back of his neck. "No. Unless you mean old Seamus Craigie. He's a strange one all right. Been loony ever since his wife left him twenty years or so ago.''

"Is he native?''

"Native as they come.''

Josh shook his head. "No, this would be someone who came here in the past forty years. He'd be seventy-three now. He'd also be extremely protective of his privacy and probably fairly reclusive.''

Bert laid the blue cloth down and crossed his arms over his burly chest. "You know how many people that could be? Son, there's a lot of islands out there. Does he have a family? Living with relatives?''

Josh shrugged. "I don't know.''

"Well, that doesn't help much.'' Bert looked thoughtfully across the water. "My wife and I opened up the lodge to paying guests about ten years ago when we got sick of the city. Been coming up here every summer for most of my life, and I suppose if anyone knows the man you're looking for it'd be me. Could be Matthew Trundle over on Rove's Island, but I believe his family comes from Nova Scotia. Then there's Miss Winnie on Sandrock. She's got a brother that stays with her most of the year now. He's about seventy. Collects bugs or butterflies or something. Taught at some college in New England.''

Bert hesitated for a moment, then added, "And there's Sam. Sam Barnes runs a diving school from Drury Island, but he's not exactly what you'd call reclusive. Anyway, he's not as old as you say. Not much more than my age.'' He chuckled.

Josh's jaw was firm. "Is there anyone else?" he pressed. "Anyone at all you can think of?"

Bert squinted, shook his head and picked up the blue cloth. "Sorry, son. Wish I could help you, but I just can't think of anyone like the guy you're describing."

With a nod at Allie, he turned back to the engine.

"If you think of something," Josh said, scribbling a phone number on a scrap of paper, "we're staying at the Royal Windsor in Vancouver."

"I'll ask around some and give you a call if something occurs to me." Bert took the paper and gave them a friendly wave.

"Well, that was a washout," Josh said as they made their way to the car. Already he was planning their next step. "We're going to have to try something else. Titles of ownership aren't going to do us much good. He'd have been too careful for that."

"Mmm," Allie muttered thoughtfully as she reached for her door.

Josh looked at her over the roof of the car. "What is it?"

"What?" She returned his gaze frowning. "I don't know. Something. I just— Oh, never mind. Something Bert Noonan said struck me as odd, but now I can't remember what it was."

"Well, what do you think about driving along the coast tomorrow? Calentro's got to get his supplies from somewhere. Eventually we're bound to come across someone in some little town who knows him."

"If he's here," Allie said.

"Yeah." Josh turned the key in the ignition. "If he's here."

FOR TWO HOURS Allie had lain on the bed in her hotel room, sipping glasses of chardonnay from the bottle she'd ordered from room service and trying to read one of the books on the islands off the coast of British Columbia that Josh had bought at the bookstore. The remains of a large pepperoni-and-mushroom pizza grew cold on the table under the window where they'd eaten, and she could hear Josh moving around in his room on the other side of the connecting door.

She couldn't seem to keep her mind on the book. For the third time she reread a paragraph, then tossed the book aside in disgust and had another sip of wine.

It was ridiculous, she thought. Utterly, completely ludicrous. They were two grown people, adults who cared about each other. What were they doing hiding from one another behind a closed door?

Standing up too quickly, Allie felt the room tilt. As she steadied herself on the bedside table, her fingers brushed the wine bottle, and she decided what the hell. She poured another glass and drank three huge gulps. She was tipsy, she knew—brave with the fruit of the vine. She was probably going to regret this, just as she regretted most things she did after three glasses of wine.

With momentary courage, she marched across the room, anyway, and flung open the door.

Josh was sitting on the bed. His chest and feet were bare, and his hair was messy from having run his hands through it repeatedly. He glanced up at her with a smile, then must have noticed the expression on her face. His smile faded, and he closed his book, marking his place with a finger.

"Allie?"

"We have to talk, Josh."

Even under the influence of the wine, she could see his face stiffen and his eyes grow distant and uneasy. She could sense his displeasure from across the room. Still, she stepped boldly forward.

"Do you like me, Josh?"

Josh looked up at the ceiling, held his breath, then steadily looked at her and said in a voice that rang with tolerance but suggested exasperation, "Yes, Allie. You know I like you."

"Do you think I'm sexy?"

"Allie."

"Do you?"

Josh lowered his book and started to rise from the bed. "I don't think we should have this conversation. Not now. How much wine have you had?"

"Oh, I see," she said querulously. "That's your excuse for not wanting to talk about it *this* time. Well, my question has nothing to do with wine. I want an answer."

Josh stood and scowled at her. "Well, you aren't going to get one. We already talked about this, Allie. You know as well as I do that there can't be anything between us but friendship."

"Bull."

"What?"

"You heard me. Bull." Her face felt flushed, and she raised her chin, glaring at him. "There's plenty between us, Joshua Mercer. And it's not just friendship."

"I think you should go back to your own room and—"

"No, I won't. You can at least give me the courtesy of telling me why you're acting this way."

Josh turned away from her. "Acting what way? We're friends, Allie. We're doing a job together."

"Then why did you make love to me?"

For a long, terrible moment her cry hung in the air. She could see his chest rise and fall rapidly, and his face looked haggard. He shook his head as though to refuse her question, then raised his hands, palms up, to her.

"Dammit, Allie. I'm a man. You're an attractive woman. What don't you understand?"

His answer struck her hard, effectively deflating her anger. As quickly as her resolve had come to her, it dissipated, leaving her limp and drained. He didn't love her, she realized. He had only slept with her out of physical need.

"Where are you going?" Josh asked, his voice rough.

"I don't know." Pulling open the door to the hall, she paused. Without looking back at him, she added, "For a walk. For a Coke. I don't know. Somewhere."

Without giving him a chance to reply, she shut the door.

Riding down to the lobby, Allie studied her face in the shining wood that paneled the elevator. Her reflection was foggy and indistinct. Exactly the way she felt. Her heart ached, her head throbbed, and she didn't know if she would ever be able to come to terms with what she felt for Josh.

How many times did he have to tell her? she asked herself as she stepped off the elevator. How many times did he have to say he felt nothing for her before she started to believe him?

She was an idiot. She'd wanted so badly for there to be something between them that she'd imagined the whole thing, pretended there was more than—

Crossing the lobby to the front doors, Allie came to an abrupt halt. Astonished, she retraced her last few steps and peered in amazement into the large, high-ceiling hotel lounge. Squinting in disbelief, she slowly crossed the room, unsure whether to believe her eyes, all thoughts of her troubles with Josh momentarily forgotten.

"Elsa?"

The old woman turned to her and smiled. "My dear," she said. "I thought that was you coming out of the elevator."

Allie opened her mouth, then closed it, stupefied.

With a shy smile, Elsa patted the plush cushion of the sofa beside her. "Won't you sit down? You look a bit...peaked, if you don't mind my saying so."

"What are you doing here?" Allie finally managed.

"I'm staying at the hotel."

Allie stared at her. "Okay. *Why* are you here?"

"I followed you. No, no. That's not exactly right. I made some good guesses and a few telephone calls." Elsa blinked behind her thick lenses, and her look was appraising. Under a pink coat with a white fur collar that hadn't been in style for thirty years, she wore a simple white dress, obviously her Sunday best. A white handbag was tucked safely close beside her. "Did you have a fight?" she asked with concern.

Weary and confused, Allie dropped to the sofa. "The world's gone mad," she murmured.

"Not at all. Everything is going exactly as it's supposed to. I know you don't think so right now, but believe me, you'll understand someday." Picking up a crystal flute of green frothy liquid from the table before them, the old woman asked, "Would you like a cocktail? They make excellent grasshoppers here."

Allie gave a feeble wave of her hand. "No. No, thank you. I don't think another drink would do me any good."

"Oh." Elsa sipped the green concoction delicately. "One of *those* fights."

Allie shot her a look.

"My dear, I was young once, too. Allie, isn't it? Yes, I thought so." She sighed and set down her glass, folding her hands in her lap. "So what are you going to do about him, Allie?"

Allie felt a little like Alice in Wonderland and decided that blue-eyed, white-haired Elsa did look a bit like a rabbit, especially in her furry pink coat.

"About who?" Allie asked in confusion.

"Your young man, of course. He's terrified, you know."

"He is?"

"Oh, yes. Completely petrified. Poor thing, he must be miserable."

Allie lowered her head to her hands and shook it. The wine, she decided, must have been stronger than she'd thought. "He's not miserable. He's irritated, and he's embarrassed for me."

"Embarrassed?"

"Because I'm making a big deal about..." Allie paused and studied Elsa. "What *are* you doing here?"

"He's neither irritated nor embarrassed," Elsa said, ignoring the question. "He's in love, and he doesn't know what to do about it."

Closing her eyes, Allie tried to get a handle on the conversation. When she opened them again, Elsa was smiling at her.

"He's not in love," Allie said. "Not with me, at any rate."

"Of course he is. Desperate with it. Probably has been for years." Picking up her drink, she gestured at Allie with it and said with firm conviction, "You're going to have to push him, my dear."

Allie watched her take a dainty sip. "I have been pushing. If I push any harder, I'm going to push him right out of my life."

Elsa smiled sweetly. "Then you're not pushing in the right places."

"I'm not?"

"No, indeed. Forget about subtlety. It's lost on most men. Seduce him brazenly. That's what I would do."

Dumbfounded, Allie gazed at the elderly woman with her soft white hair, frank blue eyes and candid smile.

"You would?"

"Definitely. Without restraint—that's important. Attack with everything you've got before he realizes he's being charged and can rally his forces. Don't give a man the chance to gather his wits. That's what I always say."

Crossing her arms, Allie leaned back in the sofa and considered. "Just go right up there and . . ."

Elsa patted her hand. "The 'and' will come naturally enough, I should think."

They sat in silence for several minutes, with Allie trying to gather her thoughts and Elsa taking small, ladylike sips of her drink. Finally Allie turned to her and asked, "Why did you follow us?"

"Because I have faith in you," Elsa said.

Allie was beginning to get a headache from Elsa's cryptic answers. "Faith in us about what?"

"That you'll find *him*. I wanted to do something about that report, myself, after Lena died. I would have. She *knew*, you see. She knew it was finally the one that would lead her to him. But I'm too old to go traipsing around islands, as you can see. And then, of course, there wasn't any money left to hire anyone to do my traipsing for me."

Allie was beginning to see the light. "So when Josh and I turned up, you decided to tell us about the report so that we would continue the search for you."

"Exactly. It's what Lena would have wanted. I hope you don't mind my following you. When you find him, I'd like to see him. I'd like to tell him about her and about how her love never wavered. He'll want to know that she died thinking of him."

The old woman's loyalty touched her, and Allie laid a hand over Elsa's thin gnarled fingers. "We'll find him for her, Elsa," she promised.

Elsa smiled. "I do hope you find him soon."

"So do I."

With a final sip of her drink, Elsa reached for her handbag, fumbled with her cane and waved off Allie's move to assist her. Slowly she got to her feet. Gazing down at Allie, she said, "I can tell that you understand her."

"Lena?"

Elsa nodded, her face serious. "She never stopped loving him. Not ever." Hanging her purse in the crook of her arm, she leaned on the cane. "Don't give up on him, my dear. Whenever you think you might, remember Lena and don't give up on him. There's too much at stake, isn't there? And besides, you've loved him for such a long time."

Surprised, Allie asked, "How can you tell? How did you know that?"

Elsa gave her a fond smile. "Your eyes, my dear. The whole soul is visible in the eyes for those who care to see it."

With amused affection, Allie watched the old woman slowly, awkwardly hobble away. With a quick laugh of delight and renewed determination, she quickly rose and headed across the lobby for the elevators.

IN HIS DARK HOTEL ROOM, Josh shifted irritably under the sheet, kicking at it impatiently with his feet. Thumping the pillow twice with his fist and screwing it viciously into a contorted ball, he crammed it under his head.

It was no use. He couldn't get comfortable, he couldn't sleep, and he couldn't seem to get Allie's face, downcast and hurt, out of his mind. Ever since he'd heard the door of her room quietly open and listened to the sounds of her getting ready for bed, he'd lain awake, gnawed by guilt. For nearly an hour now, he'd listened to the silence in their suite and tried to think of something, anything, but Allie.

Why did she have to keep bringing everything up, throwing his weakness and his mistake in his face again and again? He felt guilty enough without her constantly reminding him he was a thoughtless, selfish jerk.

Restless and surly, Josh yanked at the sheet and twisted in the bed. He'd wanted to tell her the truth. When she'd asked him why he'd made love with her, he'd almost told her that he loved her so desperately he could almost die from it. Fortunately he'd realized just in time what those words would do. They would only have made things a hundred times worse. If he told her how he felt, she would really latch on to him, and nothing he could say would convince her to let go.

It was all his fault, he berated himself again. He was the one who'd done this to her. He was responsible for the terrible state they were in. If he'd just let her go her own way and stayed out of her life and her business...

But no, he'd thought he knew what was best for her. So he'd schemed and connived to get rid of the Dentist. Naturally she'd turned to him for comfort and—damn him to hell—he'd given it to her. Only Allie wasn't made like that, he reminded himself. She didn't do things the way he did, the way other women he'd known did.

One night of passion, and Allie was committed for life. He'd always known it. Yet like a self-serving brute, he'd taken what she offered, knowing all the while he had nothing to give in return.

She was looking for a husband, and a father for her children, for God's sake, he groaned silently. That's what she wanted. That's what she deserved. But he couldn't be those things—not to her, not to anyone. Hadn't he always known he was cut from a different cloth? He might despise the notion, but he knew his father's blood flowed in his veins. He had only to look back on the countless women he'd left behind to know the truth. He had only to remember how he had failed his mother—perhaps even more completely than his father had—to see the sort of man he really was.

Tormented by his conscience, Josh flopped onto his side and pummeled his pillow again, then suddenly froze, listening intently. His eyes stared straight ahead at the wall, and he blinked in disbelief. Still and unmoving, he heard again the unmistakable sound of the connecting door to Allie's room opening. Stunned into immobility, he strained his ears and heard a footfall.

Before he'd had a chance to collect himself and sit up, he felt the sheet stir and the mattress move as she slipped into his bed beside him. Her slender arms came around his waist, and with a jolt of alarm, he felt the soft brush of her hair against his back and the warmth of her lips against his shoulder blade.

With a low murmur, she snuggled her soft, delicious curves close, her hands brushing lightly down his chest to his stomach, to his . . .

Josh's heart slammed into his chest, and the breath in his lungs turned to fire. Traitorously, his body heated, responding instantly to her touch. Warning sirens went off in his head, jarring him into action, and he threw off the sheet, flipping onto his back.

"Allie," he choked, "what the hell do you . . ."

She was leaning on one elbow beside him. Her full breasts brushed his arm, and she was smiling down at him with the secretive, teasing half smile of seduction, power and knowledge that women have smiled at men for centuries.

Good God, Josh thought. "Allie—"

But she'd placed a hand firmly in the center of his chest and was pulling herself up to cover his mouth with hers. The taste of her lips stifled his words, and he struggled and grasped at his few scattered remnants of control.

"I think you're right," she whispered against his mouth. "I don't think we should talk about it anymore."

"No, Allie. I think we *should* talk about..." Josh's words sputtered and faded as she suddenly sat up, swung a leg across his waist and straddled him. Her hair cascaded around her shoulders like dark flames of fire licking at her smooth white skin. Her breasts rose, full and perky and teasing, and her hands slid across his stomach to his chest as she lowered herself toward him for another kiss.

"Allie." His arms felt unaccountably heavy as he raised his hands to encircle her waist. He planned to lift her up and off him. He meant to place her to his side and have it out with her. He had every intention of putting a stop to the dangerous game she'd started, but then she began to kiss him, urgently and without regard for what she was doing. Her body stretched over him, the excruciating soft skin of her inner thighs pressing against his legs and her nipples grazing his chest.

With a groan of agony, Josh felt his hands grip her waist, pulling her down, closer and closer, until her soft, dark wetness touched him.

Running a hand up her back, he tangled his fingers in her hair and drank in the honeyed dew of her kisses. When she trailed her hand down his side, exploring, searching and finally touching him, he shuddered with the violent intensity of desire that roared through him. Her fingers held his erection, directing him to her soft warmth.

He fought for self-discipline, desperately trying to regain his sanity, but it was no use. She was moving too quickly, propelling him too rapidly into that irreversible storm of longing where only his need for her mattered. When she guided him to her, he felt his last reserve crumble. When she lowered herself on him, her breath coming fast and shallow, her tiny mews of passion fueling his own desire, he gripped her hips more tightly and thrust up and into her. He felt her body tense around him at his invasion, felt her tremble under his hands, and then she was moving, rising and falling on him, her slick wetness, her moaning cries and her clutching hands driving him closer and closer, faster and faster to the edge.

When he saw her back arch, heard her call his name and felt her body quiver and tense as passion consumed her, he felt his own body begin to slip over the brink into the soundless darkness where exquisite fire thundered and roared, rushing him away.

CHAPTER ELEVEN

ALLIE SNUGGLED CLOSER into her pillow and smiled
sleepily, not yet quite fully awake, but savoring again
last night's triumph. Morning light streamed cheerfully through the window, lighting her room, and she
heard Josh moving in his room next door. He stumbled against something and muttered a curse. Her grin
spread.

She'd broken through his barriers, just like Elsa had
told her she would. But while the older woman had
been thinking in terms of World War II strategies—
rush the beach and drive straight to the goal—Allie
had decided on a more modern technique.

After their lovemaking last night, hours after she'd
first crept into his bed and when Josh was finally
drifting off to sleep, she'd crept back to her own bed,
her skin still tingling from his touch and her lips full
and bruised from his kisses. The best way to handle
Joshua Mercer, she had determined, was guerrilla
warfare. And so she'd stolen into his room, sabo-
taged his self-restraint and his stubborn reluctance to
admit there was more than just friendship between
them, then quietly slipped away in the night.

Guerrilla tactics, she knew, required repeated for-
ays into forbidden territory. It was a slow wearing
down over time. She was, she told herself now, posi-
tively looking forward to the task.

When she heard Josh call her name from the door, she rolled over and gave him a wide, sensual smile.

"Hi," she said.

Josh looked disconcerted and uncertain. Awkwardly he stood in the doorway and gazed across the room at her, still not quite believing he'd woken up to an empty bed this morning.

She was smiling sweetly at him, all rosy-cheeked and innocent, and he fumbled with the doorknob unhappily.

"Allie—"

She cut him off, "Isn't it beautiful today?" she said, throwing her arm toward the window. "It's gorgeous. And I'm starving. Did you order any breakfast yet?"

"Allie—"

"Let's have a huge old-fashioned breakfast, Josh," she sang gaily. "Eggs and bacon, hash browns and toast. Oh, and order some orange juice for me, would you?"

He felt like a man who'd just been bested without even knowing he was in the fight. Somehow things were coming unglued. He was losing control of the situation. He'd been blindsided, and he wasn't even sure now how she'd managed it.

"Allie—"

"So what's on the agenda for today?" she asked breezily, rising naked from the bed. Pausing at the doorway, she rose on her toes and gave him a quick resounding smack of a kiss. "Are we going to travel up the coast?"

Defeated and confused, Josh could only watch helplessly as she started for the bathroom. Carelessly she turned back to him at the door. His mouth went dry at the sight of the slender length of her body and her soft curves.

"Breakfast, Josh," she prompted. "I'm dying of hunger." She shut the bathroom door behind her.

For another moment Josh stared at the door, as his sense of having been outmaneuvered grew stronger. He didn't understand what game she was playing with him, but he had a sneaking suspicion she was winning hands down. Sighing submissively, Josh went to the phone and called room service.

IN THE BATHROOM, Allie lingered in the shower, luxuriating in the steamy water and taking her time washing her hair. Thank God for Elsa, she thought. The old woman was a wonder of sound advice. The look on Josh's face this morning told her clearly that he was going to be like putty in her hands.

Poor Josh, she thought, smiling a little wickedly to herself as she dried off a leg and patted her hair with a towel. He didn't stand a chance.

When she pulled open the door, tucking a towel around her and humming lightheartedly, Allie heard a knock on Josh's door and headed for his room.

"Oh, good," she called. "Breakfast. I haven't been this hungry since—"

Stopping in the doorway, Allie felt her face drain of color. Josh was staring at her, his own face set and dark. His hands hung at his sides, and his powerful shoulders were squared and taut, as though he was poised for battle.

In the hallway, Walker glanced from Josh to Allie and back again, his handsome face growing hard and accusing. Unconsciously Allie tightened the skimpy towel that covered her.

"I see," Walker said, stepping into the room and sneering at them. He directed his frigid gaze to Allie. "Now I really see. When I called your brother and he couldn't tell me where you were, I knew something was happening. Then I got this—" he raised his hand, and Allie saw he held the letter she'd written him "—and I thought you'd been forced to write it. That *he* made you do it."

Allie took a step forward, all her cheerfulness washed away by surprise and by remorse. "I'm sorry," she said gently. "I know I should have called you or even waited until I returned, but I thought it would be best—"

"Best?" Walker spat. "Best? Do you know who he is, Allison? You want to destroy everything we had for some lowlife like him?"

"Walker," Allie began regretfully. "You and I really didn't have 'everything.' I mean, there was never anything like that between—"

Shaking with fury, Walker took several steps toward Josh, ignoring her. His face was twisted in anger. "I know about you," he hissed, pointing a finger at Josh. "I know all about you. You think I didn't do some checking up on you myself? You think I'd let you go off with Allison without knowing anything about you?"

"Walker!" Allie gasped, shocked.

"I know all about your past," Walker went on, still pointing his finger at Josh's impassive face. Bitterness made Walker's voice quake. "And it's a dirty, unsavory little story, isn't it? No wonder you never talk about it."

Terrified, Allie glanced at Josh, but his face remained completely still and unreadable. Steadily he returned Walker's narrow-eyed glare. Only his hands at his sides had moved, and they were clenched.

"Walker," Allie warned in alarm, taking a step toward them.

"Because you *don't* want to talk about it, do you?" Walker continued, resentment making his voice malicious and high-pitched. "No, the great Joshua Mercer wouldn't want his public to know about South Chicago, would he? Did you tell her that? Did you tell Allison about all the arrests for shoplifting and theft? Did you tell her about the fights? How about the one where you almost killed another boy in high school? Does she know about what you did to your mother?"

Josh blinked, and his body jerked.

"No, I'll bet you didn't." Walker smirked, sensing blood instantly. "You wouldn't want Allison to know how you nearly beat your own father to death or how your poor mother took her own—"

"Walker, stop it!" Allie screamed, throwing herself between the two men. "Stop it! Stop it this instant!"

Hostility contorted Walker's handsome face into a horrible mask of hatred as he took in her disheveled hair and the towel slipping from her still-damp body.

"Get your things," he snarled. "I'm taking you back with me."

"No, you aren't," Allie stated levelly and shook off his clutching hand. "You'd better go now, Walker. I'm sorry this had to happen. I'm sorry if I led you to believe there was a future for us. But you'd better go now, before you say anything more."

Across Allie's buffering body, Walker glared viciously at Josh. "You're just a worthless, pitiful nobody, and someday the world will realize that."

Glancing down at Allie, he curled his lips in distaste. "And you, Allison. I'm glad I found out in time what you are. Nothing but a tramp."

Allie barely realized that she was being picked up and set to the side, so quickly did Josh move. He was still turning away from her when he laid a single punch to Walker's midriff.

Walker doubled over, coughing and sputtering. Astonished, Josh stood at the ready, his feet planted and his fists raised, but Walker remained hunched over. Josh stared at the Dentist, then back at Allie, the fury on his face fading and surprise taking its place as he watched the Dentist clutch his stomach.

"I barely touched him," Josh explained in an awed voice. "I swear, I hardly hit him. I wasn't even in position."

Allie gaped at Walker, then at Josh, and swallowed. "Walker?" she called, approaching him with obvious reluctance.

Walker stood straighter and shoved away her hand. "You'll pay for this," he threatened, backing toward the door and the hallway beyond. "You'll both pay for this."

With a shrug, Josh shut the door on him.

"I'll sue," the Dentist called through the door, his voice a spiteful whine. "I'll sue you for assault, Mercer."

Crossing his arms, Josh tilted his head in disbelief, then shook it. Allie was clutching her towel to her, her eyes wide and her face pale.

Turning to her, Josh said unevenly, "Well, maybe from now on you'll listen to me when I tell you some guy's a jerk. You sure picked a winner that time."

Falling back on his bed, Allie groaned, "I'm sorry, Josh. I'm so sorry." She covered her eyes. "His face. I never knew. I never guessed. His face, Josh..."

Josh studied her sprawled across his bed. "Sometimes people surprise you, Allie, and not always in the best way."

"He looked like...like he hated us. Me."

Josh was silent for a moment. "Some men don't take losing a woman very easily."

Allie sat up. "And some do?" she asked.

Josh didn't look away from her, but neither did he answer.

A knock at the door made Allie jump. She stared at it.

Josh held up a reassuring hand. "Breakfast," he said. "That's all it is. Only breakfast." Striding to the door, he opened it on a waiter and a cart of covered plates. Accepting two trays, Josh turned back to her. "It's breakfast, Allie," he repeated strongly. "Relax."

"I'm sorry. It's just that Walker looked so angry."

"He was angry. If it makes you feel any better, we can leave the hotel right after we eat. I want to drive up the coast and scout out some of the towns Calentro might visit."

Allie gave him a fearful glance. "Do you think Walker might hang around the hotel waiting for us?"

"No," Josh said, feeling fairly certain about this point. He placed the trays on the table and motioned for her to join him. "My guess is he's already halfway to the airport and his attorney by now."

"I just can't believe it," Allie said in a small voice. She picked without interest at her eggs. "I just can't believe it."

Josh thought about the vicious spite on the Dentist's face. For the first time he was glad he hadn't kept his promise and gone to Charleston to talk to the man. With that feeling came a small lightening of the heavy burden of guilt he'd been carrying with him for days. It was only a small piece of a mountain of remorse, but as it fell from his shoulders, relief stirred through him like a light and welcome breeze.

Josh watched Allie pick at her toast, crumbling it into small pieces and lining them, untasted, around the edge of her plate.

When she looked up at him and caught him watching her, she smiled. "I almost forgot, Josh. In all the... excitement. You'll never guess who's staying at the hotel."

"Allie, I don't think he'll stay—"

"Not Walker. Elsa."

Josh stared at her, speechless.

"That's right. Elsa." Allie looked a little smug. "I saw her last night in the lobby. She was just—"

"You saw her last night?" Josh sputtered. "Why didn't you say something?"

"Do you want to hear the story or not?" Allie demanded.

With great effort, Josh bit his tongue, leaned his elbow on the table and put his chin in his hand. "I'm listening," he said.

"Good. Well, I was just coming out of the elevator when..."

AT ONE O'CLOCK that afternoon, they stopped in the small town of Falstaff for lunch, taking the sandwiches and fruit they'd bought at a store to a quiet spot by the water and sitting on the grassy embankment that sloped down to the strait. The water sparkled under a cloudless blue sky, and the grass was warm from the sun.

Allie nibbled her ham sandwich, took a sip of her canned soda and watched the waves rippling across the water. Beside her, Josh ate silently, his eyes thoughtful and distant. All morning, they'd been quiet, not talking much as they watched the passing scenery through the car windows, but at least it wasn't the strained silence of the past few days. Somehow, Allie guessed, the encounter with Walker had thrust them together as allies against a hostile force. Their silence now was familiar and companionable.

They'd left the hotel soon after Walker and headed north up the coast. Although they'd stopped and questioned every likely source in half a dozen small towns and hamlets along the way, no one had recognized the description they'd given of Sid Calentro.

Yet it wasn't thoughts of Sid and Lena or even of Walker that engrossed Allie and caused her silent meditations. All morning she hadn't been able to forget something Walker had said and the look on Josh's face at his words. All during the drive up the coast, she'd thought only of Josh.

She wanted to ask him what those words had meant, but she didn't know how. Finally, laying aside the uneaten half of her sandwich, she simply turned to him and said, "What did Walker mean, Josh? What did he mean about your not wanting people to know about you?"

Beside her, Josh stared at the sunlight glinting off the calm water. She heard his quick muted rush of breath, and with surprise and sudden inspiration, she knew he'd been thinking about the very same thing. A cold shiver tingled through her, and she waited breathlessly for him to speak.

"He was just angry," Josh said at last, tilting his head to look at her. "He didn't know what he was saying."

Allie refused to be put off so easily. "That's not true, Josh. I saw your face when he said those things about your father. About your mother. What did he mean?"

For a while Josh sat on the grass beside her, not answering. On his knees, he clenched together his strong, capable hands—hands that hit so powerfully and jabbed so expertly that she'd always known they'd been used for far more than mere sport, hands that had always touched her so gently and held her so tenderly that she had never feared their strength. The handsome lines of his face were stark with tension. No boyishly charming smile softened the hard angles of his jaw and cheekbones or relieved the unyielding fierceness of his mouth.

She didn't really expect him to answer her. He'd never told her much beyond the barest facts about his childhood, about the years before he'd gone to college and met Tory and their lives had become intertwined. So when he actually began to speak, she listened with trepidation.

He spoke slowly, as though reluctant to answer but compelled by something stronger. The words seemed wrung from him. "It was a long time ago, Allie. Another lifetime." He paused. "Then again, maybe it was only yesterday."

She wanted to lean toward him and cover his hand with hers, but she could only stare in apprehension.

"You couldn't understand the world I grew up in. No one could, unless they'd lived in it themselves." He closed his eyes briefly, as though remembering. "He was right. The Dentist—Walker—he was right. I did do things then that I'd rather not think about, that I'd rather no one ever knew. It was a crazy world back there, and a lot of what I did was done so that I would be accepted." He turned to her and smiled grimly. "Being accepted didn't mean you were liked. It meant you could survive."

She did reach out then and touch his arm. "You were young then, Josh. You were a child."

He shook his head. "No one stays a child for long in that environment. You can't. I knew what I was doing. I knew why I was doing it. It was just the way things were. It was a different world, and I had to live in it. I don't blame myself, Allie."

"Don't you?" she asked softly. "Aren't you blaming yourself now?"

He stared at her, his eyes so dark they were almost black—black, bottomless pools of memories and pain.

"I blame myself for thinking I was better than the place I grew up in. I blame myself for not accepting it, for thinking I could change it. That's what I blame myself for. That world—" he raised a hand from his knees and gestured, as though South Chicago lay just ahead of them "—simply exists. Maybe it's the natural order of things. But I didn't understand that. I tried to change it, and all I did was make a mess of it."

Allie shook her head, not understanding. "I think the natural thing would be to *try* to change it."

Josh gave a soft unhappy laugh. "You don't understand. I couldn't change it, because I was part of it. I was always part of it." He turned his gaze away. "I still am."

"No. No, you're not."

"Oh, yes, I am. I've just gotten good at pretending I'm not."

Allie let her hand fall from his arm. "Is that why you never told anyone when your mother died? Is that why you didn't want us to be with you? Because you didn't want us to see where you'd come from?"

Josh shook his head. "No, it wasn't that. It was because I didn't want anyone to know that I'd never left, that I'd never really changed. That I was still the same person I was back then." He paused, then with sudden bitterness added, "My father's son."

Stunned, Allie watched him in silence.

"He beat her," Josh stated matter-of-factly. "He beat me. When he wasn't in prison, that is. I stood up to him one day. I *didn't* almost kill him, however. Walker was lying about that. I might have wanted to, but I only hit him once. Then he went away, and as far as I know, he never came back."

For a moment a quick succession of memories of a very different world fluttered through Allie's mind—memories of her family, the happy times they'd spent together, the love and laughter and closeness that bound them together. Sadness, like a wave of pain, filled her.

"Oh, Josh," she said with a sigh, "you aren't anything like that. How can you say you're like your father? You've never struck a woman in your life. I know you, Josh. You would never harm a child. You aren't anything like he was."

"There are other ways of tearing a person apart than just with these." He raised his hands, palms up, and stared at them as though surprised to see them. Quickly he folded his arms, hiding his powerful hands. "There are other ways of destroying a person's life."

"Josh—"

"She killed herself, Allie," he went on, ruthlessly now, as though he meant to force her to listen. "My mother took her own life, not because of anything *he* had done, but because of what I had done to her."

Allie felt her throat constrict. She shook her head in ardent denial. "No," she protested.

"Yes, Allie. It's the truth."

"No. I know you, Josh. I *know* you. You wouldn't do anything to harm someone. I know you wouldn't."

"Maybe not intentionally, but I can't help it, Allie. I can't help but harm them."

Sick with anguish for him, Allie fought to reach through his pain. "Josh, you can't mean—"

"I do mean. You've got to listen to me, Allie. You have to," he demanded. His eyes on her were piercing and intent.

Still shaking her head, Allie gasped, "Why are you doing this to yourself, Josh? And why are you telling me this?"

"Because," he said levelly, "you need to know. Once and for all, Allie, you need to know what kind of man I really am. I saw you today in the hotel room. I saw the look on your face after Walker left. You were closing a chapter. I know what you've been doing these past few days, Allie, and I can't let you do it. I know what you want and what you're hoping for, and I've got to show you how wrong you are. You've got to see what I am, who I am. You've got to give it up, Allie, because it's no good. It never was. It never will be."

For a long moment Allie couldn't seem to gather enough breath to speak. Finally she managed to whisper, "That's what you want? You want to bury yourself in the past? You want to keep up this fantasy that you're still living in the world you grew up in and can't ever escape? Don't you see it's not true, Josh? The past doesn't have that kind of hold on people."

Suddenly rising to his feet, Josh looked down at her with tormented dark eyes. "Yes, Allie. On some people, the hold is that strong."

Spinning on his heel, Josh strode through the grass toward the car, angrily knocking a tree branch out of his way and tearing open the driver's side door with a furious yank.

After a few stunned moments, Allie gathered up the remains of their lunch and slowly followed him, her thoughts jumbled and confused and her heart aching for the man she loved so desperately and didn't know how to begin to reach. As she made her way among the trees, she thought about her dreams—the hopes he'd mentioned. She wanted a life filled with love and laughter, the kind of life she'd grown up with and seen her mother and father, her brother and his wife, live. Her dreams were those of a family and children and a husband who waited for her each night in bed.

For one terrifying moment she saw the differences in the worlds they had come from. The world she had known and the world in which Josh had battled to survive were miles apart. Perhaps, she wondered in sudden hopelessness, perhaps the worlds they'd come from were too far apart ever to bridge.

With that thought, the bitter impossibility of her situation came home to her once again. She was lost, she thought. Between her dreams and Josh, there was nowhere for her to turn, no way for her to save herself. Because, like Sid Calentro's steadfast lover, she, too, didn't know how she could ever stop loving.

IT WAS ALREADY DARK when Josh turned the red sports car south and headed back to Vancouver. Wearily, Allie leaned her head against the seat and watched his profile. They'd been polite and friendly with one another all day. Neither had mentioned again their talk at lunch. It was almost as though, Allie thought, Josh had turned back the hands of some inner clock in his mind, willing them to return to the way they'd been.

It'd been the same four years ago after Cleveland. He'd done his best to pretend that one night of wild and fevered passion had never taken place. But it hadn't been easy for her then, and it wasn't any easier now. The only advantage she had this time was a better understanding of him and a firmer determination not to back down.

Watching as he steered down the highway, she wondered how successful Josh himself actually was at pretending everything was the same with them. His hands gripped the steering wheel tightly, and though he turned to shoot a quick smile at her, his eyes were watchful and wary. There were worlds beyond those shadows in his eyes, she knew—worlds as shrouded and tortuous, as unfamiliar and perilous, as the deepest, wildest forest.

"That kid at the gas station in Middleton got me thinking," Josh said, shifting in his seat. "Tomorrow I think we should hire someone to take us to some of the islands. I know we can't check all of them, and we won't. It does make sense, though. The people most

likely to know Calentro would be the people who lived
out there on the islands, too.'' With a wave of his
hand, he indicated the straits somewhere across the
forest to the west. ''Do you think you could handle
riding in a boat tomorrow?''

Allie gave him the easiest, lightest smile she could
manage. ''I do not get seasick, Josh. I never have.''

''Uh-huh.'' He turned his eyes back to the road.
''We'll see about that. If you'd rather not risk it . . .''

''I'll be fine,'' she insisted. ''Really, the way you go
on sometimes, you make me sound like an invalid. I'm
very capable, you know.''

''Oh, I know,'' he said, and gave a laugh. ''I do
know that.''

Allie caught the faint nervous uncertainty in his
laugh, and she studied him in the lights from the dash.
A tiny ray of hope peeped out of the gray depression
that had settled over her this afternoon, and she smiled
inwardly.

Maybe Joshua Mercer wasn't as sure of himself as
he pretended to be, she thought. With renewed interest, she went back to her plans for tonight's transfor-
mation into guerrilla-warrior seductress.

''ARE THERE ANY MESSAGES for me?'' Josh asked the
desk clerk. When the man went to check, he turned to
Allie. ''You look beat. Why don't you go on up to the
room? I want to buy the local papers and get some
take-out food for dinner. I'm sick of room service.''

''All right.'' Allie stepped back from the counter.

''There's a deli down the street. What do you want?
Pastrami or ham and swiss?'' he asked, naming her
two favorite deli sandwiches.

"Pastrami," she said. "And a pickle if they have the big crisp kind."

"Coming right up," he said, turning back to the desk clerk.

Allie watched him for a second longer, then trudged across the lobby, glancing automatically and in vain for Elsa's humped back and soft white face. The long day and the endless, fruitless questioning of people who were either too suspicious or too full of gossip to give them any useful information had worn her out.

She hoped a bath and a meal would revive her. She was going to need all her energy tonight, she thought with a secretive smile. The tactics she'd come up with were sure to dissolve even Josh's most stubborn denials. All that business about South Chicago was not going to do him any good. He could punish himself and wear himself out with self-accusations if he wanted, but she wasn't going to be a part of it.

There *was* a way to bridge the gap between them, she knew, and little, old white-haired Elsa had told her how. Relentless ambushes in the dead of night when his defenses were down would eventually make him crumble. Josh wanted her, Allie told herself on the elevator ride to the tenth floor. She knew he did. She was just going to have to show him that prevarication wasn't going to help him any longer.

Slipping her key in the lock, Allie pushed open the door to her room and reached for the light, just as it dawned on her that something wasn't right. Before she had a chance to pull back through the open door, a rough hand gripped her wrist, dragged her into the dark room and shut the door behind her with a soft click.

"Walker," she breathed, anger and fear rising in her simultaneously.

"Afraid not," a low male voice rumbled close to her ear.

The man pulled her back against him and covered her mouth with a hard hand. The smell of onions and mustard assaulted her nose, and she began to fight wildly against his hold on her.

"Keep her quiet," she heard a second voice growl from across the room.

Terror swelled in her, and Allie kicked and thrashed at the man until he increased the pressure around her ribs, squeezing the breath from her body. Allie squirmed weakly, but his hand on her mouth and his other arm crushing her body in a viselike grip finally convinced her of the futility of struggling.

"Bring her over here," the second voice ordered, and she was half-dragged half-carried toward the bed.

As her eyes adjusted to the darkness in the room, she began to make out shadowy figures. A massively built man with a head like a bullet stood beside the bed. With shock, she saw the darkness by the hall door stir, and she could faintly make out a tall, lanky man across the room. The man who had seized her, she guessed, was neither as tall as the man by the door nor as large as the one by the bed, but there was an iron-hard strength in the arms that held her and a cold brutality in the pressure he applied to her rib cage.

She murmured against his hand in pain and began to cough, choking for air.

"Ease off her, Luther," the big man commanded curtly.

The pressure on her ribs lessened fractionally, and Allie breathed in deeply. Her heart thudded, and her body shook uncontrollably. In fear, she waited for the big man to turn to her, and she tried to steel herself for the blow she was sure would come, but all three men stood in absolute silence, not moving.

She realized suddenly what they were waiting for, and with mindless terror, she made another attempt to rip herself from the bruising hold.

"No," she whimpered as the man once more tightened his grip. *No, Josh,* she moaned silently.

"Quiet," the big man snarled.

The fingers on her cheek dug into her flesh, and Allie swallowed her next groan with a jolt of pain. In a wave of dizzying panic, she heard the distinct click of the key turning in the lock of Josh's room next door, followed instantly by a second, terrifying click very close to the side of her head.

Her knees nearly gave out from under her, as she saw the thin crack of light under the connecting door. Josh had turned on a lamp.

"Allie," Josh called out, "their pastrami looked like hell. I got you ham and swiss, instead. Allie?"

"Josh, no!" she tried to scream as the connecting door began to swing open, but the words were a mere gurgle, trapped in her throat.

"Allie, what the hell are you—"

The light blazed on, momentarily blinding her, and Allie slumped limply back against her captor.

"Mercer," the big man said, holding a gun within inches of her temple. "Put your hands on your head and walk slowly into the room."

CHAPTER TWELVE

DAZED, JOSH STARED at Allie, his eyes quickly scanning the room and taking in the three men and the gun. She tried to speak to him with her eyes, to tell him to turn and flee, to let him know how much more frightened she was for him than for herself.

"On your head, Mercer," the big man barked again, glancing pointedly at the gun he held on Allie.

Immediately Josh raised his arms, folding his hands on top of his head. "Let her go," he said calmly, only the gruffness of his voice giving away the depth of his rage.

"Maybe," the big man said. "Maybe I will. Maybe not."

He gestured to the tall man who stood by the door, and leaving his post, the man pulled a chair forward and pushed Josh roughly into it.

"I got a problem here, you see," the big man began again almost conversationally. "This is my problem. You been giving us a helluva chase, Mercer, and I'm sick of it."

Silently Josh returned the man's stare, his own eyes filled with contempt. "Let her go," he repeated forcefully.

"So what I'm going to do, see, is this," the man continued. "I'm going to give you a chance to make it up to me. You lead me to Calentro and don't pull any more shit like sneaking away, and maybe I'll let the woman live. How's that?"

"I don't know where he is," Josh growled.

The man shrugged. "That's not my problem. I guess you're just going to have to keep on looking real hard so you find him for me, aren't you?"

Fury turned the skin around Josh's mouth white, but he said nothing.

"See, Mercer, the thing is, if you don't find him, I'm going to kill you. The woman, too. If you try to slip past us or pull a fast one, I'll only kill the woman. Sort of as a way to encourage you to keep on looking."

"What do you want with Calentro?" Josh asked. "Or is it Joey Riazzi who's so interested in him?"

The big man blinked at Josh, then looked at the tall man who still stood beside Josh's chair. A silent order passed between them, and the tall man suddenly turned and, drawing back his arm, threw a punch into Josh's sternum.

Crazed with fear, Allie struggled against the arms that pinned her.

Josh's shoulders had slumped forward at the impact, but his hands didn't leave the top of his head, and he didn't make a sound. Slowly, his face a mask of cold determination, he sat up again.

Lowering the gun from Allie's head, the big man tucked it in a side holster under his jacket, brushing his hands together as though cleaning them of dirt.

"If you know so much, smart guy, then you know what's good for you. You just find Calentro for me. And don't forget—every step of the way, we'll be right behind you. Just look over your shoulder, and I'll be there." He adjusted his jacket. "If you try to give us the slip, we'll find you. And I know you wouldn't want anything to happen to your lady friend."

He turned then and studied Allie's terror-stricken eyes. She stared back at him, at his beefy face with the smashed and disfigured nose and the small, ferretlike eyes.

"She's a pretty one, too, huh? Only, I don't think you'd like her as much without a face."

Josh tensed in the chair. "I'll find him," he said, his voice raw and ragged with hatred.

The big man turned and smiled. "I hope so," he said.

Without another word, he started from the room. The hands around Allie slackened, then pushed her roughly to the bed where she sprawled onto her face. Weakly she pushed against the mattress to sit up, just in time to see the door closing behind the man who had held her. He looked back once, and she met icy blue eyes. Then the door clicked shut.

"Josh!" Allie cried as he bounded out of the chair toward her.

"Allie. Oh, Allie," Josh groaned, wrapping his arms around her and dragging her to his chest. He laid his cheek on her hair. "Are you all right? Did they hurt you? God, Allie, are you hurt?"

Shaking her head, Allie sagged against him. "No. No, I'm all right. Oh, Josh!"

She was trembling, unable to stop. The terror that had paralyzed her overwhelmed her now, and her teeth began to chatter. Clutching at Josh, she buried her face in his shoulder.

"What are we going to do?" she moaned. "Oh, Josh, they were horrible. I was never so scared in my life. What are we going to do?"

Brushing back her hair with slow soothing strokes, Josh said grimly, "I don't think we have much choice, Allie. We're going to have to find Calentro."

FOR THREE HOURS Allie paced the floor of her room, ranting and raving and resorting to every means of argument short of calling Josh names. Stonily Josh sat on the bed watching her stride back and forth in front of him, trying not to let the dread in his gut show on his face.

"You can't!" she shouted. "You can't just find him only to lead those... those killers to him. You can't do that, Josh."

Josh sighed. "What other option do we have, Allie? If I have to choose between Calentro and you, there *is* no choice for me."

"We could go to the police. To the FBI."

Wearily Josh leaned back against the headboard. "How many times do we have to go over this, Allie? This is the mob. That was Victor Lazano, one of Joey Riazzi's men. And I'll bet my last buck that the guy who hit me was Web Scarpini. These aren't just small-time crooks, and it's not only those three we have to worry about. There's a whole organization behind Joey Riazzi. The FBI can't protect us from them all. If we don't give Riazzi what he wants, we're dead. It's that simple."

"I won't," Allie wailed. "I won't, Josh. I won't lead them right to Sid Calentro, knowing they're going to kill him. I'd never be able to live with myself. Oh, can't you see?"

"I see. I see perfectly. You haven't quite grasped the reality of the situation here. They meant business,

Allie. And death is not some make-believe game. Dead is dead.''

Furious, Allie stopped in the center of the room, hands on her hips, eyes flashing. ''That's unfair, Josh. I know that we're in big trouble this time. I'm not stupid. But I'm not a murderer, either. I'm telling you, there's got to be a way. There was with Trimaldi.''

''That was different. Trimaldi didn't know about the story we were doing until it was almost done. By the time he was ready to strike, it was all over. The FBI moved in, and there wasn't anyone left who cared enough to retaliate. Besides, the Riazzis are bigger and more firmly entrenched than Trimaldi ever was.''

She was pacing again, her auburn hair flying around her and her stride purposeful and unyielding. She was a pain in the neck sometimes, Josh thought, but she was quite a woman.

''There's got to be a way. There's got to be something we can do. Hide from them. Or scare them. Or trip them up somehow. Couldn't we have those men arrested? No, no. You're right. There'd just be more of them where those three came from. What if we...''

In the torrent of words that spilled from her, Josh heard a single word. It caught him, tugged at him, and he sat up, thinking hard.

''... and then we could disappear for a while,'' Allie was saying. ''Oh, I don't know. Where would we go?''

''Maybe,'' he said softly.

She stopped abruptly and stared at him.

''Maybe,'' Josh murmured again thoughtfully. ''There might be something in that.''

''What? What?'' Allie cried hopefully, crossing to the bed and kneeling beside him. ''What is it, Josh?''

"Something you said. Something about scaring them."

"Scaring them? You mean like guns and body-guards? That might deter them, but—"

"No." Josh looked at her intensely, the idea slowly taking shape in his mind. "There might be a way. There just might be."

"How?"

"It would depend on a lot. We'd have to lose those three goons. We'd have to find Calentro. And then, after all that, we'd have to stay alive long enough to make sure."

"Make sure? Make sure of what?" She clutched his sleeve. "What are you thinking?"

"I'm thinking we'd have to make it more danger-ous for them to kill us than to keep us alive."

Soundlessly they stared at one another. Josh saw her search his eyes. The hope and the trust he read on her face almost made him reject his idea.

Yet when she nodded and quietly said, "Tell me," he took a breath and began.

IT WAS ALREADY well past noon when a bright patch of afternoon light fell on Allie's face, warming her skin and urging her awake. Drowsily she rubbed her cheek against the smooth fabric of Josh's shirt and squinted at the light. Sometime after five in the morning, they'd fallen asleep, still sleepily reviewing, testing and refining Josh's plan.

It was simple. If it worked, they would hold back from Josh's book an important piece of information about the Riazzis, obtained from Sid Calentro. Allie hated the notion. She wanted to stick the Riazzis with every damning piece of information they had. But Josh's reasoning, she'd finally admitted, was sound.

That one piece of information—and Josh was certain Calentro had plenty to give them—would be their ticket to freedom. Calentro's, too. As long as they were alive, Josh said, the information would remain safely in a bank vault somewhere. However, if anything happened to any of them, the information would be published overnight in every newspaper in the country.

But since they hadn't yet slipped away from the three men who'd visited them last night, nor yet found Calentro or obtained any information from him at all about the Riazzis, their odds weren't good. In fact, Josh had firmly stated, their plan had a major hitch. If any one of those pieces of the puzzle failed to fall into place, they were doomed.

Shifting on the bed beside Josh and curling her body against his, Allie thought about all the things that could go wrong. It was risky, she knew. They were taking a deadly chance. But the alternative was too horrible to contemplate. They would find Calentro, she reassured herself now, and they would fix things with Joey Riazzi. They had to.

She was snuggling closer to Josh, her fingers slipping to the curling hairs on his chest and wandering to the button on his shirt, when he suddenly gripped her fingers, rolled over and gazed at her, completely wide awake.

"What are you doing?" he demanded.

With a bewitching smile, Allie raised her face to his and would have kissed him if he hadn't held her away with his other hand.

"Allie, what are you doing?" Josh repeated, his voice gruff. "I thought we'd talked about this."

"You talked about it, Josh," she murmured, and pressed her body along the hard length of him. "Umm. I love the w   you—"

Sitting up, Josh pushed her away and glared at her. "Dammit, Allie. I told you yesterday. It's impossible."

Taken aback, Allie stared at him.

"You can't do this," he said, his voice a little pleading. "You can't do that to me, Allie."

"Why?" she finally asked. "Because you like it too much? As much as I do? Because you can't help yourself, either?"

A muscle in Josh's jaw twitched, and his eyes were troubled. He gazed helplessly at her.

"You do like it, Josh. I know you do. So why not—"

"Stop it, Allie. I told you yesterday—"

"What you said yesterday about your past and what happened to you—it doesn't matter. It doesn't matter to me."

Josh turned away. "Well, it matters to me," he muttered. Suddenly he jumped off the bed, almost flinging himself away from her. "Goddammit!"

"I understand, Josh," Allie said, her voice urgent. She had to tell him, she knew. This time she had to get through to him. "I understand everything now. You think you failed your mother. I don't know, maybe you did. I doubt it. But even if you did, that has *nothing* to do with us, Josh. It doesn't matter anymore. This is you and me."

"It matters," he said from between clenched teeth. He walked back and forth in the narrow space between the bed and the window, as though desperate to escape. "It's all that matters."

"No. No, it isn't. What matters is..." Her voice faltered. She wavered on the edge. She paused at the very brink of full confession, knowing if she finally said the words, there would be no going back. Heedlessly, she flung herself over. "All that matters is that I love you, Josh. That I've always loved you, and no one else. All that matters is that you love me. All I want is for you to love me."

Josh's face became rigid and pale at her words, and he staggered, swaying as though she'd hit him.

"You do love me, Josh, don't you?" she pressed him.

"Allie, don't—"

"I know you love me, Josh. Don't you?"

"Please, Allie—" His voice was ragged.

"Tell me, Josh. Just once. Tell me."

Balling his hands into fists at his sides, Josh stared at her, his breathing harsh and shallow. For a moment she thought he would turn and run from the room.

Then, as though the words were being torn from his soul, he groaned, "Yes. Yes, I love you. I love you." He wheeled toward the window and threw aside the curtains. Bracing his arms on the windowsill, he bowed his head. "Is that what you want to hear? I love you. All right? I love you, Allie. I've loved you forever."

Allie closed her eyes tightly and clutched her hands together. "That's all that matters, Josh," she whispered. "That we love each other."

"No." The single word rang out like a curse. "No, that isn't all."

When he turned back to her, his expression was one of deep despair. "All my life I've always gotten what I wanted, Allie. I wanted my father gone, and I made him leave. I wanted to go to college, and I fought my way there with my fists. I wanted to be accepted by your brother and his friends, and I played along so that they would think I was one of them. I wanted a story, and I trampled over anyone I had to to get it. I wanted a book—this book—and I did anything I had to do to see it happen. Happen *my* way."

Allie watched him with compassion. How could she make him see he wasn't the monster he thought he was?

Josh seemed to struggle with himself, then said, "I've loved you for years, and I didn't want any other man to have you. So I did whatever I had to do to get rid of them. I called Tory, Allie. I told him to lie to you about him and Val having a problem so you would come out here. Then once you were here, I used your brother again. I *used* him, Allie. I told him to tell Walker you were at the hotel. With me. I *wanted* Walker to know you were with me."

Shocked, Allie stared at him. Then she saw the truth behind his words—the truth he refused to acknowledge. "Because you love me," she said simply.

Raising his face to the ceiling in appeal, Josh groaned. "Dammit! Can't you see, Allie? Can't you see what I've done? Can't you see the kind of man I am? You want a husband and a father for your children. I've always known I couldn't be that. I can't be those things for you. I can't give you what you need. I can't be the man I know you deserve, the kind of man who will make you happy."

"Josh," Allie said firmly, "I don't want you to *be* anything. I only want you to love me. That's all I want. The rest, well, the rest just comes. I just want us to love each other. We've been doing it for years. Why not do it openly?"

"Because I can't love you!" The ragged cry was ripped from him. "I chased my father away, and I couldn't give my mother what she needed, Allie. She killed herself. Do you hear me? Out of loneliness and neglect, without hope or comfort, she killed herself."

"I'm not your mother," Allie said.

Josh scarcely paused. "I chased away every man who ever came into your life, Allie, knowing all the time I could never give you anything in their place. You can't love me, Allie. For God's sake, you can't. Don't you see? I loved her, too, but I couldn't take care of her. I wasn't even there for her when she died. I can't bear to do to you what I did to her. It's the only thing, the one thing, I refuse to take. It's the one time I will *not* have my own way. I won't do that to you."

A hot flush began to rise in Allie's pale cheeks, and she got to her feet. With the bed between them, she faced him, emotion making her voice shake.

"*You* won't?" she cried. "What do you mean *you* won't, Josh? Haven't you learned anything at all? Haven't you looked at your life and seen the one thing that keeps tripping you up?"

For a long moment he watched her, then he looked away. "I've manipulated and schemed everything, Allie. All to get what I wanted. Well, this time I'm not going to do it."

"But you are, Josh," she said, her voice level and accusing. "That's exactly what you're doing. You're still manipulating me."

"No," he insisted. "I'm trying to protect you. I'm trying to protect you—from me."

"Well, I don't want your protection. How's that? Thank you very much, but you can keep it."

"You don't know what you're saying."

"I know perfectly well what I'm saying. You're trying to control me, just like you've tried to control everything. But you can't, Josh. You can't control us all."

"I'm only trying to do what I know is best," he growled. "That's all, Allie."

"But I don't need you to decide that for me. I'm a person, Josh. A grown person. An adult. I don't need you to decide what's best for me. I can do that for myself. I have done that."

"But I *know,*" he said more quietly. "I know about myself."

"You are so damned arrogant! You think you're all powerful, but you're not. Josh, if your mother wanted your father back, she would have gone and found him. If I wanted those men in my life—if I'd wanted Walker in my life—I would have done just that."

"No, you wouldn't have. I made it impossible. I've had a lot of practice."

"Oh, for heaven's sake!" Allie flung up her hands. "You are such a thickheaded, stubborn man, Joshua Mercer. A man who's just too full of himself. Stop trying to decide what's best for me. Respect me enough to trust me to make my own decisions and to choose what's right for me. You're manipulating still, Josh. And I won't have it. I know exactly what I want. I want you."

"You don't understand—" Josh began, but she brushed off his words.

"I love you, Josh. I love you, I love you, I love you." She sang the words. "Nothing you can say, nothing you can do, will ever change that. That, Joshua Mercer, that is one thing you will never ever be able to twist or contort to fit your need to be in control. Because you can't control it. I love you, Josh. I've loved you for years. I've loved you when you were struggling and when you were on top of the world. I've loved you through everything. I will *always* love you. So, live with it."

With anger and frustration consuming her, Allie raced for the door, snatching her shoes and her purse from the floor. "I'm going out for lunch," she said, her eyes flashing. "I'm going alone. You aren't invited. I can't talk to you anymore. Not now."

Slamming the door as hard as she could, Allie stormed down the hall to the elevator.

WHEN ALLIE STEPPED angrily off the elevator, she noticed that the lobby of the hotel was crowded with hundreds of newly arrived conventioneers, still pouring off buses and jamming the front desk. They milled in tight packs and clustered in noisily chattering groups, calling loudly to one another across the lobby and overflowing the restaurant. The ground floor of the hotel was a surging sea of humanity.

Resigning herself to a long wait for a table, Allie gave her name to the restaurant hostess and went to sit on one of the chairs in the lobby. Only half-hopeful, she searched the huge room for a glimpse of Elsa, but the old woman seemed to have vanished since their talk the other night.

As she slumped against the cushions, Allie replayed the scene that had just taken place upstairs, wondering whether she should feel glad or discouraged. After ten years Josh had finally told her that he loved her. But in the very same breath he'd insisted that it didn't matter.

Her friendship with him had never been easy, she reminded herself. Why did she think a love affair would be any different?

She tried to concentrate on the hurdles he seemed bound and determined to set up. She tried to think about how difficult it was going to be to convince him that he didn't need to protect her from himself—that he'd never had to. But instead, all she could hear were the three words he'd finally said to her, the words she'd longed to hear for so many years—"I love you." And as she remembered the words, a smile played on her lips.

Josh loved her.

Nothing in the world, she told herself, could come between them now. She wouldn't let it. If she had to, this time she would do some manipulating of her own.

Her chair faced a deep cushioned sofa, and now a middle-aged couple sat down on it. They didn't so much as glance in her direction, and it was obvious they had eyes only for each other. With a wellspring of newfound joy rising in her, Allie smiled at them.

They cuddled and kissed, holding hands like teenagers in the first throes of passion. For all she knew, Allie thought, they were. When love was involved, age was relative.

As though a tiny bell rang in her memory, Allie suddenly paused, frowning. Age *was* relative, she repeated. Age was...

Then she remembered. In a split second she knew. She remembered what she'd thought was so odd about

Bert Noonan. She remembered his words as clearly as if he stood before her now. He had thought that Sid Calentro, a seventy-year-old man, was nowhere near his age. Yet Bert was certainly in his late sixties.

At the time she had thought Bert was splendid. That afternoon, she had almost laughed aloud at his refusal to consider himself old. Then she had forgotten it.

But now it came back to her with all the force of a bolt of electricity. She heard his words again, and she knew. Whether by instinct or intuition, she knew with utter, complete certainty.

She had found Sid Calentro.

JOSH LEANED against the windowsill and scowled out at the brilliant blue sky above Vancouver. He felt tied up in knots and confused by the emotions that stormed through him.

She loved him. She said she'd always loved him. He wanted to see past those words. He wanted to put them aside and remind himself again how impossible it was. He could never give Allie what she needed. Even if he tried, he'd spend the rest of his life walking on eggshells, dreading the moment he'd have to face the fact that he'd failed her, knowing in his heart every minute of every day that the moment would surely come.

He cursed himself for having said those three words to her. He had sworn at his mother's grave that he would never again say them to a woman—not if he really meant them. Not if they really mattered.

Now he'd broken all his rules. He'd mixed things up so badly between them, there'd be no sorting them out.

Yet Allie loved him.

Elation coursed through Josh, lifting his soul like a buoyant, bright balloon. Then he took hold of his thoughts. What was he thinking? He knew what was coming next. He could sense it just as he could sense the moment an opponent came in for that final knockout blow.

There was no going back now. He realized that. They'd said too much these past few days. This time it wouldn't take them two years to go back to the way they'd been. No, this time it would take an entire lifetime, and then they still wouldn't be able to completely repair the damage. Their friendship as it had been was over, he told himself. Either he left it, walked away and never looked back, or he could go on. There were no other choices.

He could take that step, Josh thought, the step she was taunting him to take, and damn them both. Or he could give her up. He could go forward, or he could leave. But he could no longer stand still. It was too late.

In an agony of indecision, Josh pushed away from the window. Pacing the room, he struggled with his thoughts, then finally ran his hands roughly through his hair and headed for the shower.

AFTER SHOULDERING her way rudely through the crowds around the pay phones in the hotel lobby, Allie made a call to Bert Noonan, listening with her heart in her throat, then carefully writing down the telephone number he gave her. With shaking hands, she dialed the number.

The conversation was brief, almost stilted. She'd scarcely mentioned the name Sid Calentro before a heavy silence descended over the wire. Then a second

voice came on the line, offering to answer all her
questions if she'd cooperate. He gave her instructions
in a staccato rush. Nodding, she wasn't even given a
chance to reply before the line went dead.

Ten minutes, the voice had said.

Nervously now, with one eye on the wide glass front
doors of the hotel, Allie pushed past the crowds of
conventioneers in a struggle to reach the bank of hotel house phones along the wall. A crowd waited five
deep for the four telephones. Anxiously Allie glanced
at the doors, at her watch, then at the phones.

"Excuse me," she said, trying to still the panic in
her voice. "I desperately need to call one of the rooms
here. It's an emergency."

"Lady," the fat man in front of her said, "it's always an emergency."

"No, really. It's vital."

With a disbelieving sigh, he waved her in front of
him.

It took several minutes to cajole, plead and beg her
way to a phone. By the time she dialed Josh's room
her palms were sweaty and she was cursing herself for
not having chosen to take the elevators. She could have
been upstairs by now, she told herself, but then she
would have run the risk of missing the people she was
to meet.

She heard the phone ring twice. Three times. Six
times. Dry-mouthed, she hung up and dialed again.
Still no answer.

Frantically she hung up and pushed back through
the crowd, ignoring the grumbles and insults cast her
way. Dodging and weaving through the teeming mass
of conventioneers, she elbowed her way toward the
front desk, ripping a sheet of paper from her purse

and scrawling furiously across it as she worked her way closer.

"Hey, watch it," a woman with a hawk nose and crimped hair complained. "Wait your turn."

"Please," Allie gasped. "It's important. You can't believe how important."

Just then the desk clerk peered across the counter at her, glaring. "Miss, you'll have to wait your turn. Everyone here is in a hurry, and it isn't fair to our other guests for you to—"

"I just have a note!" Allie cried. From the corner of her eye, she saw a white van with green lettering edge up to the front doors, and she felt her nerves breaking.

"Please," she begged, her voice shrill. "Room 1089. Please, I need you to give this to the man in room 1089. It's urgent."

"All right." The clerk sighed and took the note. "Who's next?"

With her heart pounding, Allie turned from the desk, dashed across the lobby for the front doors and didn't see the clerk lay the scribbled note on top of a pile of receipts where it was instantly lost.

CHAPTER THIRTEEN

JOSH WAITED in his room until three o'clock for Allie to return from lunch, wondering if she had called while he was in the shower to apologize for storming out. He'd heard the phone ring, then stop, then ring again. Although he'd jumped out of the shower and dashed to the phone—dripping wet and with shampoo running into his eyes, yet ready to be gracious—when he picked up the receiver, the line was dead.

As a gesture of appeasement, he'd taken the khakis she'd bought him from the plastic wrap provided by the hotel laundry and put them on, adding the plum-colored corduroy shirt she'd given him. He didn't think plum was much of a color for a man, but he guessed that wearing it would set a certain amiable tone when she came back. It was hard to maintain a chilly distance with someone who was wearing your most recent gift to them. Then he'd settled down in a chair by the window and tried to finish the book on the Gulf Islands he'd started the day before. When she hadn't returned after two hours, he gave up pretending to read and headed for the door.

Mobs of conventioneers thronged the hotel lobby, swarming like locusts and creating a din that was enough to set anyone's teeth on edge, let alone a man whose editor had just flung herself out of his room in disgust. Every seat in the restaurant was taken, with people standing and talking between the tables, and it took Josh several minutes of impatient searching to convince himself that Allie wasn't there.

Momentarily stymied, Josh stood in the middle of the milling conventioneers and thought. She'd probably gone shopping, he concluded, remembering the last time she'd disappeared. It made sense. Often when conflict was in the air, Allie vanished into the nearest department store, only to reappear a few hours later laden with packages, a good deal poorer and mysteriously revitalized. It wasn't a therapy he understood, but it seemed to work for her.

She'd certainly been upset enough for it. When she'd swept out of the room earlier, she'd shut the door with a finality that had made him wince.

No, he reassured himself again. No, she'd be back. She'd only gone shopping to calm herself down. She was furious, but she'd been angry at him before. She always came back.

In an effort to further ease his anxiety, he waited in line at the front desk, asking for his messages when he finally got to the counter. Yet, although he made the desk clerk check twice, there were no messages for him.

Frowning, he made his way back to the elevators, pushing through the crowd with surly ill humor. Would she have left a message for him? he wondered. He'd made a big stink about it the last time she hadn't, and with anyone else, he'd assume the same thing wouldn't happen twice. But this was Allie. And she'd been mad enough to spit nails when she'd stormed out.

Annoyed with her for going off without a word, Josh pushed open the door to his room, almost expecting to see Allie waiting for him in there. But both rooms were empty. His brow furrowed with concern he could no longer suppress as he sat by the window and picked up the book. But instead of opening it, he stared out the window at the city below and wondered where Allie was.

BY SIX THAT EVENING, Josh was restless and jumpy with waiting, his nerves strung so tightly they felt ready to shatter with a touch. He'd nearly worn out the carpeting with his pacing and had run his hands through his hair so many times it was standing in tortured disorder.

If Allie had only gone shopping, he reasoned, she would have been back long ago. But where else could she have gone? Anxiety gnawed at him, and Josh swung his arms to loosen the growing tension in his muscles. Think, he commanded himself. Think rationally and coolly. Think only about the facts.

The facts, he thought. All right. She was angry at him. She'd wanted to make love, and he'd put her off. No, that wasn't completely true. He'd put her off, all right. But that wasn't what she'd been so mad about. She loved him, she'd said, and she didn't want him to protect her any longer. Yes, that was it.

But that was ridiculous, he wanted to cry out. Allie didn't know what she was asking. She wanted him to love her. Well, of course he loved her! He'd loved her for years. But she had meant more than that. She wanted more than that from him.

The facts, he demanded sternly. He was only going to look at the facts, and the facts were that she had said she only wanted him to love her.

But it was never that simple, was it? If he went along with it, she would start to depend on him. She would grow closer to him, and he would feel more responsibility for her than he already felt. He would be afraid every day of his life that he would let her down and disappoint her. He would live in fear of hurting her.

Fear. Pulling himself up short, he murmured aloud in surprise, "Only the facts."

Blood began to pound in his ears, and he stared blindly at the room. The facts were that he was afraid—him, Joshua Mercer, the man who always prided himself on never being afraid of anyone or anything. He was afraid of a little redhead with a dazzling smile and a whole world of tender love to give. He was afraid of her—of what he might do to her, of what she could do to him.

The facts were that, to keep his fear at bay, he'd told her his love for her didn't matter. He'd rejected the possibility that there could be more for them and brutally swept away all her arguments. He'd been so damned frightened of what it meant to love Allie that he'd rejected the very love she was offering him.

She'd left him, he realized in a blinding flash of insight and pain. Allie hadn't gone to lunch. She hadn't gone shopping. She'd left him, and like a damned idiot, he'd just let her go. His one hope was that he could guess where she'd gone. There was only one place she would have run to.

Galvanized by sudden decision and spurred by anger at himself, Josh scooped his keys off the bedside table. Briefly he paused, staring at the phone in indecision. He knew the danger. He knew the risk he'd be taking if he picked up that phone. Over the years, he'd learned enough about the FBI and how they worked to know, if he made the call, they'd locate him within the hour. The whole game would be up.

A memory of the sound of the door slamming behind Allie reverberated through his mind, and Josh snatched up the receiver and dialed.

It was answered on the fifth ring.

"Hello?"

"Val. Val, listen to me. It's Josh. I can't talk long. You understand. Tory explained to you. I need to know if Allie is with you."

"Allie?"

"Is she there yet?"

Val's voice was hesitant with surprise. "No, she's not here. I thought she was with you."

"Listen to me, Val. Tell Tory that when Allie gets there, he has to keep her there. Do you understand?"

"But, Josh, Tory isn't here. The team's in Kansas City. He won't be back until tomorrow."

Josh yanked a hand through his hair. "Then you'll have to do it, Val. No matter what she says. Keep her there."

He couldn't be sure, but Josh thought he heard a faint click on the line.

"I've got to go now. Just make sure she stays with you, Val."

"What's going on, Josh?" Val demanded. "What's happening—"

He hung up, grabbed his backpack with his books and notes, and headed for the door.

Within minutes, without daring to look behind him, Josh was in the red sports car and pulling out of the hotel's underground garage. He ground the gears and tried not to think about how everything was spinning out of control. Between the FBI trailing them and Victor Lazano and his buddies threatening their lives, they were in one helluva mess.

But somehow, at the moment, that didn't seem to be the worst of his problems. Somehow, the most important thing was that he find Allie.

AT SIX-TWENTY-SEVEN that evening, Special Agent Zimmerman burst through the door of the nearly empty office on the third floor and clattered down the aisle to the desk in the middle of the room, waving several sheets of paper.

With weary frustration, Steve Johnson looked up.

"We got him, Johnson."

Johnson gazed at the man in disbelief, then sprang to his feet, sending a sheaf of papers fluttering to the tile floor. "What? Where? Where is he?"

"In Vancouver. He finally called the brother. The boys traced the number. The Royal Windsor Hotel." Zimmerman grinned. "He's a sitting duck now."

"Thank God," Johnson muttered, flipping through the transcript of the phone call. He paused to read through the short conversation. "The woman's not with him?"

Zimmerman shrugged. "Sounds like it."

"All right. Where's Haywood?"

"Down in the commissary. Want me to go get him?" Zimmerman made a move to leave.

"Yeah. We're going to need permission to go up there."

Zimmerman halted and looked back at him. "Go up there? Why don't we let the Canadians handle this for us?"

"Because I want this guy myself."

Zimmerman shook his head. "But that could take hours to arrange. Maybe longer. We'd need permission from the Canadians. We'd need their cooperation. Mercer could be long gone before we managed to set it up. I think you're taking a big chance by—"

"That's why I'm running this operation and not you," Johnson interrupted curtly. "Rule number one, Zimmerman—never send another man to do a job you know you can do better."

Zimmerman exhaled rapidly and shook his head, but he only replied, "Whatever you say, Johnson. I'll get Haywood."

DUSK HAD SETTLED over the quiet neighborhood like a gauzy veil, and the concealing darkness of night had rapidly followed. From his vantage point behind the hydrangea bushes in the backyard, Josh could watch the comings and goings in front of the house, as well as the back patio and door.

A single light glowed in the kitchen window above the sink, and nearly half an hour ago another had flicked on in the second-floor master bedroom. Glancing at his watch, Josh read the glowing numbers.

Nine-thirty. Time to make his move.

Cautiously, his ears straining for the smallest rustle or snap of a twig that would tell him he was being followed, Josh crept toward the house, keeping low to the ground. Knowing Val might have locked the back door and not wanting to make any more noise than necessary, Josh stopped under the master-bedroom window. He picked up several pebbles from the flower bed at his feet, then tossed them at the window.

At the third pebble, he saw Val brush the curtain aside and look out. When she finally glanced down and saw him, he waved wordlessly at her. Even from that distance, he could see her eyes widen. The curtain fell back into place, and she disappeared.

He was waiting by the back door when she pushed it open, his finger raised to his lips in the universal sign for silence. With a quick glance over his shoulder, he slipped through the door and sat at the kitchen table. He put his head in his hands.

"What's going on, Josh?" Val demanded. "I've been worried out of my mind all night. Where's Allie?"

Josh's head snapped up. "Allie? She's here, isn't she? She's with you."

"No, she's not. Josh, what's happening?"

Standing up so quickly he tipped over his chair, Josh gaped at her. "She has to be here. I know she's here."

Val moved forward and righted the chair, then gently pushed him back into it. "She's not, Josh. I think you'd better tell me what's going on. Why did you think Allie was here? She was supposed to be with you."

Dazed with confusion and growing dread, Josh closed his eyes. "She *was* with me. We had a fight. It was... We had a rotten fight, Val, and she stormed out. I waited for hours for her to come back. When she didn't, I knew she'd left me for good this time. I knew she'd come here. Where else would she go?"

"Oh, Josh." Val lowered herself into a chair, pulling her robe closer around her. "When are you two ever going to learn? Why can't you just admit the obvious? That you're in love with each other."

Josh started to speak, but Val held up her hand to stop him.

"I know. I know. I promised myself I would never do this. I hate people who interfere. But I just can't keep my mouth shut any longer. It makes me want to scream watching you two dancing around each other like you're on hot coals. For ten years I've been waiting for both of you to come to your senses, but I see that hasn't happened. It just burns me up, Josh, the way you're letting her go off with that man from Charleston. I can't understand how you could possibly let her—''

Josh cut off her tirade. "She's not going. She's not moving to Charleston. I don't know what she's doing. I don't even know where she is. I blew it, Val. I made a mess of everything.''

Val stared at him.

Josh rubbed his forehead. "I told her I loved her.''

"You told her you loved her?'' Val's expression was a mixture of relief, surprise and pleasure.

"Yes, I told her. But I said it wouldn't work. And now she's gone.''

Val made a face. "Oh, Josh. You *are* an idiot sometimes.''

"I know that.'' Josh stood up and crossed the room. He came back to the table, but didn't sit down. "I think I really hurt her this time, Val. I think I made the biggest mistake of my life. She said she loved me and —''

Val sat back. "She said it, too? For heaven's sake, that *was* monumental conversation.''

"It's not a joke, Val. She told me she loved me, and I practically threw a fit. I told her I couldn't do it. I told her it was impossible.''

"I take it back. You're not an idiot, you're a full-blown moron. Why on earth did you say that, Josh?''

"Because I thought it was true," he said miserably. "I still think it might be. How can it work? What do I have to give her, Val?"

"Your love, you dope. That's what a woman wants most of all. As long as the man she loves gives her his love in return, she can handle just about anything else. The rest is just icing. But in your case, I can't believe it would even be a consideration. I mean, you've been friends for over ten years. You already have a lot of other things in common."

"But that's as friends," Josh protested.

"Everything you and Allie have as friends will carry over. Believe me. It's not like you have to give up one relationship for the other. Think of it as sort of an...extension."

Josh fell back into his chair. "At the present moment, Val, none of this matters much. She's gone, and I don't know where she is. She's just vanished."

Sitting up, Josh felt terror sweep through his veins like ice water.

"What is it?" Val breathed, seeing his look. "What, Josh?"

"Oh, God. Oh, my God." Unsteadily, Josh got to his feet. "Victor Lazano. What's wrong with me? Allie's right. I *am* arrogant. I thought it was because of me, but what if she really did go to lunch? What if all this time..."

Thoughts too terrible to contemplate rushed through his mind, draining his face of color. "They got her, Val. Those bastards must have gotten her."

"What? Who are you talking about? Josh, you're scaring me."

But Josh was already heading for the back door. "When Tory comes home tomorrow," he ordered, "tell him to call the front desk of the Royal Windsor Hotel in Vancouver. I'll leave a message for him there."

Val was up and at his side, holding him back by his arm. "Josh, tell me what's going on. Is Allie in some danger?"

"I can't talk now, Val. I've got to get back to the hotel. Please," Josh said, prying her fingers away. "I've got to find her. I can't stop to explain."

"Josh!" Val shouted, but he was already running across the patio and into the darkness of the yard.

AT TWO THAT MORNING, FBI agents Zimmerman and Johnson stood in a suite at the Royal Windsor Hotel while members of the Royal Canadian Mounted Police systematically searched the two rooms.

"There's nothing here," Zimmerman admitted cautiously.

Glaring around him, Johnson kicked at a discarded shoe. "Dammit," he snarled. "I can't believe this. Where the hell are they? It's already late."

Zimmerman tried to look patient. "They'll show up. They've left clothes and other stuff behind. They wouldn't have done that if they were running. If they had learned we were coming, they would have had plenty of time to pack." He didn't add that it was Johnson's fault so many hours had elapsed since they'd traced the call.

Johnson narrowed his eyes at Zimmerman, anyway. "I want men posted in the lobby downstairs, another man at both ends of the hall and men at all the exits."

"Right," Zimmerman said. "Where do you want me?"

"In here," Johnson snapped. "With me. We're going to be the welcoming party. When Mercer walks through that door, we'll be here to greet him."

"With smiles on our faces and open arms," Zimmerman joked.

Johnson only glared at him.

OUTSIDE THE HEAVILY curtained window of the bedroom, Allie could hear the muted rhythmic wash of the surf on the narrow beach far below. Once more she closed her eyes, but sleep refused to come. Ever since she'd climbed into that van and been driven in swift silence to a boat, which took her to the island, no one had spoken to her or explained what was happening.

It was spooky, she thought. She wished Josh was with her. The huge hulk of a man who had been her guide and who'd introduced himself simply as Simon hadn't been very communicative. On the trip she'd chatted nervously, growing more and more uneasy with every mile they put between her and Josh.

She told a silent Simon about Riazzi's three men and her hope that they weren't being followed. He'd only nodded silently, which she'd found somehow reassuring and frightening at the same time. She got the distinct impression that, by simply telling Simon about Riazzi's men, there was nothing more to worry about from that quarter. Their friends from New Jersey, she guessed, were in for a surprise, not necessarily a pleasant one. It wasn't a line of thought she wanted to pursue.

When they reached the island, Simon drove her in a small vehicle about the size of golf cart to a large gray building that was partially concealed by trees and shrubbery. Unadorned, square, and constructed of granite, it reminded her more of an unattractive government building than a private residence.

Simon had led her through quiet halls to a terrace that overlooked a cliff and gave a good view of the strait. There he had silently watched her devour two pieces of excellent quiche, a spinach salad and three helpings of raspberries and cream. When she'd tried to explain about Josh, he had stared blankly at her until her words finally died away. When she'd asked when she could talk to his employer, he'd said only that he was gone until tomorrow.

Fat chance, Allie thought now, hugging the pillow to her. They were probably just stalling, checking out everything they could find about her. She was in trouble, she knew. She'd landed herself in a real mess, and this time Josh wasn't around to help her out of it.

In the evening, after Simon had brought a dinner tray to the room she'd been given, she'd found out just how sticky a situation she was in. Until that point, she'd been pleased with her success and excited about what might happen. Then she'd decided to go in search of Simon to beg for a second helping of rice pudding. That was how she learned her door was locked. From the outside.

There was no phone in the room and no way to escape unless she wanted to hurl herself suicidally out the window and into the strait at the bottom of the cliff. She was a prisoner. But the worst part was, when Josh got her note and followed her, he would become a prisoner, too.

IT WAS AFTER MIDNIGHT as Josh drove toward the hotel, and the streets of Vancouver were quiet and empty. Streetlights cast pools of light on the pavement and across dark shop windows. No pedestrians strolled the sidewalks. For this reason he was surprised to see so much activity around the Royal Windsor Hotel. The circular drive to the front doors was a jumble of buses and taxis, and the curb along the street was crowded with waiting cars.

Then he remembered the convention. Cursing his luck, Josh nosed the sports car into the traffic, inched around a taxi and rolled toward the entrance to the underground garage. Out of nowhere, a station wagon piled with luggage and conventioneers cut him off, narrowly missing his front bumper. With a rude hand gesture, Josh threw the car in reverse to back out of the snarl of cars and buses. Desperate to get into the hotel and up to the room so he could begin his search for Allie, he gunned the engine.

From behind him, Josh heard the screech of brakes and the blast of a horn. A white van came to a shuddering stop just inches from the sports car, then backed up with a squeal of tires and whipped around him.

"Stupid idiot!" Josh yelled. "Don't you know how to—"

He stopped and stared. The van was dodging a bus, heading for the cross street ahead, when he remembered why the green lettering on its side seemed so familiar. Barnes's Diving School. Of course. Bert Noonan had said someone named Sam Barnes ran a diving school off one of the islands.

Well, the guy was certainly driving like a bat out of hell, Josh thought. Almost like a getaway car leaving the scene of a crime.

Like the windows of a slot machine clicking one by one to a winning row, Josh saw each piece of the story fall into place and knew in the space of a heartbeat that he'd hit the jackpot. Without a second thought, he threw the car into gear and tore after the van.

Already the other vehicle was several blocks ahead and putting distance between them quickly. Josh pressed the accelerator, and the little car leapt forward. Three lights down, he slammed on the brakes and screeched around the corner. Far ahead, he could see the taillights of the van, speeding down the street.

The highway, Josh told himself. The van was heading for the highway. More confident now, he pushed the car as fast as he dared, swerving as he took the ramp to the highway leading north. Careful not to close the distance between them, unwilling to let the driver of the van suspect he was being followed, Josh slowed the car a bit.

It was a disastrous mistake. Several miles up the road, at the crest of a hill, the red taillights disappeared. With his heart in his throat, Josh stepped on the accelerator, but it was no use. He'd lost the van. How, he didn't know. It must have turned off somewhere, and he'd sped ignorantly by.

There was only one thing to do. Unless the van's presence at the hotel was the coincidence of the decade, he thought he knew who Sam Barnes was. With Allie missing, Josh had only one goal in mind—to get to that island. And he knew just the man to help him.

BERT NOONAN PEERED sleepily at Josh through the screen door of the lodge, rubbing a hand over his face. His gray hair was disheveled and his pajama top askew, yet the next moment recognition lit his eyes and he grinned.

"Well, if it isn't the writer. Come on in, son. What're you doing out at this time of night? Don't you know decent folk go to bed with the sun around here?"

"I'm sorry to wake you," Josh apologized, stepping through the screen door Bert held open. He raised his hands as though to gesture with them, then dropped them helplessly to his sides. "I need your help," he said without further preamble.

Bert squinted at him, the smile fading from his face at the serious tone of Josh's voice. "Tell me what the problem is and we'll see."

"It's a long story," Josh began.

Bert nodded without surprise. "I'll make some coffee."

CHAPTER FOURTEEN

ALLIE SAT at the wrought-iron table under the brightly striped umbrella and stared at the elderly man who had walked leisurely across the lawn and paused beside the table. He was tall and thin, his expensive silk trousers and the sweater casually thrown across his shoulders conveying an impression of elegance. Under a thatch of snow-white hair, his face was deeply tanned from many hours in the sun and heavily scored by lines of age and worry, but his dark eyes were sharp. They surveyed her with lively interest as he pulled out a chair and sat beside her.

Allie returned his gaze, her heartbeat unsteady and her emotions a jumble of awe, fear and resentment. She lowered her untasted glass of orange juice to the table.

"You locked me in," she said accusingly.

She thought she detected a flash of amusement in his eyes. "My apologies. It was an unfortunate but necessary precaution. Can you understand?"

Allie sighed. "Yes, I suppose so. Am I a prisoner?"

He smiled. "I don't know. Are you a threat to me?"

"Is there anyone who isn't?"

At that, he laughed. "Miss Allison Shannon," he said, not answering her question. "I'm pleased to meet you."

He didn't bother to introduce himself. He didn't have to. She knew perfectly well from the second she saw him crossing the lawn that she was in the presence of the long-lost, illusive Sid Calentro.

The short, wiry man who had brought her breakfast earlier appeared on the patio. Balancing a tray, he quickly descended the steps to the grass. Expertly he laid out a second breakfast in front of Calentro, then left without a word.

"It's some diving school you have here," Allie commented dryly, watching Calentro spoon up a grapefruit section. "Does anyone on the island actually dive?"

He chewed slowly, swallowed and dabbed his mouth with the corner of a linen napkin. "A few of the men do in their off-hours. It's a good front. At least, it has been for the past twenty years. No one questions the men coming to the island. Simon even gives lessons occasionally."

Although she'd been preparing herself the past twenty-four hours for this moment, Allie still couldn't quite believe she was sitting here, chatting with Sid Calentro over grapefruit and coffee. "You know why I'm here?" she asked.

"Yes, it wasn't hard to find out. Your colleague, Joshua Mercer, wants to write a book. And you, my dear, want to publish it."

"That's not all. I haven't just come to you about the book. We need your help with something else, as well." Allie paused, then added, "The Riazzis."

"Simon told me about that. I don't think you need to worry about those three any longer. They weren't permanently removed. I don't believe in that. Never have. But they'll be seriously incapacitated for a while."

"That won't help," Allie insisted. "There's more where they came from, and I don't think the Riazzis are going to stop trying. Think about it. If I was able to find you..." She paused, her implication clear. "They want to know where you are, and I don't think they'd flinch at murder to find out. They'd gladly kill me and Josh for that information."

"The Riazzis always were barbarians." Calentro took a sip of coffee.

"There's only one way to stop them," Allie went on. "And that's to hold something over them. Without some damaging information about the Riazzis, we're all goners. With it, however, we have a fighting chance. We can negotiate. We can tell Riazzi that, as long as he leaves us alone, that information will never be published."

Calentro leaned his elbow on the table, resting his cheek on two fingers. Allie could almost see the rapid analysis he was making of the situation.

After scarcely a minute, he nodded. "Yes, that's not bad. That would probably work. I think I could tell you a story or two that Joey Riazzi would rather stay secret." He looked thoughtful. "We could tell him the truth about Vito Giuseppe."

"The truth?"

"Yes." Calentro paused with his hand on his coffee cup and considered her at length. Finally, as though making up his mind, he nodded. "It was Frank Riazzi himself who killed Vito, but not because of the hearings. Neither Vito nor I would have told them anything. We knew better than that. We'd have been dead within twenty-four hours. That wasn't what it was about."

"Then why? What happened?"

Calentro smiled faintly. "Frank Riazzi thought Vito was casting glances in his wife's direction. Of course Frank always was rather stupid. Vito had cast quite a bit more than his glance. I can't believe Frank never wondered why Joey didn't look a bit like him. But some men are that way. They see what they want to. I had the unfortunate luck to walk in on Frank while he was finishing off Vito. Wisely, I ran. I don't know if I ever really expected to get away. But we disappeared so fast I think they lost our trail."

"So Joey Riazzi is actually Vito Giuseppe's son?" Allie asked in astonishment.

Calentro grinned. "I don't imagine Joey will be too happy about it, thank goodness. But family honor, even among that bunch, will prevail. The last thing he wants is gossip about his mother. I don't expect you'll have any trouble from Joey once he's been told you have that kind of information."

"But will he believe it?" Allie asked.

"All he has to do is look in the mirror. Just in case, I have a few letters Maria Riazzi wrote to Vito that will dispel any lingering doubts. In fact, if you don't mind, I think I might like to contact Joey myself."

"You think this will stop him?"

Calentro nodded. "I know the Riazzis and their family honor. It'll stop him."

Relieved, Allie smiled and picked up her orange juice. "Well, that's settled then," she said, feeling pleased with herself.

Calentro picked up his spoon and ate several more grapefruit sections. "Actually, I'm afraid it's not settled," he finally said. "I've agreed to help you with the Riazzis. It's obviously in my best interests to do so. But as for the book..." He laid down his spoon and spread his hands. "You must see my position. It would be dangerous for me to agree to that. It would be the end of any peace or anonymity I have. I'm sorry. No book."

Allie set her glass down on the table and nodded slowly. "I was afraid you were going to say that."

"It would be cutting my own throat. If it got out that Lena and I are still alive, we'd be hounded by every police force and television crew in the country."

With a twist of compassion, Allie noted Calentro's use of the present tense when speaking of Lena. Of course, she thought, he didn't know.

Leaning back in his chair, Calentro studied her, his dark eyes assessing. "What I'd like to know," he said, "is how did you do it? It's been forty years, but I didn't think I'd grown that careless. How did you and your colleague find me?"

Allie bit her lip. "Albert Freuboldt."

Calentro looked puzzled.

"Lena's agent. Apparently she'd written to him."

The old man smiled faintly. "Ah. Of course. I should have known she wouldn't listen to me. So she's been writing to him."

Allie took a deep breath. Her hands were clasped tightly under the table. "Joshua Mercer found out about the letters, and we traced them to Seattle. Lena and Elsa had been living there, and they had information that suggested you might be up here."

Calentro turned his face away, and in that moment, he looked every bit of his seventy-three years. He seemed to be studying the trees a few yards away, but she could see that his eyes had misted over, as though he was remembering—and longing. His hands trembled slightly.

"Why didn't you try to find her?" Allie asked unexpectedly.

Something in her voice—a thin note of appeal, a faltering sadness—made him turn back to her. "I did. I've never stopped trying."

Calentro's gaze was intent, and Allie could read the hope in his weather-beaten face. This was the moment he had been waiting for and savoring, she understood, and the one she'd been dreading.

"You've seen her, then," he said.

Sadly Allie shook her head.

"But you've talked with her. You know where she is."

Again Allie shook her head, not trusting her voice.

"I don't understand." Calentro gave her a sharp look. "You said you had her letters. You said she was in Seattle and thought I might be here. If she didn't tell you, who did?"

Allie stared at her plate. "Elsa."

"Elsa? Then you didn't see Lena?"

Closing her eyes and running the tip of her tongue over her dry lips, Allie wished somebody else—anybody else—could say what she had to say next. She took a deep breath.

"No, we didn't see her. I'm so sorry. Lena died two years ago, Mr. Calentro." When she looked up, his face had crumpled and his old, dark eyes dulled. "I'm so sorry."

Suddenly Calentro gave her a grim, tight-lipped smile. "You're wrong. She's not dead."

This was horrible, Allie thought. She couldn't stand it.

"I'm so sorry. I wish—"

"She's not dead," he said again. He smiled and shook his head at her, utterly confident. "I would know. She's still alive."

"We saw where Elsa buried her," Allie said softly. "I do know that she never stopped looking for you. Elsa said that she was hopeful right up until..."

Allie's voice faded, and she looked away from the stubborn disbelief on the old man's face. He was smiling at her pityingly.

"Tell me where you saw Elsa," he urged quietly. "She might be able to lead me to Lena."

Allie shook her head, distressed and aching for him. "She was living in Birmingham. But she followed us to Vancouver. She's staying at our hotel."

Getting to his feet, Calentro looked years younger. "Thank you," he said with great feeling. "I have a few calls to make. If you'll excuse me." He headed purposefully for the house.

"Mr. Calentro," Allie called, twisting in her seat.

He paused and turned around.

"Elsa..." Allie bit her lip. "She's going to tell you the same thing. I think you'd better prepare yourself for that. I know you don't want to believe Lena's dead. I understand that. But I have to warn you that everything I've told you came from Elsa."

He smiled at her, a warm and genuine smile. "Thank you, my dear. But I think I know—"

"Mr. Barnes!" someone shouted. "Mr. Barnes!"

Allie stared across the lawn.

"Mr. Barnes!" Simon called again.

Sid Calentro stepped down, frowning. Three men who appeared to be bodyguards trotted across the lawn with Simon, herding two prisoners between them. Prodding and shoving, they bustled their reluctant captives forward. Allie felt her mouth go dry as she recognized Bert Noonan and Josh.

"Mr. Barnes," said Simon, "we caught these two in the south cove a few minutes ago." He glanced uneasily at Allie. "Looks like they came prepared."

In explanation, Simon dumped the contents of a duffel bag onto the ground. A couple of shotguns, ammunition, flashlights and two radios tumbled out. Josh looked ill. There was a raw abrasion under his right eye, and his shirt was filthy and torn. Bert Noonan didn't look much better. Leaves clung to his hair, and his face was gray.

A soft moan escaped Allie's lips, and she rose to her feet. "Josh," she said, making a move toward him.

Simon's huge hand blocked her way. Across his arm, she could see Josh shaking his head in warning, his eyes dark with worry and barely suppressed anger.

Anxiously Allie pushed at Simon's arm. "Get out of my way!" she snapped.

When Simon didn't move, she turned to Calentro, who was still frowning from his place in front of the steps. "Mr. Barnes," she said with careful emphasis. "This is the man I was telling you about. I'm sure you'll want to talk to him."

Calentro studied her, and she saw his eyes light with amusement. "All right, Simon. Apparently our visitors aren't familiar with our customs." With his eyes still twinkling, he addressed Josh. "Normally people announce themselves before coming to the island, and if they bring along anything, it's usually a good vintage to accompany dinner, not a portable armory. But then, maybe you had something in mind besides a friendly visit?''

Josh remained silent.

"Thank you, Simon," Calentro said finally, waving off the four men. "Would you mind finding a safe spot for our friends', er, luggage?''

Scooping up the guns, Simon and the other bodyguards stuffed them back into the duffel bag, casting suspicious sidelong glances at Josh and Bert Noonan. They seemed reluctant to leave.

"That's all," Calentro said. "You can go now. I don't think I'll need you. Will I?" He directed the last question at Josh, who was beginning to look confused.

"Allie," Josh said, ignoring Calentro's query. "Are you all right?''

"Yes. I'm fine." She paused. "What are you doing with Bert Noonan, Josh? Didn't you get my message?''

"Message?''

"Yes. I told you to call here. Simon would have picked you up. You didn't have to bother Mr. Noonan.''

Bert was gaping at them, his head swiveling from one to the other as though he was watching a tennis match.

"Allie—" Josh pointed at Calentro "—do you know who that is?''

"Of course I do. That's why I'm here. That's why *you* should have been here yesterday.''

Josh rubbed his eyes tiredly. "Wait a minute. You weren't kidnapped?''

"No, of course not. I told you exactly where I was going in my mess—"

"I didn't get any message, Allie. You didn't leave one."

"I did, too."

"No, you didn't."

"I most certainly did."

"I'm telling you there was no message."

"There was. I left a—"

Calentro had crossed to the table and sat down, watching them. "Excuse me," he interrupted, holding up a hand. "Before you two come to blows over this, would someone please explain to me what's going on?"

"Me, too," Bert Noonan muttered.

"I thought you were in danger," Josh told Allie. "When I couldn't find you, I thought something awful had happened to you. Then I saw the diving-school van at the hotel last night, and I figured everything out. I thought Calentro had somehow grabbed you."

"Ah," Calentro said in sudden understanding. "The boys from New Jersey. You saw the van because we were . . . well, giving them a lift, you might say."

Allie stared at Josh's disheveled clothes and the darkening bruise under his eye.

"So you decided to storm the island with Mr. Noonan," she said. She sat back down in her chair and lowered her head to her hands.

"In a way," Josh admitted. He glanced from Allie to Calentro and back again. "What in the world's going on here?"

Calentro raised his hands and smiled. "Don't ask me. I only own the place. You people just keep dropping in. Uninvited, I might add. And you, Bert. Did you really think I'd kidnapped a young woman?''

Bert Noonan shuffled his feet and jammed his hands in his pockets. "Well, Sam—I mean, Sid. Whatever your name is.''

"Sam is fine.''

"It was a pretty convincing story." He stared at Calentro. "All these years we've been pals, I never guessed.''

"Yes, well." Calentro looked chagrined. "I hope we can still go fishing together.''

"Josh," Allie said, sitting up, "I told Mr. Calentro everything. He's willing to help us with the Riazzis.''

"But not the book," Calentro reminded her. "Although if any more people have followed you here, you might as well publish it. Half the population seems to be turning up on my island as it is.''

"Might there be room for one more?" a woman's familiar husky voice asked from the trees not far from the table.

The group around the table froze, every one of them recognizing the sultry voice that seemed to have risen from the grave. Staring, her heart in her throat, Allie watched the woman step out of the shadows.

She was older now. Much older. Her hair was white, but thick and pulled back into the chignon she'd been so famous for. Although tiny cobwebs of wrinkles creased her once smooth skin, the perfect bones of her face and the brilliant blue of her eyes were still the same. Even in her late sixties, she was slender, and her slow, distinctive walk was so like her walk in the movies that Allie fell back into her chair, stunned.

Sid Calentro had sprung to his feet, his face paling under his tan. His hand gripped the table, and Allie saw it was shaking.

"Lena," he said simply.

She smiled then, the exact same smile that had caused film critics to label her "naughty" forty years ago. When she reached the table and stood before Calentro, she didn't touch him, but only continued to smile up at him, her face glowing with joy. It was a grand entrance.

"My God," Josh murmured. He pulled out the chair beside Allie and lowered himself heavily to the seat, staring at the elderly couple. "I can't believe it."

"Elsa," Allie said softly, watching the transformed woman. "She fooled us all along, Josh. It was an Academy Award performance."

WHEN THE EXCITEMENT had calmed to a mere fever pitch, they finally pieced together the whole story.

Elsa, Lena told them tearfully, had died two years earlier in Seattle. Between all the money she'd spent looking for Calentro over the years and the cost of caring for Elsa during her illness, Lena was left with very little to live on and nothing with which to continue her search.

"You two," she said, glancing at Josh and Allie, who were holding hands, "were my last hope. I'd been disguising myself for years, and it wasn't hard to convince you I was Elsa."

"It was a magnificent performance," Allie said with admiration.

Josh nodded, remembering. "That's why it always took you so long to answer the door. Your disguise."

Lena smiled. "I knew you wanted to find Sid and needed very little encouragement. So I told you everything I knew, prayed the information was correct and hoped you'd be the ones to finally find him for me. I guessed you'd go to Vancouver, and luck was on my side this time. You were staying at the first hotel I checked. I watched you from the lobby. Last night, when I saw you race off after that van from the hotel, Joshua, I had a taxi follow you to Bert Noonan's, then hired a boat and followed you here. In the confusion, no one saw us pull up on the other side of the island."

Smiling and fighting back her tears at the same time, Lena laid her cheek on Calentro's shoulder. He held her against him as though he would never let go, stroking her arm with his hand. Yet his eyes were on Josh.

"What happens now?" Calentro asked.

Josh could feel their eyes on him, waiting. He knew what Calentro was asking. He didn't answer.

Beside him Allie removed her hand from his as though in protest, but Calentro said first, "I can't stop you from writing this book, but you must know what it would mean. It would be the end of my home here. Lena and I will be together—and I've got you to thank for that—but if you publish this story, we'll be forced to start running again. You must see that they'll look for us—the FBI, the Riazzis, every thrill seeker and media person in the country. They'll know we're alive, even if they don't know where we are. And they'll never stop looking for us."

Rising roughly to his feet, Josh met Calentro's eyes. "I'm a journalist," he said slowly. "I write the truth."

Calentro looked away, caught Lena's troubled gaze and nodded. "Then we'll have to find a new place to hide."

Turning, Josh left the table and strode across the lawn. Allie watched him go, her heart aching for him and the terrible decision he faced. When she felt Lena's hand touch hers softly, she nearly jumped.

"Go after him," the older woman said. "Talk to him."

Allie shook her head. "I won't try to talk him out of this. It's his decision to make. You don't understand what this book means to him. You just don't know."

"Yes, I think I do," Lena said quietly. "But there's something more important involved, isn't there? He's so close, my dear. He's so close to believing in much more than he ever has before." Lena turned to Calentro and reached for his hand, her eyes on his although she still spoke to Allie. "Don't give up on him now, my dear."

ALLIE FOUND JOSH standing on the beach at the bottom of the lawn, hidden from the house by a dense stand of trees. He didn't seem to notice that he was ankle-deep in water.

"Josh?"

He turned to her, his face blank but his eyes dark with worry. Allie scrambled down the bank and stood in the water beside him.

Without speaking, he reached for her hand, held it, then pulled her against him.

"I was scared out of my mind," he said after a while. "I thought something terrible had happened to you. I thought you'd been kidnapped."

Allie leaned her cheek against his chest. "I'm all right, Josh. Nothing's happened to me."

With his arm around her shoulders, he gazed out across the water. "If anything ever happened to you..." He left the sentence unfinished. "The truth is I thought at first you'd left me."

Allie smiled into his shirt. "I didn't leave you. I couldn't. I love you, Josh."

She felt him go still beside her, then he held her shoulders and turned her toward him.

"After everything I said to you," he asked, "you still love me?"

"Of course I do. After ten years, I guess I just can't help myself anymore."

His smile was tentative and uncertain. "What am I going to do, Allie? What are *we* going to do?"

Raising his arm so that she could snuggle under it, Allie shook her head. "I don't know. But we're friends, Josh. Whatever we do, whatever happens, we'll see it through together."

His arms tightened around her, and it was a while before he said thickly, "Whatever else happens, I do know one thing. I love you, Allie."

THE SMALL ROOM in the basement of the nondescript building in Seattle was cramped and stuffy. Allie's head ached from the warm closeness and the glare of the fluorescent lighting. Beside her, Josh sat perfectly still, apparently oblivious to the uncomfortable chairs they sat on or the rude way they'd been hustled through corridors and down to this room. Across the scarred table from them sat two FBI agents. The picture IDs pinned to their jacket lapels gave their names—Johnson and Zimmerman.

The agents had been waiting at the hotel for them when Josh and Allie finally got back. Without explanation, they'd been bundled into separate cars and driven in silence back to Seattle. It was the most nerveracking trip Allie had ever made.

Now they were settled in an overheated windowless room, and she kept glancing nervously at Josh. They hadn't committed any crimes, Allie knew. But she was scared to death for Calentro and Lena. Whatever Josh said here, she knew, would determine the elderly couple's fate. It would also determine whether Josh wrote the book he longed to write.

"Why did you and Miss Shannon go to Vancouver?" the tall, lanky agent named Johnson demanded for the second time. He seemed, Allie decided with instant dislike, pompous and overly pleased with himself.

"Vacation," Josh answered simply.

The agents smiled, but not pleasantly.

"Come on, Mercer. You can do better than that."

Josh sat a little straighter in his chair. "You still haven't told us what this is all about. If you're arresting us for something, I want to see my lawyer."

The shorter agent glanced at Johnson as though for confirmation, then said, "You aren't under arrest. Yet. We simply want to ask you some questions. If you cooperate, you'll be free to go."

"So tell me again," Johnson asked. "What were you doing in Vancouver?"

Allie remained silent. Josh shifted in his chair.

"We were vacationing," Josh repeated.

"Come on, Mercer. We all know better than that. You're working on a book about Sid Calentro. Where is he?"

For the briefest of seconds, Josh looked at Allie. Then he smiled in amusement. "Sid Calentro's been dead for forty years, boys. We all know that."

Allie hadn't realized she'd been holding her breath until air suddenly rushed into her lungs. He'd done it. He'd made his decision, and she wanted to kiss him for it and weep for him at the same time.

"He's alive," Johnson insisted. "And you know where he is."

"Someone's been pulling your leg." Josh grinned. "The guy's probably dust by now. Yes, at one time I did consider writing a book on him, but the data is too scarce and most of the people I'd need to interview are dead." He shrugged. "Sorry I can't help you. Anything you want to know about the Trimaldis, though, I'll do what I can."

Johnson scowled, then fixed his stare on Allie. "Where's Calentro?" he asked her.

Allie blinked. She hated lying, so she tried to get out of it by simply not answering the question. "Sid Calentro?" She turned to Josh. "Was he an actor? You know, that comedian?"

"No," Josh answered kindly, as though they went through this all the time. "That was Sid Caesar."

"Oh."

Johnson was still watching her, his eyes cold and furious. "Think about what you're doing, Miss Shannon. Sid Calentro is a cold-blooded killer. If you know where he is and aren't telling us, it makes you an accessory."

For the barest second, Allie hesitated. Then she remembered Calentro's smile and his statement about Riazzi's three men. *They weren't permanently removed. I don't believe in that. Never have.* He could have had those three men killed, she knew. In fact, he could have killed her and Josh to protect himself and to keep Josh from writing his book.

Yet he hadn't. He'd let them leave, a little sadly, and only asked Josh to call with his decision so that he and Lena would have plenty of time to disappear—if necessary.

Allie shrugged casually at the agents, despite her sweaty palms, and tried to think of how Val might answer the question. "I thought an accessory was something you put an outfit together with."

"He means you could also be held accountable for the actions of a person you're protecting," Josh explained patiently, as though he truly believed she didn't understand.

"Oh." Allie tried to smile across the table.

Johnson turned back to Josh in disgust. "Do you realize that this conversation is being taped? If you even *try* to publish a book about Calentro after what you've said in this room, you *will* be arrested." He smiled icily. "Now, why don't you just tell me everything you know, then you can go home and write your book."

Allie's breath caught at the agent's threat. Her heart in her throat, she looked at Josh.

He sat in stony silence, then gave Johnson another smile. "I don't know what you're talking about. I'm not writing anything at the moment. I'm certainly not doing a book on Sid Calentro. Although I have been gathering some notes on Robert Mulhanney and the Denver serial killings. Say, neither of you guys worked on that case, did you?"

Zimmerman twisted in his chair. "Well, yeah. Actually, I did. That was a helluva—"

"Zimmerman," Johnson hissed. He glared at Josh, knowing he was beaten.

JOSH AND ALLIE were finally told by a furious and stymied Johnson that they could leave. Suffering from a splitting headache, Allie trudged beside Josh down the long tiled hallway to the front doors of the building. There, she was swept off her feet in a crushing hug.

"Allie!" she heard her brother cry. "You're all right!"

Tory set her back on her feet and swung around to face Josh. "What have you been doing to her, Josh?" he barked. "What kind of mess did you drag my sister into this time?"

With a tired, exasperated expression, Josh merely pushed open the front doors, nodded politely at Val in passing and stepped out into the Seattle night.

"Josh," Tory demanded, following him. "I want to know what's going on."

"Later, Tory," Josh said.

"No, now."

"Tory, please," Allie began. They were making a scene in front of the FBI building. Great, she thought. Now all four of them would be arrested.

"Val called me in Kansas City, practically hysterical," Tory said, stepping in front of Josh. "Allie was missing, she said. I had to come home right away. Then when I get home, the FBI calls to tell us the two of you are being questioned and could we please come pick you up. Now, I think that deserves an explanation."

In the harsh streetlights, Josh looked at Allie, his face nearly gray with exhaustion. "It's a long story,

Tory. Too long for me to start tonight. So you might as well just punch me now and get it over with."

Tory stared at him in bewilderment.

"I've been sleeping with your sister," Josh explained. "And I don't intend to stop."

Beside her, Val laughed and raised her hands to her mouth. Tory turned slowly to Allie, his face blank with surprise.

"Allie?" he asked.

Allie shrugged. "It's true, Tory. I've been seducing your best friend."

Taken aback, Tory blinked rapidly at them. "Well, I'll be damned." He suddenly grinned. "I guess the baby'll have an uncle, after all."

"Now, wait a minute," Josh began. "I never said anything about marrying Al—" He stopped.

Allie was squealing and laughing with joy. She hugged Val, then her brother, and jumped around the sidewalk, unable to contain herself. "I knew it!" she cried happily. "I knew it. I'm going to be an aunt."

Tory accepted another wild hug from her, then his smile began to fade, and he turned back to Josh with a dangerous expression. "What's this about not marrying Allie?"

CHAPTER FIFTEEN

JOSH NESTLED DEEPER into the mound of blankets and listened to the light patter of rain on the bedroom window. The morning light was gray and weak, struggling through an overcast sky. As he had every morning for the past three weeks, Josh waited in bed for the creak that told him the front door of the Tudor house was opening, then the thump as it was banged shut, followed by the quick tap of Allie's disgustingly cheerful footsteps as she ran lightly up the stairs.

It was too early in the morning to be chipper, Josh thought with a grumble, and he rolled onto his stomach and burrowed further into his pillow to hide from her. Too late. Like a fresh ocean breeze, she blew into the room, her hair and face damp from the rain and her cheeks flushed pink from her early-morning run along the shore. With a playful laugh, she threw herself on the bed and sprawled across him. Josh buried his head under the covers.

"Good morning, Josh," she sang lightly.

"Allie, cut it out," he complained. "You're all wet."

"Am I?" She giggled and squirmed on top of him, covering the only part of him that was visible—his cheek and left ear—with wet kisses. "It's wonderful out, Josh. Windy and wet. I think we should build a fire in the living-room fireplace and stay in our pajamas all day."

Josh swatted at her hand, which was tickling the back of his neck. "We don't wear pajamas."

"All the better." Straddling him and the layer of blankets around him, she waved several envelopes near his head. "Want to know what the postman brought?"

"No."

He could hear her ripping open an envelope, then silence as she read. She was as light as a child, but the pressure of her legs around him where she sat on his back was starting to wake him up more fully than any gentle teasing.

"Another threatening letter from Tory. Wants to know when you're going to marry me and stop embarrassing the family." She tossed the envelope aside. "Hmm. This one looks like your electricity bill."

"Allie," Josh muttered into the pillow.

"An overdue notice from the library." He heard the mail fall on the floor beside the bed. She bent over him, nibbled on his earlobe, a strand of her wet hair lying against his shoulder, cool and slick, teasing him out of the last drowsy realms of sleep. Finally he couldn't stand it any longer and rolled onto his back, carrying her with him.

Every morning it seemed to take less time to tug her running shorts and T-shirt off her. He must be getting good at it, he thought as he pulled her naked body under the covers with him. At any rate it was his favorite part of her morning workout.

Her skin was warm from exercise, and covered with a thin sheen of salty moisture. Her slender arms and legs tangled with his under the covers, and he claimed her mouth with his.

Waking up this early in the morning, he amended, wasn't really so bad. It definitely had its pleasant side. Beneath him, Allie moaned softly, and she wrapped her arms around his neck.

"You're a devil," Josh murmured against her mouth. "I can't keep my hands off you, and you know it."

"I was wondering about that." Her voice was soft with laughter.

"Wondering?" Josh pretended scorn. "You know exactly what you do to me, and every night and morning for the past three weeks, you've snuck in here and proved it."

"Mmm." She raised her chin so he could kiss the hollow at the base of her throat. "If you want me to sleep on the sofa like we'd arranged—"

"No, you don't." Josh stopped her from sliding away with a large hand on her hip. "Now that you're here, I'm not letting you go."

With a gentle caress that made him shiver, she ran a hand down his back. "So it's working, is it?"

"I don't know exactly what *it* is. But, yes, I'd definitely say it was."

"Guerrilla tactics."

"What?"

"Nothing." She smiled at him. Her auburn hair lay in a damp, dark red mass around her, soaking his pillow. He lifted a tendril and brought it to his face, enjoying the feel of its wet silkiness on his cheek.

"Josh?"

"Mmm." He brushed a hand down her shoulder to the soft skin above her breast.

"I think I might have found an apartment."

That stopped him. Uneasily, he gazed into her green eyes. "An apartment?"

"Well, I know this is only a temporary arrangement. I appreciate your giving up your privacy until I could find another place, but I know you want to—"

"What?" Josh broke in, his voice unexpectedly gruff. "What do you know I want?"

Allie's eyes widened a fraction. "To have your privacy back."

He was leaning over her, balancing his weight on his arms, careful not to crush her. Under him, he could feel each soft curve and delicious hollow of her body, and suddenly he wanted only to make love to her. He didn't want to talk anymore.

"Josh!" Allie pushed at his shoulders and turned her face away from his hard kisses. "What are you doing? That hurt. You're squashing me," she cried, a little alarmed at the sudden intensity with which he'd covered her body with his.

Her voice stopped him, and he drew back. "Why don't we?" he asked quickly, almost desperately. "We'll build a fire and sit by it all day, pajamas or not."

Allie stared up at him in confusion.

Running a hand through his hair, Josh rolled to his side and leaned on an elbow beside her. "Maybe I'll even go running with you tomorrow."

"What? You hate running in the morning."

"And I think we should try to make pancakes again. They weren't that bad last time. We could probably get the hang of it after a few tries."

Allie pulled herself up to sit back against the pillows. "Josh, what in the world are you talking about?"

He tried to look away from her but couldn't. "I just don't... Don't go, Allie. You don't have to find an apartment. You can stay here."

Her eyes registered surprise. "Here? But you've been walking around this house as grouchy as a bear all week. I thought I was in your way, that you were—"

"I'm always grouchy when I start working on a new book," Josh interrupted. "You know that. Stay here, Allie. You don't have to go."

Her face softened, but then, unaccountably, she seemed to draw back from him.

"Why, Josh?" she asked. "You said you could never live with anyone."

"I know." He looked away. "But I've just gotten so used to you being around. You said you wanted to start a novel. That you weren't going back to Grauber. Well, you could write here. We could work together."

Allie remained silent, her eyes uncertain.

"I don't want you to leave, Allie. I don't think I could stand the silence. I like having someone in the house. I think I'd feel—" he hesitated "—lonely on my own."

A flicker of hurt crossed her face, so quickly he wasn't sure he'd really seen it. She suddenly threw the blankets off and started to rise.

"Then maybe you should get a dog," she snapped unexpectedly. Standing beside the bed, she reached for her running shorts.

Josh was baffled. "Allie—"

"No, Josh. I'm going to go and look at that apartment today." Fumbling ineffectually with the shorts, she suddenly dropped her hands and stared blindly at them.

Josh knew then. Of course he did. He'd always known what she wanted to hear—and what he wanted to say. He just didn't know if he could make himself do it. He'd lived so many years with regret over his mother, so many years of doubting his own ability to love, and so many years of fearing he would hurt Allie.

He had a lot of years to overcome in one sentence, in one heartbeat, in one quick, cautionless plunge. Hesitantly, with his heart hammering in his ears, Josh reached out and offered her his hand.

"Allie," he began, thinking that these were the most difficult words he'd ever said in his life. "I love you, Allie. I want you to stay because I need you. I won't ever be happy anymore unless you're with me. I don't know what will happen or if I can be the man you deserve. But I do know I can't live without you because I love you too damned much."

Allie gazed at him, taking in his words. She seemed to sway away from him, and her eyes grew shiny with unshed tears. For the longest, most awful moment of his life, Josh felt the silence stretch to eternity, and he thought with sudden terror that she was going to turn and walk away from him.

Then, she reached out and placed her hand on his. With a muffled groan, Josh pulled her down to him and knew they'd crossed a final hurdle. He found himself suddenly wondering why they'd waited so long.

In the end, it had been the easiest thing in the world to do.

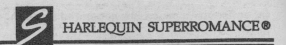

COMING NEXT MONTH

#606 SHADOWS IN THE MIST • Karen Young
Ryan O'Connor and Joanna Stanton had been divorced for
fifteen years. But when she showed up on his doorstep, running
for her life, he could hardly refuse her sanctuary. Then came his
grandmother, his editor, a fourteen-year-old boy and his dog—and
now that he thought about it, there was *something* about the boy....

#607 RIVALS AND LOVERS • Risa Kirk
(Women Who Dare)
Gene Logan was a champion rider who wanted to *win*.
Ross Malone wanted to keep her safe—a task that was much
harder than it sounded. If he withdrew his support, he'd lose her
trust, and if he encouraged her, he might lose Gene herself.

#608 BRINGING UP FATHER • Maggie Simpson
(Family Man)
Nick Lupton had always allowed his wife to make the decisions
concerning their son's upbringing. Now Vicki was dead, and Nick
was all Billy had. But Nick was too busy fighting demons of his
own. Until Betsy Johnson, Billy's principal, began breathing down
his neck about Billy's failing grades. Just as Nick thought life
couldn't get much worse...it suddenly got much better.

#609 TRUTHS AND ROSES • Inglath Caulder
Librarian Hannah Jacobs was happy with her life, just the way it
was. At least until Superbowl hero Will Kincaid came back to
town. After a knee injury put an end to his football career, Will
needed time to find a new future. For Hannah, however, Will's
arrival brought the past rushing back—a past she'd spent ten years
trying to forget.

AVAILABLE NOW:

#602 ROSES AND RAIN
Karen Young

#603 INDISCREET
Catherine Judd

#604 SINGAPORE FLING
Lynn Leslie

#605 I DO, I DO
Pamela Bauer

MILLION DOLLAR SWEEPSTAKES (III)

No purchase necessary. To enter, follow the directions published. Method of entry may vary. For eligibility, entries must be received no later than March 31, 1996. No liability is assumed for printing errors, lost, late or misdirected entries. Odds of winning are determined by the number of eligible entries distributed and received. Prizewinners will be determined no later than June 30, 1996.

Sweepstakes open to residents of the U.S. (except Puerto Rico), Canada, Europe and Taiwan who are 18 years of age or older. All applicable laws and regulations apply. Sweepstakes offer void wherever prohibited by law. Values of all prizes are in U.S. currency. This sweepstakes is presented by Torstar Corp., its subsidiaries and affiliates, in conjunction with book, merchandise and/or product offerings. For a copy of the Official Rules send a self-addressed, stamped envelope (WA residents need not affix return postage) to: MILLION DOLLAR SWEEPSTAKES (III) Rules, P.O. Box 4573, Blair, NE 68009, USA.

EXTRA BONUS PRIZE DRAWING

No purchase necessary. The Extra Bonus Prize will be awarded in a random drawing to be conducted no later than 5/30/96 from among all entries received. To qualify, entries must be received by 3/31/96 and comply with published directions. Drawing open to residents of the U.S. (except Puerto Rico), Canada, Europe and Taiwan who are 18 years of age or older. All applicable laws and regulations apply; offer void wherever prohibited by law. Odds of winning are dependent upon number of eligible entries received. Prize is valued in U.S. currency. The offer is presented by Torstar Corp., its subsidiaries and affiliates in conjunction with book, merchandise and/or product offering. For a copy of the Official Rules governing this sweepstakes, send a self-addressed, stamped envelope (WA residents need not affix return postage) to: Extra Bonus Prize Drawing Rules, P.O. Box 4590, Blair, NE 68009, USA.

SWP-H794

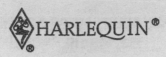

WEDDING SONG
Vicki Lewis Thompson

Kerry Muldoon has encountered more than her
share of happy brides and grooms. She and her
band—the Honeymooners—play at all the
wedding receptions held in romantic Eternity,
Massachusetts!

Kerry longs to walk down the aisle one day—
with sexy recording executive Judd Roarke. But
Kerry's dreams of singing stardom threaten to
tear apart the fragile fabric of their union....

WEDDING SONG, available in August
from Temptation, is the third book in
Harlequin's new cross-line series,
WEDDINGS, INC. Be sure to look for the
fourth book, **THE WEDDING GAMBLE,** by
Muriel Jensen (Harlequin American Romance
#549), coming in September.

WED3

This summer, come cruising with Harlequin Books!

PORTS OF CALL

In July, August and September, excitement, danger and, of course, romance can be found in Lynn Leslie's exciting new miniseries PORTS OF CALL. Not only can you cruise the South Pacific, the Caribbean and the Nile, your journey will also take you to Harlequin Superromance®, Harlequin Intrigue® and Harlequin American Romance®.

- ◆ In July, cruise the South Pacific with SINGAPORE FLING, a Harlequin Superromance
- ◆ NIGHT OF THE NILE from Harlequin Intrigue will heat up your August
- ◆ September is the perfect month for CRUISIN' MR. DIAMOND from Harlequin American Romance

So, cruise through the summer with LYNN LESLIE and HARLEQUIN BOOKS!

CRUISE

FL

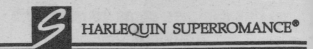

HARLEQUIN SUPERROMANCE®

The O'Connor Trilogy
by award-winning author KAREN YOUNG

Meet the hard-living, hard-loving O'Connors
in this unforgettable saga

Roses and Rain is the story of journalist Shannon O'Connor.
She has many astonishing gifts, but it takes a near-death
experience and the love of hard-bitten cop Nick Dalton to show
her all she can be. July 1994

Shadows in the Mist is Ryan's story. Wounded in his very soul,
he retreats to a secluded island to heal, only to be followed by
two women. One wants his death, the other his love.
August 1994

The Promise is the story that started it all, a story so powerful
and dramatic that it is our first featured Superromance
Showcase. Laugh and cry with Patrick and Kathleen as they
overcome seemingly insurmountable obstacles and forge their
own destiny in a new land. September 1994

Harlequin Superromance,
wherever Harlequin books are sold.